Sarah Goodwin completed the BA and MA in Creative Writing at Bath Spa University. *The Yacht* is her fifth novel to be published with Avon, following several years as a self-published author. She lives in Cornwall with her family and a very spoiled dog.

Also by Sarah Goodwin:

THE YACHT

S.L. GOODWIN

avon.

Published by AVON
A division of HarperCollins*Publishers*
1 London Bridge Street
London SE1 9GF

www.harpercollins.co.uk

HarperCollins*Publishers*
Macken House
39/40 Mayor Street Upper
Dublin 1
D01 C9W8
Ireland

A Paperback Original 2024
2

First published in Great Britain by HarperCollins*Publishers* 2024

A catalogue copy of this book is available from the British Library.

ISBN: 978-0-00-867105-1

This novel is entirely a work of fiction. The names, characters and incidents
portrayed in it are the work of the author's imagination. Any resemblance to
actual persons, living or dead, events or localities is entirely coincidental.

Typeset in Sabon LT Std by Palimpsest Book Production Limited,
Falkirk, Stirlingshire

Printed and bound in the UK using 100% renewable electricity at CPI Group (UK) Ltd

This book contains FSC™ certified paper and other controlled sources
to ensure responsible forest management.

For more information visit: www.harpercollins.co.uk/green

This novel is dedicated to my brave and beautiful
Auntie Nicki, who passed away in August 2023.
She will be forever missed.

CHAPTER ONE

I had to work late on the night before New Year's Eve, which wasn't that shocking. It was business as usual according to the company. Any normal person was at home in the days between Boxing Day and New Year's, living off Celebrations and increasingly ripe brie. But 'normal people' don't work in management at call centres or supermarkets, or any of the other places that just have to be open so that one or two lonely members of the public can have someone to whinge to. I didn't have the excuse of kids or a partner at home to spend the time off with, so my festive period was up for grabs as far as Rin, my manager, was concerned. I didn't really mind that much though.

No, that's actually a lie; I did mind quite a bit. I just hadn't said anything. None of the arguments I'd had with Rin had ever made it out of my head. In my shower I could come up with all sorts of things to say to him. In reality, though, if my manager told me to do something, I'd do it, and keep my irritation between me and my shampoo bottles.

As I was the only person on the 'late-late shift', I rattled around the otherwise empty call centre for three hours after the last person headed off. I was mentally going over all of the ways I could have better used this time, given that I had a twelve-hour car journey ahead of me. Though to be honest, I wasn't exactly looking forward to that either. Obviously. Twelve hours in my car, not including sleep and rest breaks, sounded like Hell, quite frankly. If I'd had the money to fly and then take an extortionate taxi journey from Nice airport to Ventimiglia, I'd have done so. But 'twas the season for insane prices so, by car it was.

At least it would be worth it – or so I told myself as I imagined the next twelve hours. At the end of it I'd be spending a glittering weekend on board a private yacht with my best friends. I just had to not think about the drive back in time for work afterwards. Which would likely be undertaken with a hangover.

If anything, being alone in the office was a last chance to relax. Free access to the coffee machine and thermostat was also a bonus. I mostly read on my Kindle and chain-drank mochas with extra shots to keep myself awake.

I got exactly two calls in all that time. One from Rin, to make sure I was actually still working, and one on my mobile, from Libby.

'Hi, babes, just wanted to double-triple-check that you're still coming to my party and that your car hasn't died or anything,' she said breezily. In the background I could hear scraping, banging and raised voices, none of which seemed to faze her.

'I am on my way as soon as my shift ends. I'll be with you tomorrow night, fresh from one of France's charming laybys.'

Libby laughed. 'And you've got a dress for the party? You don't need to borrow anything? Because I can have someone go out and—'

'Party outfit is ready and waiting in my car.' I had spent months agonising over what I was going to wear to Libby's New Year's Eve party. I think I'd actually started worrying about it during last year's party. That time, I'd made the mistake of wearing something from the high street, and when Libby had asked me where it was from, she looked appalled. 'They sell suitcases, Hannah,' she'd chided. As though I'd announced that my eveningwear came from Lidl. *So does Louis Vuitton*, I'd thought but managed not to say out loud.

My dress for this year was silk at least, and from a good designer, even if it came via the charity shop. I thought it was suitably classy for the night, if a little too small and with a tiny repair under one arm. One I hoped no one would notice.

'What's all that noise?' I added, trying to distract Libby from her offer to buy me a dress, especially given that I was already planning to wear the designer heels she'd gifted me. Her presents were always over the top, pricewise, and I felt embarrassed that I couldn't reciprocate.

'Noise? Oh, it's the staff.' She lowered her voice a little before adding, 'Olly hired these caterers to stock up the yacht in advance and we're having them move a few things around, too, just some last-minute changes to the layout. You don't know the Italian for "be careful, that's fucking expensive", do you?'

'Never had the use for it,' I said, trying to work out what time it was where they were and hoping she was paying them well for the bother. 'Well, I can't wait to see it.'

'It's going to be amazing, but I swear if they break one more glass, I will kill everyone here and then myself. See you soon! Mwah!' Libby rang off and I sighed, feeling more apprehensive about the party than I had before. With so few guests there would be nowhere to hide, and it was obvious she wanted everything to be perfect.

Whilst I filled out my 'end of shift handover', I sent a text to Harry asking him what he was wearing. I was hoping he'd go for his usual, as it would keep the attention off of me. Harry had, since our uni days, kept up a somewhat grungy look – bleach-splattered plaid, shredded jeans, leather and slogan t-shirts I'd made at various stages in my amateur crafting career. Underneath it all, he was a sarcastic ginger nerd with arms like knotted rope and a cherub nose he'd pierced three times in an attempt to 'butch it up'. I'd once told him he looked like a plumber that had fallen through an Urban Outfitters and he'd thrown a chicken drumstick at me.

Nowadays, though, he probably got his leather jackets from Bottega and his 'subversive' slogan tees from Moschino instead of from my bag of half-priced 'rejects'. Last year we'd have been in the same boat. This year he'd hit the big time with the budget to match. His welded junk sculptures were finally finding an audience and he'd packed his electrician job in to become a full-time darling of the art scene. His work was selling for almost disgusting amounts of money and I'd seen him on the TVs in our reception area, being interviewed on the news. I was happy for him, honestly. He was doing what he'd always wanted and earning a fortune, just like the rest of them. Which left only me in the 'don't quit your day job' bracket.

Whilst both Maggie and Libs had more money than I

could ever hope to set eyes on, let alone spend, Libby was rich-rich. She and Olly had a mansion in the country, townhouses in London and Paris, villas in Italy and Spain and, apparently, a yacht. Olly's family had some kind of title, which I could never remember, but he'd not had much in the way of actual cash when they'd met. Just an enormous estate and manor house, which his parents couldn't afford to heat. Libby's grandad had founded a bunch of nightclubs and 'gentlemen's establishments', which it took me years to realise meant 'strip clubs'. When he died, she inherited a cool quarter of a million and Olly used that to invest in property. He managed to get tons of other people to invest with him – in a way which never managed to sound completely legit – and he'd come out of it with a profit of over two million.

Every year Libby threw a New Year's party, and I always got an invite. A throwback to our uni days when we'd reconvene after Christmas. Libby would have spent two weeks skiing in the Alps or sunning herself at a private resort whilst sleeping with a cocktail waiter and learning how to jet-ski. Maggie would be full of gossip (and goodie bags) from Christmas parties in New York and Paris, where champagne flowed like the tears of out-of-vogue designers, and naked models rode horses through hotel lobbies. Then there would be me and Harry, fresh from spending a fortnight with our families – Harry's parents fought constantly, and my mum was too busy mourning memories of Christmas with my dad to really spend it with me. By the time New Year's rolled around, both of us were desperate for a good time and Libby's party always delivered.

Libs would splash out on a hotel suite, holiday home or,

once, a church about to be converted into flats. She'd invite fellow students and Harry's tradie mates, and we'd get hammered, dance and generally make sure the police got called on us by three a.m. Libby had once had the idea to make 'indoor snowmen' by hiring a film-studio-grade snow machine, which got her banned from a well-known chain of hotels. Worth it though.

This year the party was on Olly's yacht.

Normally I was lost in a sea of guests at the yearly event, each year's party being bigger than the one before. Two years ago, we'd been at a castle in Scotland haunted by paid actors I actually recognised. Between the arrival of a full roast deer and a game of 'murder in the dark', which had involved blood packs, pyrotechnics and a stunt performer taking a dive into the moat from a turret, I'd barely spent one collective hour with Libby.

This year, the guest list had been slashed right down, with Libby describing it as 'more intimate and elevated'. I suppose it was because a yacht was obviously smaller than a castle, and I felt a bit honoured that I'd made the cut. It was actually kind of incredible that no matter how much our lives diverged, Libby kept this tradition going. Like she knew how hard this time of year was for me and never wanted me to spend it alone, especially since losing Mum.

Maggie and I both knew Libby from way back. We'd all grown up together after meeting at the same girls' school. I was in on a scholarship, naturally. My parents were a bus driver and a dinner lady respectively, at least until Dad died. But back then it didn't matter so much. It wasn't until I got a bit older that I began to realise just how different our families were. And once I became aware of it, it only ever seemed to get worse. There was a scary point where Libby and Mags were considering Oxbridge or studying abroad, and I thought I would be forever left behind. Thankfully, Maggie's exam results and Libby's behavioural record kept them closer to my level, and with my excellent results in art and a battery of loans, we ended up all going to the same place. Mostly because I wanted to go where they were going, and Maggie wanted to copy whatever Libby did.

Maggie – the daughter of a semi-successful model and the owner of a French fashion magazine, which closed its doors in the late-nineties – had always been a bit touchy over her parents' sliding fortunes, especially when competing with Libby. Mags had used their names and her 2:1 in textiles to get a foothold in fashion, but I sometimes thought she was waiting for the bottom to fall out of it all, just as it had for them. I also wondered if that was the attraction of her fiancé, Leon. If everything turned sour for her, she'd still have his name to fall back on. Thinking about Leon . . . He would – unfortunately – be at the party, too. Not only because of Maggie, but also because he knew Olly.

Harry was the final guest. He'd entered our uni friend group through Libby. They'd dated for a week during our first year, until she moved on to someone else and he dropped out to do an apprenticeship with an electrician instead. I honestly don't know if we'd have ever seen Harry again after that, had he not moved into the off-campus house he did. It was shared with a load of other apprentices and trade college blokes, but it was also near the clubs and, crucially, nowhere near nosy campus security guards and visiting parents. Harry's house quickly became our go-to for pre-club drinks and post-club passing out during our first year, and he became a part of the group by extension. So much so that by the time we moved off campus ourselves, it never occurred to us to stop inviting him to things.

Harry's response pinged through.

Worried I'll show you up? If it makes you feel better, I'll leave my ermine and diamonds in the Rolls.

I snorted. Same old Harry; that was a relief.

My car was parked underground and it was the only one still there, save for the security company's van. I shivered my way over to it. Ermine didn't sound like a terrible idea, now I thought of it. I was going to be freezing if it stayed like this when I had to pull over for a nap. Not to mention if we had to spend much time outside on deck once I was dressed for the party. I considered popping home for a blanket and maybe a jacket, just in case, but no, I was already pressed for time as it was.

And who cared if I was going to freeze my butt off? I would be drinking expensive champagne and eating tiny daubs of things off tiny circles of other things and having a lovely time with my friends. We'd tell stories about uni and bemoan the near decade since graduation, and the looming dread of turning thirty. For one weekend I would leave call centre Hannah behind and revert back to the old me, the one only Libby and Mags could bring out. The me who had time and energy for art and dancing and giggly confessions in a toilet cubicle. As much as I fretted over the party, it was a yearly trip back to a time when I was genuinely happy. I wasn't going to pass on that. Ever.

Inside the car I cranked the heating as high as it would

go, hoping to at least keep myself lukewarm. I had a travel-mug of office coffee in the cup holder and a long drive ahead of me. The best of Dolly Parton clicked into place in the tape player – a reminder that I'd had the same car since those long-lost uni days – and I reversed out of my bay, heading for the road.

CHAPTER TWO

I made pretty good time, all things considered. It helped that the roads were fairly deserted. Even with the motorway not being as packed as normal I kept to a brisk fifty-nine miles per hour. Mostly because my car felt like it was shaking apart if I went faster.

I caught a quick hour of sleep on the ferry crossing and then spent the remaining half hour wondering if saving thirty quid was worth the wasted time. I should have taken the tunnel. The ferry was pretty grim actually – with it being so late, most of the passengers were drinking or asleep in the soft-play area.

Finally I trundled into France feeling, if anything, more tired for having had a taste of sleep. I wound both the windows down to try and keep myself awake.

An hour or so into my journey towards what the internet had promised me would be a good place to spend the night for free, my phone rang again. The phone was in its cradle on the dash and I put it on speaker. It was Harry.

'*Bonjour, madame – comment allez-vous*? That was all my French, by the way, so, appreciate it.'

'It's going fine, Harry,' I said, rolling the windows up so I could hear better. 'And it's "mademoiselle" for unmarried women. Libby's a madame.'

'She certainly is – can you believe she just re-sent me the dress code? Like that's going to make me follow it.' I heard rustling, which sounded suspiciously like he was in bed.

'I was about to turn in,' he said, apparently reading my mind, 'but I thought I'd make sure you didn't get lost and end up in Amsterdam. Because in that case I would come and join you.'

'You wish. Nope, I'm in France and on my way – so there is no chance of you escaping from Olly.'

'Pity.' Harry sighed. 'Though I think you mean Olly has no chance of escaping from me. He thinks I'm the worst person alive, whereas I just think he's a tosser.'

'Be nice.' I yawned. 'It's his boat, remember?'

'Tosser *is* me being nice. I didn't want to shock and horrify you whilst you're driving. What's the view like?'

'Uh . . . dark and full of moths?'

'Stop it, you make it sound so romantic,' Harry gushed. 'However will I sleep now?'

I giggled. 'Goodnight, Harry.'

'*Gute nacht.*'

'That's not French,' I said, but he'd already hung up. I rolled my eyes.

To pass the time, I wondered what we were actually going to do on this yacht. Libby had been frustratingly light on the details, but surely we couldn't be going that far, not if Olly wanted to enjoy the party and not spend the whole weekend sailing. A little cruise and maybe a band on deck to play us into the New Year, that was probably the idea. Though that sounded a bit sedate for Libby. Three years ago she'd thrown her party at the Royal Opera House in London. We'd spent the night in the Paul Hamlyn Hall with acrobats and silk dancers performing over our heads, hanging from the ironwork of the enormous conservatory-esque structure. She had something more planned; I could feel it.

Even my anticipation of what was to come couldn't keep me awake forever though, and I yawned my way to the spot I'd picked for a few hours of sleep. France was a bit more relaxed on parking up and camping than the UK, or so I'd read, and I'd chosen a decent-looking public car park, which had no signs forbidding drivers from sleeping there. It was screened from the road by some trees and on the other side two hiking paths wound their way into a pine forest. At least they did on the map. I couldn't see anything once the car was parked. I'd have liked a toilet, or even a streetlight, but it was free, unlike a hotel, so I was going to make the best of it.

In the back I pulled a sleeping bag over myself and contorted my body to the shape of the seats. I wished I'd brought something to cover the windows with as I kept peeking at them to see if anyone was looking in. A few times I thought I heard someone moving about outside, but when I sat up to look there was nothing. Somehow, in all my planning, I'd not considered how scary it would be to spend the night in my shitty car in a foreign country. I lay there for hours but couldn't make myself relax.

Part of me wanted to call Harry for some reassurance but it was too late to be bothering him. Not that he'd have minded. I'd once called him to come and get me at one in the morning when my car broke down in Swindon. He'd turned up with a coffee and a smile. That was Harry. He was the person Libby, Mags and I knew we could call in a pinch. The entire time we were at university, if something broke, needed moving or we were pissed and couldn't find a taxi – Harry was there. I hadn't seen much of him lately, as he'd been busy with work, but he was always calling just to say hello when he had downtime, and he always picked up when I rang for reassurance or to whinge about work.

I finally managed to get to sleep, only to be jolted awake to blinding sunshine. I sat up, banged my head on the roof of the car and struggled to remember where I was and why. Someone was yelling outside – a woman, followed by a man yelling back. It was an American couple, arguing about where they were or where they ought to have been. The woman who'd woken me was beating a folding chair into submission and her husband was, from the smell of things, making coffee. My mouth watered.

After stretching the kinks from my twenty-nine-year-old spine, I got into the front seat and winced at my reflection. A pale, shadow-eyed woman looked back at me, her hair a tangled mess and her face indented with the shape of a seatbelt catch. Lovely. I'd have to find somewhere to get cleaned up before heading to the party.

I checked the time and swore. I'd slept for ages. It was already nearly noon and I still had to get to an entirely different country.

I had toyed with the idea of doing some sight-seeing on my way to the yacht, but I was so tired and so late that I could only muster the strength to locate the universal golden arches of McDonald's before heading for the Italian border. I ate hash browns whilst navigating the unfamiliar roads and wiped the grease on my leggings. Libby would have been horrified.

Having parked up just north of Dijon to take advantage of the National Park and its camping areas, I had a seven-hour drive ahead of me. Not counting the pit stop at McDonald's, a quick sandwich and refuel at a petrol station and finding a place to get changed ahead of my arrival at the party.

I ended up putting my party clothes on in a public toilet and doing my makeup in my car. Not exactly a glamorous start, but no one but me was going to know. And all things considered, I thought I looked OK.

Finally I reached Ventimiglia, the city where Olly's yacht was currently moored. It was already dark by this time, but I couldn't help but try to soak in the sights as I drove through. The rambling caramel-coloured stone buildings reminded me a little of Bath, as did the winding streets. But there was no mistaking the tiled roofs, arches and thin steeples as anything other than Italian.

The marina was embedded in a district completely packed with hotels and restaurants, all of which were mobbed. It was past nine at night on New Year's Eve and everywhere I looked there were people nonchalantly stepping out in front of my car. It was chaos. Normally I thought of myself as quite a confident driver. I'd done my fair share of French camping trips both solo and with Nicola and Rosemary, friends from my crafting group (both older ladies, who were as overworked as I was), and my ex, Jimmy, had once asked me on a road trip through America, but I'd turned him down flat – couples' trips were a no-no. Still, after a day of non-stop driving, even I was losing my cool a little. It didn't help that the roads were lined with parked cars on both sides and so many side roads were gated and covered with Italian signage.

Once I found the parking area I more or less abandoned my car. I just wanted to get out of it and not see it for a few days. After paying for parking, I got my overnight bag out of the boot, along with my hostess gifts for Libby. Despite the fact that I was only staying for two days I'd slightly over-packed – the bag was heavy and annoying to carry. I debated wearing my memory foam trainers until I got to the boat but that was hardly the aesthetic Libby would be going for. They didn't fit in my overnight bag, so I left them in the car instead.

The marina was circular and like nothing else I'd ever seen. It had a paved dock that curved away from the car park in both directions, dotted at intervals with flawless white boats, bobbing in the calm water. The stars stood out, sparkling like nuggets of ice, and I craned my head back to take it all in. Even the moon, a razor sliver overhead, was clear and bright. It really was beautiful. I'd have hung around to take in more of the view, but the temperature was in the single digits and I just wanted to get inside. Which meant finding Olly's yacht.

The criminally expensive shoes Libby had gifted me had not one millimetre of padding anywhere in them; it was like wearing plastic heels from a child's princess costume. I winced my way over the uneven street and down some truly dicey stone steps. The sea air was so clean and so coldly crisp that it made my heart and lungs ache. I drank it in anyway and felt calm for the first time since leaving work the night before. The only thing spoiling it ever so slightly was the deep bass of someone's music, which I could almost feel in the stones of the wharf.

'Oh my God – Han! Han! Over here!'

I tensed and my eyes darted down the row of boats. Each one was different, strung with fairy lights or with glowing windows, the decks covered in prayer flags, bay trees, deckchairs or planters of waving dark plants. At the very end of the row, though, was a boat that dwarfed the lot of them. On the top deck, waving at me in the white beam of several spotlights, was Libby.

I carried my bag to the gangplank leading onto the lower deck. It was the largest of the three decks on the yacht and lit by spotlights that revolved on their own, reminding me of old-timey film premiers. Strings of glittering beads hung overhead, dripping down like bedazzled spider webs, interspersed with monogrammed bunting – gold thread on white silk combining Olly and Libby's initials. There was a certain wedding vibe to it all and I wondered if it meant that they were going to renew their vows at midnight. The path towards a set of glass doors was strewn with white petals and what looked like flakes of gold leaf.

More spotlights slashed through the darkness on the upper deck where Libby had waved from. The mid-deck was mostly taken up by a glassed-in room, the glass gently pulsing with light, like it was rigged with fibre optics. Behind the glass, the shapes of white and gold balloons were pressed against the windows near the ceiling.

The lower deck had its own glassed-in room, and at the rear, spot-lit from a dozen angles, was an honest to Jesus helicopter, white and gold to match the boat itself. Was that intentional or a happy accident? I rolled my eyes. Of course it was intentional. Who wouldn't colour coordinate their helicopter to their yacht? What were we, savages?

Be nice, Hannah, I warned myself. At least until I could get Harry alone for a bit. He was the only person I could speak my mind to when the sheer over-the-top nature of Libby's life became too much to witness. Though for all I knew, Harry might have already ordered his own helicopter, now that he was raking it in like the rest of them.

'Hannah!' Libby shouted as she threw open the double doors of the glassed-in room and dashed towards me, holding out her arms for a hug, her heels sending up a wave of petals. As she put her arms around me, I felt a cold dribble of spilled champagne soak through my blazer and onto the shoulder of my dress. She twirled me on the deck and placed sticky lip-gloss kisses on both of my cheeks. 'Mwah, mwah – so glad you're finally here! You took ages!'

I caught a waft of cigarette smoke mixed in with her perfume. Had she started smoking again? She'd given it up years ago because Olly thought it looked common. Maybe he'd changed his mind – that, or she didn't care anymore.

She pulled back and we both did the 'outfit appreciation' eye sweep. Libby, as usual, looked amazing. Ever since school she'd been fake tanned to perfection with professionally dyed blonde hair, modelling herself after the most glamorous employees at her family's clubs. She'd only gilded her looks since then, with several boob jobs, a new bum, lip fillers, and extensions to both her hair and lashes – which, thanks to her access to the best treatments available, somehow managed to look almost natural. She could have walked right off of a *Baywatch* beach.

She was wearing a short gold dress absolutely encrusted in seed beads – it had to weigh a ton – and her tan made the white fur coat draped over her shoulders stand out brighter than the gold and diamonds around her neck. A

17

tiny bitchy part of me wondered if she'd dressed to match the yacht and helicopter.

'Look at you,' she cooed. 'God, you are so good at accessorising the basics.'

I managed a smile and took the compliment as I hoped it had been intended. It wasn't her fault that she was so blunt. She always had been. When shopping for a graduation dress she'd told me I looked 'like a frump with a hunch' in my pick and she was right. I had a great-looking graduation picture because she'd picked out an amazing dress for me.

'Come on, you absolutely have to see what we've done inside. No thanks to those absolutely appalling catering people. Let's get you a drink, too. This champagne is delish, but I am dying to make cocktails,' she trilled with a shimmy, as if auditioning for a reality show about millionaire yacht owners. She'd clearly had her share of the 'delish' champagne.

'Sounds like just what I need. This is for you, by the way.' I handed her the gift bag and she took it between her exquisite claws.

'Oh you're so sweet!' Libby opened the bag and looked down at the box of chocolates from a special shop on the high street – which I'd spent roughly five hours of my wages on – and the bottle of whisky I'd added for Olly's benefit. It was from the supermarket, but it came in a cardboard tube and wasn't the kind of thing you'd get to mix with cola. She closed the bag and smiled at me.

'You're such a sweetie. Olly's going to love this.'

I smiled and felt myself relax a little. The journey was over, and this night was my reward for crossing two countries in twelve hours.

'Let me show you through to your room so you can dump

that' – Libby gestured at my bag – 'and then we can get you a drink and get this party started!'

Libby led me into the body of the yacht, a sort of lobby with a white marble fireplace, snow-white couches and circular gold tables topped with vases of lilies. More monograms were splashed across little silk pillows. There was thankfully a fire in the fireplace and the inside of the boat was warmer than my flat at home, despite the glass walls showing a vista of the dark sea. A pyramid of empty champagne glasses stood at the centre of a larger table, ready to form a champagne fountain should the mood strike us.

'Total redesign,' Libby was saying as she tapped over the pale wood floors. 'Top to bottom. The previous owners had it all done in like, oak and studded leather. Totally literal, you know?'

'Yeah,' I said, with no clue what she was talking about. Oak and leather sounded cosier than marble and metal. It was kind of giving me 'dental hygienist turned rapper on the weekend', what with how many of the gold, marble and white leather surfaces were wipe-clean and shiny.

'The cabins are all below. She sleeps ten in five bedrooms so there's plenty of space – though the extra room is locked right now.' She shot me a cheeky smile. 'Can't have this turn into a night of bed hopping!'

Given that the guest list comprised two couples, Harry and myself, it didn't seem likely to descend into orgy territory. Still, I felt my cheeks heat up as I tried to decipher the reasoning behind her little joke. Maybe I was reading too much into it?

Libby teetered down the stairs to the cabins, laughing at herself as she staggered off the bottom step. Each step was

19

lit up from within by fluorescents, adding to the swanky dentist's office aesthetic. Continuing along the corridor, Libby threw open a mirrored door to a room housing a king-size bed half buried in sheepskins and plump cushions. The smart alarm clock by the bed was playing soft classical music and beside it was a carafe of mint water, a satin eye mask and a Jo Malone candle. My feet sank into the creamy carpet and I craned my neck to see the vanity opposite the bed, where someone had fanned out several thick fashion magazines and set the flat screen behind it to show a roaring fire.

I was only staying two nights, but I could have happily taken a three-week holiday in that room. It was larger than my kitchen and bedroom put together. Libby took my bag from me and dumped it on my bed, on top of a neatly folded robe decorated with a white rose. She also dropped the gift bag, then waved me out and shut the door.

'Right then – drink time.'

I smiled tightly. She'd probably just forgotten why she was carrying the bag, was too buzzed or drunk to remember that I'd gifted it to her. I wasn't going to let it ruin the evening.

'Lead the way. Let's get this party going,' I said.

CHAPTER THREE

'Hannah! We were starting to think you'd never get here,' Maggie called as I reached the top of the stairs to the top deck. She was leaning with both arms against the side of the boat, as if posed there for a photo shoot. Leon was the only other person up there, lying on a leather couch against the opposite railing. No sign of Olly, or Harry. I hoped to God the latter hadn't decided not to come.

'Got here as fast as I could,' I said. 'At least I can't say "I've been driving since last year".'

Only Maggie smiled at the joke, her perfectly made-up face barely moving. She clicked over to me and air kissed my cheeks. She was dressed up as extravagantly as Libby but had gone the 'less is more expensive' route. She had on a charcoal cocktail dress with raw edges and visible seams, which nevertheless would have cost more than an entire floor of my local Primark. She'd also probably designed it herself as it fitted her like a glove, showing off her slender arms and deeply carved collarbones. Her long black hair was slicked back into a ponytail any thoroughbred would

21

have been praised for and diamonds dripped down from her ears to her shoulders. They matched the butterbean-sized one perched on her elegant finger.

'You look amazing,' I gushed.

'Thank you, sweetheart – you look very nice, too,' Mags said. 'That blazer's Terrico, you know.'

'Oh, right,' I said, not having a clue who the hell that was. Probably a smaller designer, like the one she was on about last year who made everything from sterling silver chainmail.

'Hmmm, yes, if I remember correctly, they were trying a plus-size range, but it never took off. They dumped the lot on us actually – for recycling. A green initiative tax write-off.'

I pressed my lips together and nodded, not trusting myself to speak. Maggie had probably forgotten that she was the one who'd gifted me the blazer. She was like that, as vague and wafting as her designs, but I'd always been a bit in awe of her artistic nature and effortless cool. That didn't stop me feeling hurt by her forgetfulness though. I didn't care that she'd got the blazer for free – I was still using a sleep mask I'd found in a hotel five years ago, for God's sake – it just stung that she'd put such little thought into my birthday gift that only four months later she'd forgotten what she'd given me.

Maggie drifted away from me and towards the drinks cart. Leon, her fiancé, didn't bother getting up from the long leather couch to greet me. If he hadn't been actively drinking, I might have assumed he was asleep.

I'd only met Leon a few times and was always struck by how broad he was. He had the body of the rugby lad he'd undoubtedly been at university, and the pink, round cheeks and blond messy hair of a schoolboy. Together, he and Maggie looked like day and night personified. Tonight he was almost flexing his way out of a pale pink shirt, white trousers and a dark blue blazer. What bothered me was his lack of socks, considering he was wearing brown loafers. That and the sunglasses, since it was dark out – though maybe it was because of all the spotlights on the decking.

Libby poured me a glass of champagne and pressed it into my hand before refilling her own glass and leaning against the railing, one foot hooked through it like she was a kid on the playground, acting cool. Her last drink was still soaking into my dress, so I knew I wasn't going to be able to take my blazer off for a while. Which was a shame as with the space-ship-looking heaters going on deck, I was starting to feel a bit flushed.

'I suppose you had to work today, right?' Maggie winced in sympathy, draping herself next to Leon on the couch with a fresh drink in hand. 'God, remember that, Libs? All those Saturdays dragging ourselves out of halls by six to do a shift in Topshop.' She laughed, shaking her head at the very idea of doing that now. I was surprised she remembered. They'd only done it for three months over one Christmas before they both just stopped going. Like it was a gym membership they'd tried out and decided wasn't for them. I suspected even at the time that they'd only got a job because everyone else had one and they felt left out when the rest of us in halls talked about our shifts at Costa and Wetherspoons.

'Respect the grindset,' Leon said, nodding like he'd contributed something that I couldn't have gotten from Rin's inspirational calendar. 'I've been banking content for the last month so that I don't miss an upload over the season.'

'Content?' I asked, just to be polite.

23

'Leon's started a podcast,' Maggie cooed, as if praising her toddler's toilet training.

'I'm starting a movement,' Leon corrected.

'What's it about?' I asked.

'You wouldn't get it. It's not for you.'

'O . . . K,' I said, because honestly, what else can you say to that? Other than 'that sounds like bullshit'? Which is what I really wanted to say but kept to myself. Leon's appeal had always been lost on me, but I supposed Maggie saw something in him. Even if that something was that he had old money connections, just like Olly. After all, Maggie always wanted anything that Libby had.

'Cute shoes, by the way,' Mags said, gesturing to them with one talon. 'What are they – Dior? Maybe . . . two years ago?'

'Four,' Libby corrected. 'We love a vintage moment.'

How on earth had I expected to get away with it? Libby had probably clocked them the moment I set foot on board. *OK*, I told myself, *calm down. They didn't mean it.* We used to mess with each other all the time. For instance, I'd teased Libby mercilessly when she had to ask me how to use a cash point. Her dad had always just given her cash and for a solid term, every time one of us got money out, we'd call it 'raiding Daddy's wallet'. Just like we both joked about Mags who, despite having lived in Portugal for a year (or 'yar' as she would say), maintained for an entire Geography lesson that it was in Asia. This was nothing new. I just needed to get a thicker skin.

Footsteps tapped up the stairs from the second deck and Olly appeared. He was wearing an all-white outfit except for his gold watch. The combination of polo neck and pleated trousers with the white loafers was blinding amidst the spotlights.

24

Olly was pale and tall, a contrast to Leon's wined and dined, sportsman proportions. He always gave the impression that he was being held up by a single string and that without it he would clatter to the floor. It was the same kind of ethereal ease that Maggie had, but turned up to the highest possible degree – just short of needing an actual back brace. Libby always said that his family 'went back a long way' (which . . . didn't everyone's?) and that they had once been titled, or were still titled but didn't use it. Thank God, because honestly, having to call Libby 'Lady' or 'Baroness' would have put Harry in the hospital with collapsed lungs from laughing.

'Oh, Hannah – you're . . . here,' Olly said, pale eyebrows rising towards his hairline.

'Yes, I was just saying it was a long drive. I'm glad it's over.'

'Right,' he said, then looked at Libby, who slid away from the railing and busied herself getting him a glass of champagne.

'I suppose you had a quicker journey. Is that a Robinson R22 I saw? Our hotel in Bali had one,' Maggie chimed in.

Was that something new from BMW that I'd never heard of? I hoped we weren't about to launch into car talk. Mine was out of sight but I'd been driving it since our university days and both Libby and Mags loved to ask me if 'the crust-town express' was still in operation. I might have given the car that nickname myself, but hearing it from them had only become more humiliating as time went on.

'She's a beauty, isn't she? We made it in no time at all – and she's such a darling in the air. Isn't she, Libby?'

'Oh, the dreamiest. I can't believe how easy it is to get around now.'

25

Right, the helicopter. I had a sudden image of it landing in the park near my flat and Libby leaping out for an impromptu visit. Highly unlikely, of course. Not the helicopter part – the visit itself. She hadn't been to my place since uni because the few times a year she came to visit me we always met in a restaurant or at the spa – her treat.

'So convenient having the helipad on deck as well,' Olly continued. 'We're weighing anchor for a jaunt along the southern coast of France after the party, then I'll probably have the yacht sent back to England so we can fly home after we pay a visit to the house in Paris. I've no patience for sailing for its own sake.'

'Oh, are we not . . . going anywhere tonight?' I asked.

Everyone looked at me like I'd just suggested we head for the Bermuda Triangle. Leon snorted into his drink then turned his face into Maggie's neck and whispered something that made her smile.

'You know because, that's . . . I mean, because you were having it on a boat, I just thought . . .' I felt myself turning red.

Libby laughed like I'd made a joke and made a 'you're too much' wave with her hand, sliding her other arm around Olly's waist. 'We're in port for the duration. Sorry, Han.'

I stood there and sipped my champagne as they bandied helicopter brand names and yacht destinations back and forth. I had nothing to contribute to the discussion except a sense of growing unreality. Olly and Libby had been out of my league in terms of wealth for years now, but this was something else. They must have really done well for themselves since last year. A private helicopter and a yacht? Was Olly on the verge of making his first billion? More?

I could feel the divide between us stretching out like a

chasm filled with all the experiences we no longer shared, such as late buses, supermarket substitutions, rising energy bills and dying high streets. When was the last time Libby had gone to a high street and not some designer's exclusive showroom? My stomach twisted in knots. Why did I feel so embarrassed about it all when I was the normal one? The one living a quiet life? I guess because, to them, that was the abnormal thing to do. Here I was the one with the 'unique' experience.

'Are you all right, Hannah? You've gone very quiet?' Libby asked.

Did I hear Olly laugh then? An almost soundless huff of scorn? Or was it just my pricked pride deflating? Olly and Leon weren't exactly making me feel welcome but then again, they weren't my friends. Libby and Mags were. And Libby at least looked genuinely concerned.

'I'm just recovering from the drive. You know how hypnotic the road gets.' Maybe I should have added, 'sort of like how clouds get, I imagine', as an attempt at a joke. The atmosphere felt a little tense all of a sudden.

'The roads were so empty today. Good to finally test the limits of the Lambo. She doesn't get much of a real ride in the city.' Leon fixed me with a leer. Was this some kind of innuendo? If it was, I really hoped it'd be the last one he tossed my way.

'I have no idea how you've kept that car running so long, given all we put it through,' Mags said to me with a giggle. 'God, do you remember the night we missed that sign on the way home and ended up on the bridge to Wales? It took us hours to get back.'

I relaxed a little, remembering that night and all the fun we'd had together. I laughed. 'I remember you crawling into the boot to sleep on the way home and getting stuck in the hatch.'

'Ahoy!'

Recognising Harry's voice, I darted to the side rail and looked down towards the harbour road. Most of the light was coming from the boat so I could see Harry quite clearly where he was squinting up at us, waving even though we must have been a blur to him. He'd shaved his ginger beard since I'd last seen him, which was a shame as I had thought it suited him. And he was, to my relief, not dressed like Olly or Leon. In fact, I thought I recognised the t-shirt under his sheepskin jacket as one I'd made a few years ago. Back before I'd given up on my screen printing business. It was the design that had very nearly made me go viral – an image of sausage dogs watching a doggy clown make a balloon human.

'You're late!' Libby called down. 'Maybe you should take some of your art show money and buy a watch!'

'Had to stop at duty free for some wine fit for the occasion,' Harry called back. 'Swine before pearls and all that.'

I glanced back and saw Olly rolling his eyes. It was only then that what he'd said earlier really resonated with me. *Oh, Hannah – you're . . . here.* Not, 'you're finally here' or 'you're here!'. Just 'you're . . . here', like he was somehow confused by my presence. Like I hadn't been expected to come at all.

A wave of cold that even the aggressive heaters couldn't dispel went through me. I'd never felt particularly welcomed by Olly, or Leon, come to that. We hadn't really chosen each other and I understood that. They weren't my friends, they were just attached to Libby and Mags. But just then that sense that not only did I not fit in with them, but that I wasn't meant to be there, felt stronger than ever.

'I'm coming aboard!' Harry called, jogging over the gangplank.

I held my glass like a lifeline. At least Harry had arrived. To him, we were all just people with history and a shared interest in getting plastered before midnight. Something I would gladly raise a glass to.

CHAPTER FOUR

It got easier to be there after Harry arrived. Or maybe that was due to the two rounds of cocktails Libby brought out for us. Either way, things mellowed considerably.

Once Harry had thrust his bottle of Jacob's Creek – reduced sticker and all – into Olly's reluctant hands, he pulled me in for a hug and whispered, 'Ermine and diamonds, called it' in my ear. The hug was over too soon. I could have done with some more reassurance, but it was enough to break the spell the yacht had been weaving over me. I no longer felt so out of place. I was a guest, and these were my friends. At least . . . some of them were. I was going to have a good night.

'Nice shirt,' I said, gesturing at my design.

'I can tell you where I got it.' Harry grinned. 'Small company, very exclusive.'

'I heard they went out of business,' I said, trying to sound upbeat and jokey.

Harry nudged my shoulder. 'Nah, they're coming back, just you wait.'

I flushed, embarrassed at his belief in me, especially since

I had no intention of bringing my business back. I'd had my one shot at creating something that was just mine, something I could be proud of, and I'd gotten burned. Never again.

The top deck felt a little cramped with all six of us up there, so Libby showed us down to the middle deck where the control cabin was. Built on to it was a sort of viewing lounge with a modernist gold chandelier and a table laid out with hors d'oeuvres on white marble slabs. The rest of the furniture wasn't as sharply modern as that on the lower deck, some of it was even made out of wood instead of metal, though even that was inlaid with mother of pearl and what looked like ivory. I wondered if they were antiques and realised they most likely were, despite their new white and gold upholstery. There was no fireplace but there was a depression down the centre of the hors d'oeuvres table filled with clear crystals and some kind of liquid fuel, on which a wave of yellow flames danced. I wasn't sure if it was purely decorative or a take on fondue, and I was too embarrassed to ask. I'd just have to watch to see if anyone started poking food into it.

Only two of the walls were glass; the ones running down the sides. The dividing wall to the 'cockpit' – or whatever the ship equivalent was called – was floor-to-ceiling bookshelves, and I wandered over there to check out the collection. There was a bar on the wall opposite the shelves, with a TV flanked by oil paintings of the yacht itself hanging over it.

'What prompts a person to have not one, but two separate paintings of their yacht, on their yacht?' Harry murmured to me as he came to stand at my shoulder. The smell of solder and singed hair wafted from his jacket. 'Is it because from inside it they can't marvel at how fancy it looks to outsiders? Or is it in case they forget what it looks like?'

'Stop it,' I muttered, suppressing a giggle.

'Do you think there was a two-for-one on? Pay for the port side and we'll throw in starboard for free?'

I pressed my lips together, laughter lighting a tiny fire in my chest. It felt good, like a defence and a defiance against my surroundings. With Harry there it was easier to remind myself that I wasn't mad and that the Emperor really was naked – sometimes, at least.

'Do you think they have one of the helicopter, too?' I asked, enjoying this shared joke.

'Oh no, don't be childish . . . They definitely have at least two of the helicopter.'

This time a tiny snort escaped me and I quickly glanced over to see if any of the others had heard. They hadn't. Libby was effusing with Mags over an antique chaise she and Olly had had shipped in from Versailles – hopefully not the actual palace, but I wouldn't have been surprised – and Olly and Leon were in fierce discussion near the faux fire. I caught a sentence ending in 'private lunar module' and that told me all I wanted to know.

'So, what do Lord and Lady Scoffington read whilst at sea?' Harry said, pulling a book from the shelf. It shot out quickly, owing to how light it was. Harry turned the cover of *The Complete Works of Oscar Wilde* over in his hands. The gilding on the antique leather caught the light as it flopped open to reveal the stubs of pages, which had been cut from the binding. I didn't normally get too precious about books – I liked to crack my paperback spines – but looking at such a gorgeous book with nothing inside it was like seeing a family pet improperly taxidermied.

'They really make it too easy, don't they?' Harry said. 'I mean, this is just sad.'

'Harry!' Libby came rushing over and snatched the hollowed-out book from his hands, returning it to the shelf and adjusting it so it fell in line with the others. 'Don't mess with the books, please.'

'My deepest apologies,' Harry said. 'Was your interior decorator unable to find you any books that you could, I don't know, actually read?'

Libby rolled her eyes. 'Don't be so stupid. They were just too heavy, that's all. Boats have to float, you know. It was this or we'd have had to downgrade to double beds in all the rooms instead of kings. You're welcome, by the way.'

I dug my nails into my hand to keep my laughter inside. God bless Libby but she was ridiculous. This whole boat was insane. The amount of marble alone had to be close to sinking us. Were they really going to sail this thing around the coast of France and home again? Or at least, have someone else sail it home?

'What's the plan for midnight then?' Harry asked. 'We all write our resolutions on gold bricks, then chuck them in the ocean? You release some peacocks and we shoot them out of the air with diamond bullets?'

I pinched his hip out of Libby's view and he retaliated by reaching around my back and pinging my bra strap.

Libby glared at him. 'Wait and see, smart arse. Anyway, Hannah, come have some girl-time.' She pouted. 'No boys allowed.'

'Oh, no. Please let me come too,' Harry deadpanned.

'Go be with the menfolk,' I told him.

'Shan't.'

I stuck my tongue out at him as Libby towed me away.

Once we were in grabbing distance of Mags, she ushered us both out onto the deck. Spotlights out there were illuminating a canopy draped in fairy lights. Underneath it, white floor cushions fought with furs and sheepskin rugs for space. Not that we'd need them with the heaters putting out near-BBQ levels of warmth. Beyond the canopy a hot tub took up most of the rest of the space, the churning water sparkling with gold flecks. I prayed I wouldn't be forced into it. For one, none of Libby's swimwear would fit me, and for another, I had no desire to show off what forty hours at a desk per week had done for my body. Which was precisely nothing.

Libby threw herself down on the cushions and slithered into a sitting position. Two gold champagne buckets were already set out, keeping the booze frosty in front of the heaters.

I settled in on one side of Libby with Mags on the other. It was nice to be outside and away from Olly and Leon, and I felt a bit of tension leave my shoulders. Just us friends, together. I felt even more relaxed when Libby sipped champagne from the bottle and burped ostentatiously. Even Mags allowed her face to form a smile at that. Laugh lines be damned.

'Oh my God, do you remember when you absolutely let rip that night in halls and it echoed right down the corridor?' Mags said.

'And people started opening their doors to see what the fuck was going on?' I laughed.

'So like twenty people were watching when you threw up on that fake plant,' Mags finished.

'What happened to that thing?' I asked.

'I think they had to burn it.' Maggie took a swig from the bottle, eyes glittering with humour.

'No! You guys are horrible,' Libby cried in fake outrage.

'How about when Maggie went for a pee behind that car and it drove off?'

I snorted champagne out of my nose. It hurt, a lot, but not enough to quell the beginning of my hysterical wheezing.

'She didn't even notice,' I managed to get out.

'She did when she tried to lean on it and fell down.'

Mags took a slice of orange from her discarded cocktail and threw it at Libby. It landed on the front of her gold dress, leaving a sticky round mark. She just laughed harder. I'd held my breath, thinking of the stain that was going to be there come morning, but relaxed. If she didn't care, I didn't care.

'Han, which winter ball was it when you ended up in the lake?' Mags asked.

'Second year!' Libby and I cried in sync. 'Oh my God, that was nearly the death of me. Can you imagine the newspaper write-up? "Student dressed as slutty elf perishes in freak ice-skating accident."'

'Is it still skating if you don't have, you know, skates on?' Libby asked.

'Ice-shuffling then. Anyway, you dared me to.'

'I did no such thing.'

'You did! I had to skate . . . er, shuffle, across the lake and you had to . . . what was it she had to do?' I asked Maggie.

Her face screwed up in concentration, pushing back the years and the drinks of both this party and that one to get at the memory. 'I . . . think she had to get with one of the members of the band they hired? The ones who were dressed like—'

'Pick up a penguin!' Libby and I chorused, collapsing into giggles.

'Yes! And then you had to get his bowtie as proof. Which you never did. So I guess Hannah won.'

'She did not!' Libby said. 'She didn't make it over the lake. She fell in.'

'My leg fell in. The rest of me made it onto the bank,' I pointed out. The memory of that freezing water shooting up my leg made me shiver. There'd only been candy cane striped tights between me and the water under the lake's icy crust. It hadn't even felt cold; it had felt like hot needles hitting my whole leg at once. I was lucky I'd been a metre away from land and able to fling myself forward onto the snowy bank. At nineteen, I'd not really appreciated what might have happened if I'd gone in right in the centre of the lake. Still, there was no point fretting over what might have happened if things had gone differently almost a decade ago. I was fine and it was now all just a stupid story.

'And Libs didn't get the tie . . . so it's a draw,' Maggie said.

Halfway through a sip of champagne, I spluttered into my glass.

'What?' Maggie asked.

I just shook my head and laughed. Maggie had a habit of cracking me up by missing the obvious. The fact that Libby hadn't managed to get the tie meant that our competition was just that – a tie. One of those things that was only really funny in the moment, to an alcohol-fuzzed brain.

It was a fun time, sitting out there and reliving our old stories. I sat back at one point, watching Libby retelling the tale of our five-hour-long walk home from a festival, her face lit up with it, and reminded myself that this was what I still came to these things for. To sit around, get trashed, and relive those moments together. Like some kind of oral tradition passed down from ancient crones to our hysterical arses. Shared history, shared stories and sh . . . ampagne.

But, as with those times themselves, it couldn't last.

'Babe,' Olly called from the door to the viewing room. 'We're out of Moscow mules.'

'OK! I'll mix up some more,' Libby trilled back. She rolled her eyes at me, looking just like her old self for a moment. 'It's vodka, ginger beer and lime. How hard is that?'

'Don't get me started.' Maggie had picked herself up off the cushions and was brushing her dress off. 'Leon still can't work our coffee machine. It's literally one button.'

'Is that the only button he can't find?' Libby snorted.

Mags meaningfully raised one perfect eyebrow, setting us all off again.

'You're so lucky not to have to deal with that kind of thing,' Libby tossed over her shoulder at me, as we headed inside. 'Sometimes I wish I'd given up on men, too.'

Just like with my dip into the lake, that sobered me up real quick. I set my teeth and braced my newly tensed shoulders.

Our trip down memory lane was at an end and we were back to the present. Libby, Maggie and Hannah were a thing of the past. It was Libby and Olly, Maggie and Leon, then Hannah following after. The toilet paper on their shoe.

'Oi, Han,' Harry called, one hand on the doorframe as he swung into view, jacket discarded, the familiar shapes of his amateurish tattoos cavorting over his arms like a comic strip. He waved a cocktail shaker at me. 'Get over here and try this brandy Alexander. Little Lord Fauntleroy here thinks he can taste the difference between brandy and cognac.'

And Harry, thank God.

CHAPTER FIVE

Armed with a second round of fresh mules and a brandy Alexander, I settled into the viewing room and pretended not to notice the lines and smudges of white powder between the decimated hors d'oeuvres. Clearly the boys – or at least Leon, given that the residue was plain to see on his ruddy nose – had been having a little party of their own in our absence. I wasn't averse to dabbling in chemical enhancement, but the hard stuff wasn't my scene. It wasn't Harry's either, at least to my knowledge, but he was pretty laid back about what other people wanted to put in their bodies. I wasn't going to spoil anyone's time either. Instead I helped myself to some prosciutto-wrapped figs and wondered if there were chefs somewhere below us still churning out nibbles.

I was happy to just vibe to the music for a bit and drink cocktails, which really were good. It had been a long journey and I felt almost jetlagged, despite having travelled by the slowest means available.

I hadn't been keeping an eye on the time at all, so when all the spotlights started to whirl faster and flash, I at first thought I'd had far too much to drink. Which was true but not the reason for the seizure-inducing light show.

'Come on, Han!' Libby clattered to a stop in front of me and hauled me off the sofa with both hands. We nearly fell over into the flaming table and she was laughing as she steered me towards the deck. 'No lagging behind – party's just getting started!'

Out on deck the others were already assembled, the countdown to midnight flashing up in giant numbers on the fibre optic glass of the viewing room. At the touch of a button Olly turned the outside sound system up and the whole boat vibrated with music. Smoke rushed in with the sound, spilling from a machine on the upper deck in a waterfall of violet and blue vapour.

We stood in a tight knot as Libby passed out fresh glasses of champagne. Floating in each glass was a tiny pink pill, dissolving into a pastel trail as it fizzed. Ecstasy, maybe? Some kind of designer drug?

The projection had reached single digits and together we began to count down.

'Nine, eight, seven . . .'

I glanced around as we counted and saw the couples laughing, arms around each other. Time for the traditional kiss at the stroke of midnight. My eyes unwillingly strayed to Harry and I quickly looked down into my drink, debating whether or not to neck it.

'Three, two one – Happy New Year!' we chorused.

'Happy New Year, bitches!' Libby shouted over the music, before downing her glass. She pulled Olly to her with one arm and he planted a kiss on her cheek as she raised her empty glass towards the gold confetti suddenly raining down on us from the top deck.

To my left, Maggie and Leon were attached at the mouth, snogging like teenagers. Sandwiched between the couples, I felt suffocated and lonely all at once. Not having a long-term relationship, even if it was by choice, could really suck sometimes. And New Year's Eve was definitely one of those times. It was especially bad at that moment, without the usual hundred or so other guests to hide amongst, some of whom would also be single. I saw Harry through the coloured smoke, dancing with exaggerated awkwardness – too cool to ever try and do it properly.

Fountains of fireworks were going off, adding brilliant white sparks to the general confusion, and the smoke and shimmering confetti turned the deck into a chaotic wonderland. It helped me to hide the fact that I'd not downed my own drink. Instead I tipped it into the hot tub. I wasn't going to start doing random unknown drugs just because the night had fallen a little flat for me. Everyone else had taken theirs though, and whatever it was kicked in quickly. I wasn't surprised – Libby had spared no expense on the best of everything, clearly.

Soon, Olly and Libby were dancing in a clear space that had been designated as 'the dance floor'. They were ankle deep in coloured fog and the lights from several drifting flares overhead cast long shadows through the blue mist. Maggie had slipped into the hot tub – dress and all. She looked mesmerising, an oil-slick mermaid speckled with gold leaf. Leon looked set to join her, unbuttoning his shirt as she watched from the bubbling water. Harry was twirling with his arms out, head craned back to look at the sky, a cigarette weeping ash down his front. The last drunk girl at the school disco, that was him. All he was missing was 'Dancing on my Own' on the speakers and a plastic cup of spiked cola.

It was all very festive, but I couldn't get into the mood, even when Harry grinned and waved his hands at me, wafting me onto the dance floor. I gave him a smile but wrinkled my nose and ambled back to the viewing room where I collapsed onto a couch. I'd only been at the party a few hours, but I felt like years had passed. Maybe it was the journey catching up with me. Maybe it was because things weren't as crazy as I'd come to expect from Libby. She'd reined it in this year. Not that I was in much of a state to get crazy given I kept thinking about the giant bed waiting downstairs for me.

Harry appeared not long after and sat down beside me, our shoulders pressed together. After some consideration he smashed two canapés together into a sandwich. After munching for a while, he pulled a face and swallowed with difficulty.

'Not as good as it looked?' I asked, feeling sleepy and warm.

'No . . . I think there was actual gold in that. Something gritty.'

'You sure it wasn't . . .' I indicated the *Scarface* set dressing with a tilt of my head and Harry raised an eyebrow. 'Don't they say coke doesn't pair well with salmon?'

'I think that's steroids. Coke's better with camembert.'

'Ah, well, I bow to your superior knowledge . . .'

'What's up, champ?'

'Hmmm?' I said, distracted by Harry's arm coming to rest over my shoulders. 'Oh, just knackered from the drive.'

'You should've let me buy you a plane ticket,' Harry said. 'Still, you made it here and the night is . . . over, but the morning's just started – fancy a dance?'

In truth my feet still hurt a bit from the trudge down

from the car park. I should have left my Skechers on or at least brought them with me for the walk back tomorrow. I hated that I'd let my pride rule my common sense. Still, I let Harry pull me up off the sofa and out onto the deck. It was a party after all. And it wasn't like I got to see him all the time. We only got together a handful of times in a year thanks to our work schedules and budgetary restrictions. Though he didn't have those anymore. Maybe this coming year would be different.

Harry twirled me around the deck, doing a waltz that fitted with his semi-ironic gentleman act. After a while, I noticed that Maggie and Leon were dancing in the hot tub, turning in circles and doing a lot of . . . grinding. I caught Libby's eye across the dance floor and she pulled a face at the performance. A moment later Olly took her arm and they both headed down to the lower deck. Possibly for a breather and some non-alcoholic refreshment, which sounded like a good idea. I was feeling a bit dizzy and wondered if any of the other drinks had been laced as well, or if it was just the combination of tiredness and alcohol.

'I need some water,' I sort of half-shouted into Harry's ear. The music was quite loud now. I wondered if I ought to turn it down but had no idea how to go about it. Olly had used a remote before and I didn't know where he'd put it.

'I'll get you some.'

'It's fine – I'll be, like, two seconds.'

I teetered down the steps to the lower deck, thankful they were enclosed in glass or some kind of Perspex, even though it squeaked under my sweaty hands as I used it for balance. Once back in the lobby area I tried to work out where the kitchen might be. Did boats have kitchens? This one probably did, right? I was actually surprised I hadn't seen any waiters or even bar staff – normally there were masses of them at Libby's parties. Though perhaps that was part of the whole 'stripped-down guest list' thing.

The door on the opposite side to the stairwell to the bedrooms seemed a good starting place for my search, but that only led to a toilet. It held a lot of white marble and two of everything – twin cubicle loos, twin sinks, even twin white orchids and little machines for heating up towels. I contemplated swigging some water from the tap, but didn't fancy getting my dress wet or worse, getting caught slurping like a dog.

After having no luck at deck level I slithered down the glowing steps towards the bedrooms. The kitchen was the second door I tried down there. It wasn't enormous but one of every conceivable appliance had been squeezed in, from a juicer loaded with oranges to a sous vide machine, which I only recognised from watching *MasterChef*. I took a glass from a rack and approached the gleaming American-style fridge, which dominated the end wall. The front of the fridge promised to dispense not only ice but also two different kinds of water – cold and not as cold. I opted for 'not as cold' with ice to be contrarian.

Whilst I gulped my drink down, I wandered around admiring the spotless cookware mounted on the walls. I'd seen some of this stuff as prizes on American cooking shows; Japanese folded steel knives, Le Creuset (naturally) and an honest-to-God set of gold pans from Artemest. I knew for a fact that just one of those things cost over two thousand pounds. For a stew pot. Because it was so ridiculous that it had been seared into my memory. I also knew that Libby couldn't cook anything more complicated than a jacket potato and Olly apparently couldn't mix his own three-ingredient cocktails. Maybe they had a personal chef? I took a sauté pan down and tested its weight. I could probably get a great risotto out of it. My pans at home were thin and heated unevenly, leading to crispy patches and underdone areas.

'Think you can get one of those in your bag before you go?'

I whirled round and found Leon leaning in the doorway, watching me. He'd not bothered to put his blazer back on after his dip in the hot tub and looked flushed from the heat.

I forced a smile, hoping he was joking and didn't actually think I'd try and steal cookware. Or anything for that matter. But even if it was a joke, I didn't appreciate it. He stepped into the kitchen and the door swung closed behind him with a click.

'Water?' I asked, to be polite.

He nodded. I took down a fresh glass and went back to the fridge to fill it. When I turned back around Leon had crossed the room and was only a few inches away from me. I ducked to one side instinctively, already apologising nonsensically for being in his way, but he brought both arms up, essentially penning me in against the tomb-sized refrigerator.

'You know, I've always liked you, Hannah,' he said, breathing salmon and brandy cream against my face.

This close I could count the grains of coke on his sweaty upper lip. My insides turned the temperature of the glass in my hand. Shit. What was he playing at? I put on what I hoped was a flattered but amused expression.

'Might not want to let Mags catch you saying that,' I joked.

Instead of recoiling at the reminder that he was engaged

to one of my best friends, he leaned closer with a soft laugh. I felt his breath on my neck and cringed.

'Doesn't that just make it better, though? Bet you're wet through thinking about getting one over on her.'

The words were one thing, filling me with disgust so strong that I struggled to find a response, but it was the touch of his sticky tongue that snapped me out of my shocked silence. I shuddered as he slicked it up my neck, my skin erupting in goose pimples as my belly filled with acid. I shoved him, ducked under his arm and tipped the glass of iced water down the front of his trousers as I did so. My legs were shaking as I wiped my neck with my hand, tripping out of grabbing distance. I wasn't scared exactly, but I still pivoted to keep my eyes on him, suddenly worried he might come after me. I only stopped when I was within a foot of the doorway.

'Fuck!' Leon glared at me incredulously. 'What the hell did you do that for?'

My eyes were wide with disbelief. Was he so out of it that he didn't know what he'd just done? Or was this just normal for him? Did he make a habit of cornering Mags' friends and slobbering all over them? Jesus. I had to tell her. I had to get back to the others and away from him.

I was almost out the door when Leon got his arm around my waist and lifted me, laughing. I yelped and flailed out, trying to grab hold of something, but there was nothing within reach. He twisted me around and pinned me between the kitchen island and the wet front of his trousers. I felt afraid for the first time since he'd appeared behind me. What was he going to do?

'Leon!' I slapped at his chest, squeezing my eyes shut. 'Let me go! Now!'

'Hey! Calm down – look, here,' he said, like I was a stray dog, and he was trying to bribe me with a biscuit.

It took an effort to convince my eyes to open. As if what I couldn't see wouldn't hurt me.

'There, see . . . knew you'd like that.' Leon smirked, stroking a wad of notes against the tip of my nose. The cold metal of his money clip tapped my lip. 'How about we play piggy bank?'

For a moment I was too disgusted to be scared. I struggled harder, no longer worried about accidentally scratching or hurting him. When his hold on me tightened, I raised my voice and bellowed right in his face. 'Get. Your. Hands. Off. Me!'

Either the message finally got through to him or my sudden volume had him worried about being caught. Leon let me go as if I'd caught fire and pushed me away from him. I skittered over the shiny floor towards the door, knees trembling. I could feel tears starting to choke up the back of my throat.

'The way Maggie tells it, you get around enough for free – so what's the problem? You should be flattered, fat bitch,' Leon snapped as I left.

In a perfect world I'd have had a retort ready to fire back at him, but I didn't. I knew if I stopped or opened my mouth I'd just break down. Instead I blundered into the hallway and, blinded by tears, made for the door to my room. Unfortunately I couldn't remember which giant mirrored door was which and ended up trying a locked door and then ending up in the powder room instead. It had a lock on it though, so I wasn't complaining. I clicked the tiny gold bolt into place and collapsed onto a white leather pouffe.

What the hell had Leon been playing at? Why had he

thought he could do that to me and get away with it? Jesus, what was I going to tell Mags? Even as I thought it, his words 'The way Maggie tells it . . .' rang in my head. Of course she knew about my casual relationships; I didn't make much of a secret that I wasn't out for anything serious. Serious relationships were serious risks, and I didn't want to feel that way, ever. Watching Mum lose Dad had been bad enough.

What if I told Maggie what he'd done and she didn't believe me? I didn't want to believe that she wouldn't, but she'd been with him for years and we only saw one another sporadically. She probably felt like she could trust him more than me. I could almost hear her voice in my head. *Oh, Han, I really think you've had too much to drink. I'm sure he didn't mean it to sound like that.* Worse would be trying to get her to believe that he'd go after me whilst she was only one deck away – his rich, model-beautiful fiancée. She was a fashion designer, she had hundreds of thousands of pounds and a waist you could do a bracelet up around. I glanced at a mirror and saw what a mess I looked – blotchy faced and with damp patches all over my dress.

No, I couldn't talk to her right now. Maybe tomorrow, once we'd all sobered up? I could get her alone and explain it all properly. If I tried now, I'd just get my words mixed up and end up getting upset and angry with myself. I also didn't want Harry hearing about it right now. He'd probably flip out and start a fight and it would ruin Libby's party. I didn't want to do that to her, not after all the effort she'd gone to. Especially not when she'd made a point of inviting me to such a small get-together.

Slowly my heartrate returned to normal, tears drying on my cheeks. I got up and dabbed cold water on my face. My makeup was a little streaky, but I cleaned myself up as best I could. A drawer under the sink provided me with cooling eye gel and I let that work its magic whilst I took some deep breaths.

I listened for any sign of Leon outside before I unlocked the door. I wasn't really scared of him, not now that horrible moment in the kitchen was over. He'd tried to bribe me into sex. He hadn't tried to assault me or even gripped me that hard. I knew that didn't make it OK, not at all, but I reassured myself that he probably wasn't still out there, prowling around. He'd made his move and now it was over. He'd probably gone back to Maggie instead. I shuddered just thinking about it. I had to tell her once we were all a bit more with it. She deserved to know what she was engaged to.

I was about to open the door when I heard footsteps; shoes and heels. Was it Leon with Maggie in tow? Had he told her a pack of lies about me and brought her along to exact some revenge? I held my breath and listened.

'I told you it was nothing.' That was Olly's drawling voice.

'I definitely heard a shout,' Libby replied. The pair of them had obviously been in one of the other rooms and had heard me yell, though apparently not clearly.

'It was probably you,' Olly purred. I heard lips smacking and felt my face burn. They'd snuck off for a mid-party romp. If I stepped out now, they'd think I'd followed them down here like a weirdo. Fantastic.

'Sounds like everyone's having fun upstairs,' Libby said. 'I told you this would be a great night.'

I could in fact still hear the music blasting, bass humming through the boat itself like we were in the body of a giant guitar. My phone was in my room and I had no idea what time it was or how long it had been since midnight. Time on the yacht felt slippery, unreliable.

'Hmm . . . though I would've liked to have been apprised of the guest list,' Olly said. 'We did say it would be more . . . exclusive, this time. The right people, the right atmosphere.'

I felt myself stiffen, remembering the way Olly had 'greeted' me earlier. Maybe this wasn't about me though. Maybe it was about Harry. Olly had never really warmed to him. It was as if he still saw Harry as competition because Libby had hooked up with him once.

'Oh come on. I kept it small, intimate . . . no staff . . .' More lip smacking.

'I know, I'd just be having a better time if your povo friend wasn't sitting there like a starving dog all night.'

It was like being drenched in ice water. I felt my skin tighten all over and my breath hitched as humiliation and shock shot through me. I waited for Libby to say something. To snap that of course I was welcome at her party. We'd been friends since we were kids, for God's sake. She'd been there for me when my dad died. It was Libs who begged her parents to let me stay over when Mum had to go with Dad to hospital. She'd called Mags and they'd both sat up with me all night by the phone, the three of us holding hands.

'Aww, baby,' Libby chided him gently. 'Hannah's one of my oldest friends. Of course I invited her.'

My heart swooped, only to crack in two with her next words.

'She's like . . . the first cheque you frame when you hit it big. A little reminder of where you've come from. Having her here . . . doesn't it feel good? Doesn't it just make you appreciate everything we have a little more?'

49

I barely heard Olly's response or their retreating footsteps. My ears were actually ringing as blood rushed to my face. My cheeks burned with humiliation and my heart was shattered in my chest. I couldn't breathe. I slid down the wall to the floor and sat with my head in my hands. Sobbing.

I'd known for a long time, deep down, that Libby thought she was better than me. Hell, not even deep down. It was on the surface like a great big raw nerve that she occasionally ran right over in her fucking Dior shoes. Reminded of the 'gift' that was shredding my feet, I wrestled them off and threw them across the powder room.

It wasn't a surprise to learn that Libby cared about the difference between our lives. Or, to be honest with myself, that she took some kind of pleasure in that divide. I knew she liked to show off her money . . . and Olly's money now. That she didn't give me expensive shoes or invite me to blow-out parties on yachts just because she wanted me to have fun. Libby was a show-off, even before she got her own money and started moving up in the world. She'd shown off about her gap year and her exam results and every boy she brought back to halls. Like a cat dropping a dead canary in front of you saying 'look at me, look at what I've got'.

Still, I'd managed to convince myself that it was mostly unintentional. That she and Maggie were just somewhat out of touch. They didn't mean to put me down at the same time as they showed themselves off. Only, apparently, they did. Their lives were all the shinier for having my grubby nose pressed up against the window, watching it all.

Well, not anymore.

As I gathered the shoes and wiped yet more tears from my face, I made myself a promise. As soon as the sun came

50

up on the New Year, I'd be out of here. Off of this boat and out of their lives for good. I was done being someone's 'povo' mate. I was going back to my normal life to have normal friends and enjoy myself just fine without all this ridiculous gilding to make me feel worthless.

I let myself out of the powder room and started looking for my bedroom. I hadn't gone more than a few steps, though, before Harry's voice echoed down the stairwell.

'Can you just calm the fuck down!?'

The sound of glass shattering cut through the deafening music, followed by multiple voices shouting and a scream that was unmistakably Maggie. I didn't stop to put my shoes on, I just ran for the stairs.

CHAPTER SIX

Up on deck I spotted the remains of the champagne glass pyramid just in time. I'd nearly run right over it in my bare feet. The foaming champagne surf lapped around Harry and Leon's shoes as they scuffled a few feet from me. Harry's lip was split and he was warding Leon off with his hands out like a referee. Leon was drenched in sweat, chest heaving as he glared at him. Whatever Libby had given us at midnight, it apparently wasn't mixing well with the cocaine and alcohol already coursing through Leon's system. He looked like he was either five seconds away from blowing his top completely, or having a heart attack.

Libby and Mags were in a corner of the lobby, eyes wide. Several feet away Olly was leaning against a wall and watching this display like he was about to narrate a BBC documentary called 'Coke Heads in their Natural Habitat'. He seemed to be waiting for Harry's reaction, watching with flint-eyed disinterest as Leon advanced on him. Why wasn't he doing something? Anything? I took a step forward, careful of the glass, unsure if I should stand next to Harry or try and get between him and Leon, but knowing that I had to do something.

It was only then that I noticed that there was a seventh person on deck – an annoyed-looking man standing behind Harry with his arms folded. He was older than us, with grey hair standing up at all angles, and was wearing shorts, which seemed weird given the cold night. It looked like he'd just rolled out of bed, and judging by the jumper and slippers, he had grabbed whatever was available. In one of his hands I could just see the greenish glow of an old-school mobile keypad.

'You turn the music off or I'll call the police,' he shouted over the sound system, which was still blaring. 'It's not late now, it's early – morning!'

The stranger was clearly exasperated and judging from the fact he was yelling in English, I guessed I wasn't the only one present who didn't know any Italian. That or no one felt inclined to help Harry with the situation.

'We will. We will, all right? Olly?' Harry said, raising his brows in exasperation. 'A little help from the host here, eh?'

Olly performed a fully-body sigh, but reached into his trouser pocket and took out the remote. With just one click the boat fell silent. Except for Leon, whom I could now hear swearing at the stranger, calling him all sorts of names in between demands for Harry to move and for Olly to put the music back on.

I glanced at Maggie but she wasn't looking at me, or at Leon. She seemed to be watching the flames in the fireplace. It looked unlikely that she'd step in to calm her fiancé down. Honestly, I couldn't blame her. I wasn't sure there was much she could do with him in this state.

'Hey, look,' Harry said to the stranger, struggling to push

Leon away as he lunged forwards again. 'We're sorry – it's New Year's, we've had a bit to drink and it's gotten a bit rowdy. We'll calm it down and get off to bed and leave you in peace, all right?'

The man looked us over, one by one. It was easy to see how unimpressed he was with the lot of us. Despite the fact that I'd just been put very firmly into my place as an outsider, I felt embarrassed just the same. I just wanted to get off this boat and go home. If I'd been sober enough to drive I might've walked right past him and run to the car park. Hell, if I'd thought I'd be safer sleeping in my car in the middle of the city I'd have done that. It was only the memory of how scary it had been to camp out even in the quiet countryside that stopped me.

'Every year it's the same. Fucking tourists – leaving mess, making noise. This is my home, not a holiday camp. I've been awake all night and now I need to work all day!'

'We're sorry,' Harry repeated. 'We'll be gone soon and it'll all be quiet again. We're going to clean up . . .'

'For the next people to come in and do it all again?' the man said. 'It's worse every year now. All of you, piss off home!'

'We've paid to be here!' Libby yelled back, apparently finding her tongue.

'Not that we will again,' Olly drawled. 'We'll be taking our business elsewhere, as will our friends when they hear about the reception we've received here. If you want to turn away paying visitors, go ahead.'

The stranger rolled his eyes and waved a hand at them, shooing them away. 'Money is all you care about? Typical! This is why you ruin everything. You think we need your money? Fuck you!'

'Hey, fuck *you*!' Leon jeered, flinging a vase that missed

Harry by inches, crashing into the glass lobby wall and making a spider web of cracks. Leon laughed at the damage, sniffed and picked up a half-empty cocktail, downing it in one.

'Leon! That was crystal!' Libby shrieked.

'That's also my bloody window,' Olly sneered. 'Learn to aim or let the adults talk.'

I unfroze and took a few steps forward, finding my voice. 'Leon, why don't you sit down for a second? Let's calm things down.'

'Fuck you . . . bitch,' Leon snapped, tossing the empty glass in my direction. Either he hadn't meant it to hit me or, as Olly said, his aim was shit. The glass landed on the deck half a metre from my feet and exploded into shards like ice.

'Oi! Keep that up and you're going over the side, mate,' Harry said.

In response Leon looked around for another projectile. He snatched up an empty beer bottle and mimed throwing it at me. 'Try it, go on.'

Harry tensed and I saw him move forward. My heart was beating so hard I felt sick. I didn't want him to get hurt. (Though there was no denying the fact that seeing him defending me so adamantly was stirring feelings I thought I'd put behind me.)

'You're animals. Disgusting,' the stranger shouted.

'Olly, can you do something?' Libby said, glaring at her husband.

Olly finally made a move, slouching away from the wall and sidling over to Harry and the enraged neighbour. He ignored Leon completely, as if he were a small child that was a nanny's concern, not his. As he went, he pulled something out of his pocket. A money clip – gold, of course. He casually licked his thumb and peeled off some notes, holding them out to the neighbour like he was a taxi driver waiting for his fare.

'The fuck is this?' the man growled through clenched teeth. 'You think you can do what you like in our city as long as you pay us?'

'I think I'm tired of this whole thing and I want to get back to my party,' Olly said. 'Now get off my yacht.'

'I should call the police. All of you. You—'

'Go,' Olly said, tonelessly. Like he was dismissing a waiter. 'Now.'

The shift from Leon's outright aggression to Olly's tightly wound condescending approach was sharp. It didn't feel like it was making things any better though. In fact, the tension around me seemed to draw tighter, like something was about to snap.

For a moment I was sure the irate local was going to deck him. After the way Olly had spoken to him I kind of wanted to see it, to be honest. His sun-wizened face screwed up like he was considering it, but he settled for snorting up and ejecting a massive dollop of spit. It hit Olly in the centre of his chest and dribbled down his pristine white polo neck. I expected Olly to look disgusted or to get angry, but he laughed. A short, sharp bark of genuine amusement. Like an exotic bird had just crapped on him. As the man turned to go, he slapped Olly's hand and the banknotes in it were scattered, snatched up by the cold breeze.

'That guy's nuts,' Libby said, at the same time as I thought, 'that guy's my hero'.

'I think it might be time for me to turn in,' I said to no one in particular.

'Turn the music back on, Ol.' Leon was seemingly in a better mood now that the man was gone. He chugged the last of a bottle of beer and held it up high in a mock toast. 'Let's get wrecked.'

'I think you've wrecked enough of my things, Leon,' Olly said tightly.

Leon threw the empty bottle against the wall with a whoop. 'I'll write you a cheque.'

It was like watching a minor royal and a drunk rugby player go head-to-head. I might have stayed to watch if I hadn't been so emotionally overextended and worn out. I glanced over at Maggie only to find that she'd melted away at some point. To where, I had no idea, but she hadn't passed me, so she wasn't below deck. Maybe she'd decided to go back up to the top for some peace. I was kind of worried for her, given the state Leon was in. Libby was still there though, watching Olly bicker with Leon. She didn't look my way so I turned and headed for the stairs. My night was officially over. I didn't want to be around any of them right now, especially her and Leon.

'Hey, you OK?' Harry caught up with me when I was only halfway down the stairs and lightly tapped my shoulder. I turned to face him and realised that his lip was bleeding more than I'd thought – his teeth were stained with blood and it had started to drip down his chin.

'Are *you* OK?' I asked, reaching for his face. Harry gently batted my hands away.

'Ah, just a scrape. You know public school boys can't hit for shit. It's the constant wanking, it destroys the wrist bones.'

So it wasn't the stranger who'd hit him. Figured. My money was on Leon. Olly wouldn't get his hands dirty.

Though I could see him paying someone to do the fighting for him.

'I'm . . .' I considered telling him – about Leon, about Libby – but really, what would that accomplish? He'd just want to address it then and there. That was who Harry was and it was something I normally liked about him, how he didn't believe in letting things fester. Only I didn't want to prolong this awful night with questions, arguments and accusations. Right then all I cared about was getting my head down on my king-size bed. I wanted to smear my mascara all over Libby's expensive sheets with a big old cry, and then get the hell out of there once I was sober enough to drive the twelve hours home.

'I'm a bit tired,' I said. 'I'll see you tomorrow, OK?'

'All right. Listen, don't worry about things up here – I've got it handled, OK?' Harry squeezed my shoulder and gave me a bloody, but comforting, smile. It reminded me of the time we'd gone out clubbing whilst Libby and Maggie spent the summer holidays in Rome. I'd twisted my ankle and he'd carried me all the way to his place and tucked me into bed. Prince Charming with a nose ring. My heart flipped over at the memory of watching him frown in his sleep, curled up on the floor by the bed.

'Sure. Thanks,' I said, managing a smile back, my voice wobbly.

I watched him head off after Leon, who'd gone out onto the deck by the helicopter. As I carried on down the stairs I heard Olly sneer to Libby, 'I'm surprised she didn't go after the money.' Libby's playful shushing was a final slap to the face.

In my room I saw the bottle of whisky and the expensive chocolates I'd brought along with me as a gift. In three quick moves I swept them up, dumped them in a drawer and slammed it shut. Just looking at them made me feel small and stupid.

After checking twice that the door was locked and then wedging the heel of one of my shoes into the crack at the bottom as a doorstop, I got undressed. The silk dress was stained with champagne on the shoulder and damp with spilled water from the kitchen incident. Sweat patches ringed the underarms and it had left marks on my skin where it was too tight. I scrunched the whole thing up and shoved it into the gold bin under the vanity. I was such an idiot to think squeezing myself into that thrifted dress would earn me some kind of reprieve from Libby's comments. As if she wouldn't clock it immediately from miles off, because how else could I afford something like that? Maggie, with her fashion collaborations, was even worse. She could probably smell the Oxfam on me the moment I arrived.

After using the cupboard-sized wet room I got into bed. Safely tucked into my Primark PJs, I turned off the lights and lay there, wide awake and fuming. I should have said something to Libby. To all of them. I should have loudly announced that Libby was a snob and her husband was insufferable. That Maggie was snide and miserable to be around, and her fiancé had just slobbered over my neck. What had I done instead? Put myself to bed and said nothing to anyone.

I thought of all the times Libby had been there for me; Mags, too. We'd started a new school together, friends from day one simply because we were all four and sat at the same table. We played, shared toys, shared lunches. We went through puberty together – Mags gave me my first cigarette and Libby supplied the tampon for my first period when it came unexpectedly on a class trip. I'd sat between them on the coach that day and shared their headphones because I didn't have an iPod. Libby and I had worked together to shoplift a pregnancy test for Mags at age fifteen. We got properly drunk together for the first time and held each other's hair whilst we threw up. Libby tried to give Mags a bob and we all went with her to get it fixed at a salon, and when Libby's dad got remarried to a woman only five years older than her, we all got together and squeezed Nair into the woman's shampoo – a coven of three, stirring our cauldron in secret.

Those were memories I couldn't replace and didn't want to. I didn't have sisters. I didn't have my mum or dad anymore. Mags and Libby were the only people with whom I shared a history. Only tonight I'd found out that Libby thought that history was worthless. That *I* was worthless.

I had other mates at home, obviously, from work and from the craft fairs I'd done back when I was trying to build my own business. Libby and Maggie weren't just friends though. They were my oldest friends; practically sisters. I'd had wobbles before, times I felt like maybe I didn't belong with them anymore, but I'd never felt like this. My unease had usually come from not wanting to show them up. Or so I'd told myself. I'd had to get used to them having more money, more everything, than me, and I'd come down hard on myself for my issues with them, telling myself not to be jealous or ungrateful. But I saw now that what I'd really been was hurt and upset. I'd just never let myself acknowledge it before.

Lying there in that bed and listening to the music as it came on again, I decided that I was never going to see any of them again. I'd make an exception for Harry, of course.

That was . . . unless he turned into one of them. I didn't want to believe that it was possible, but hadn't Mags been generous and sweet until her dad got her in the door at a big fashion label? Teaching me to sew, helping to rework thrifted dresses for uni parties? And hadn't Libby been brutally honest but supportive until she inherited all that money and met Olly? Always there with advice, telling me to dust myself off and try again when I got stressed out over a project or failed a module?

A tiny part of me wondered if they'd ever been those things. If I'd just been kidding myself all this time. Maybe Libby and Mags had always been shitty to me, and the money thing had just made it worse. Made them worse. How long had I been making excuses for them and convincing myself they didn't mean it? I felt like an idiot. Even Harry had noticed it, had tried to ask me about it more than once back in uni. I'd just brushed it off as him not understanding how girls were together. I hadn't wanted to look weak or pitiable to anyone. Especially not to Harry.

God, he probably thought I was such a sad-sack. I cringed at the idea of him pitying me. Poor stupid Hannah who didn't even notice her 'best friends' were making a joke out of her. Not anymore though. For all the shitty things I'd gone through since setting foot on this yacht, at least I was no longer living in blissful ignorance. No, there was nothing blissful about my mood. I set an alarm for seven, rolled over into the pillows and cried until I passed out.

CHAPTER SEVEN

I'm not sure if it could be called sleep, but whatever it was left me feeling stripped to the bone and sober enough to drive. When my alarm went off I silenced it immediately, hoping I was the only one who'd be awake at this ungodly hour after the night before. I crawled out of bed with a mouth like dirt and shoved my PJs back into my overnight bag. I got changed into my travel clothes – tie-dye gym leggings and a sweatshirt from one of Mags' more affordable lines. I'd bought them myself at least, in a stupid attempt at 'supporting her'. As if she needed my support, or even cared if she got it. Once I got back to my Skechers, the heels were going in the bin up by the car park. I never wanted to look at them again. Even the idea of walking up to the car in them sounded like torture.

I was hunting around for my phone charger when I found a pair of sheepskin slippers under the bed. They were tied together with a ribbon and obviously new, probably intended to be used by guests. I paused and wondered what Libby would have to say about me pinching her guest slippers to walk home in. Then I realised I never had to find out what she thought about it. I never had to speak to her again. The feeling of relief that went through me was astonishing. I felt like I'd just dodged a twenty-year prison sentence. I put the slippers on and left the shoes on the floor of my room. This Cinderella was going back to her old life, even if that meant shutting myself back in the attic, with the mice.

With my bag clutched under one arm I crept into the corridor. Everything was silent so it was probably safe to assume that everyone was still asleep, or at least unconscious.

When I reached the stairs, I was quite glad I'd worn the slippers. The fluorescent steps were spattered with slices of orange, sticky puddles of cocktail and shards of glass. I picked my way over it all, grateful for the thick soles on the mules.

I emerged into the blinding light of morning and squinted around the lobby area. The destruction Leon had caused last night was still there. No one had made any effort to clean it up or contain the damage. Not that I'd really expected them to. Libby probably had a cleaning crew scheduled for today. A whole horde of uniformed maids and handymen to come in and scrub the place clean and fix or replace anything damaged so that her guests could trash the place all over again tonight. I hoped those people were at least getting paid double – or triple – their usual rate. The place was an absolute wreck.

Aside from all the broken glasses, vases and spilled flowers that Leon had left to get trampled together, there were jagged slashes in one of the white leather couches – caused by what, I had no idea – and the table looked like it had been dusted for fingerprints. Which it probably would be if the police saw the sheer amount of cocaine on display. It also smelled like someone had pissed somewhere in the room. A horrible old pub toilet stench. I retched as the smell hit my poor, hungover brain. I rushed to the bathroom and only just got my head over the toilet before I threw up. When I went to get some water I realised the sink was already full of someone else's red wine vomit. With streaming eyes I backed away as I tried to regain control over my stomach. It wasn't easy, as when I opened my eyes again, I noticed a used condom plastered to the edge of the marble vanity. This whole place needed bleaching to the core.

That was it, I had to leave right now or I'd be vomiting until the others woke up and found me. I'd get some water at the first shop I passed. And some paracetamol because my head was killing me. Though, of course, I remembered as I left the lobby and was slapped in the face by the cold sea air, it was New Year's Day and everything would probably be shut. Surely petrol stations had to be open though? I'd find something.

The sea breeze braced me and washed away the clinging odours of the inside of the boat. I breathed deeply and let out a long sigh. In front of me the early morning light sparkled off the grey water and I could see all the way to where the sky met the sea in a blurry line. Part of the coastline rose out of the mist in the distance. Gorgeous. Nearly worth the whole experience of last night and the twelve-hour car journey that lay ahead of me. God, how long was I allowed to be parked here anyway? I'd assumed it was free on bank holidays and I'd checked in with my debit card, but what if there was a limit? Why hadn't I tried to translate the sign?

With cold panic prickling over my skin I looked for the gangplank. I thought it had been opposite the lobby doors, but I must've remembered wrong. I circled the glass-walled room to the opposite side of the deck, beyond ready to get on the road and near some sort of caffeinated beverage.

Only, the gangplank wasn't there either. I was really irritated now. How much had I had to drink? Or was this the result of the others messing around after I'd gone to bed? It had to be around somewhere. I went back to the lobby doors in case I'd overlooked it whilst blinded by morning sunshine. But I hadn't. There was no gangplank on that side either. The view of the wide, uninterrupted ocean was where the land had been when I'd gone to bed. That distant misty coastline I'd been admiring, was that . . . the harbour?

I took a few steps to the railing and looked out across the water in disbelief. Then, as my hungover brain struggled to take in the enormity of the situation, I walked a circuit of the deck again. At least, it started as a walk. By the time I'd seen the water on all sides of the boat I was running for the stairs, bag abandoned on deck. My feet slithered over orange bits and broken glass as I stumbled into the lower corridor and started shouting Harry's name. I don't know why I was calling for him when it was Olly's bloody boat we were on. Maybe it was because he was the only one I wanted to see, even in that horrible moment where shock was turning into full-fledged fear.

I started trying doors. Powder room, locked door, linen cupboard . . . Finally I found Harry's room with his t-shirt draped over a footstool. The duvet was piled up but I could just about see his head poking out the side.

My feet thundered even over the thick carpet. Within seconds I was shaking Harry awake, less gently than I'd planned. The panic inside me was growing, leaving no space for anything else.

'Wha? Wha's happening?' His eyes shot open and he recoiled from the tiny amount of light in the room. 'Jesus fuck, Hannah! What time is it?'

'We're in the sea,' I said, my brain still trying to put words together that matched the awful discovery I'd just made.

'I know, Han. Go back to bed and sleep it off.'

'No! We are out at sea, Harry.'

That seemed to get through to him. He sat up so quickly that our foreheads knocked together.

'Fuck. Ow. What did you say?' He asked, rubbing his forehead and squinting at mine as if worried he'd hurt me.

'The boat is drifting,' I ground out, finally finding the right words to describe what I'd just seen. What I was only just starting to understand the full impact of. We had drifted out to sea, and I had no idea what to do.

Harry sprang up and ran for the stairs. I heard him swear and hoped he hadn't cut his feet on all the glass. He hadn't been gone long before I heard him running back down the stairs. He was already shouting before his feet hit the floor below.

'Olly! Libs! Wake up! Wake up, it's an emergency!' He reached a mirrored door and pounded on it with his fist. 'Unlock this bloody door and get this thing back to land!'

I heard a groan from behind the door. How long would it take to get some sense out of either of them? For all I knew, Olly had joined Leon and was sleeping off alcohol and a cocaine bender. Could he sail in that state? I had no idea, but I wasn't going to wait around and see. I took the stairs back up to the lower deck and found where I'd dropped my bag. How did you phone the coastguard in Italy? I had the EU emergency services number programmed in, just in case something happened whilst I was on the road, so I dialled it and waited. Then kept waiting. There was no reassuring ring, no voice on the other end of the line. The call just didn't connect. I looked at the screen in time to see the 'low or no signal' notification pop up before it disappeared. My heart thumped once, nauseatingly hard.

What now? Wi-Fi? We hadn't been given a code or anything when we arrived, but surely this floating hotel had internet. It had everything else. I opened the settings on my phone. There'd be a network named something stupid, I was sure. Maybe just like fifteen pound signs and a smiley face.

I stared at the blank screen for a long time, waiting for it to load. It took me several incredulous moments to realise that it *had,* in fact, loaded. There was just no wireless internet. Not even a random hotspot to pick up on. The yacht had a helicopter and a hot tub, but was somehow less technologically enabled than the Caffè Nero I stopped at on my way to work every other day.

'He's coming up,' Harry panted behind me, making me jump. I turned around and saw him standing there, red in the face from rushing around. There were still pillow creases on his anxious face and he was shivering in just his jeans, arms crossed over the wonky skull tattoo on his chest. 'Olly. He'll get us turned around and on our way back.'

I held up my phone, struggling to remain calm. 'I've got no signal. There's no Wi-Fi either.'

'What?' Harry dug his phone out of his jeans. 'You're right. Maybe it got unplugged last night. Things did get a bit crazy. Leon might've decided it looked at him funny.' The weak joke was clearly meant to make me feel better, which it did, sort of.

'Yeah, I see that. Everywhere's a mess. Did Olly decide to take the boat out whilst he was wasted?'

'No. Or I don't think so? I was one of the last ones up – too wired to sleep after all that with the local guy. Leon went looking for Maggie and I found them crashed out on the top deck just after four. Sent them off to bed, but I heard them later in the loo. Olly and Libs were already in bed by then; not sure when they went down, maybe half two? Three? I had a smoke on deck and went in. Everything was fine.'

It was about half seven by this time. We could have been on the move for hours. How long had it taken us to get this far out? How long to get us back? We both looked at the gap in the side of the yacht where the gangplank should have been. Had we drifted, or was someone playing a stupid joke?

Olly finally emerged a moment later, wearing a white monogrammed dressing gown and looking nearly the same colour as it. Libby was behind him, still in her party dress but wearing UGGs.

Olly looked out at the horizon and slowly shook his head. Libby was just as stunned. I wanted to scream at them to move already, but I also knew first-hand how overwhelming it was to see all that water, everywhere. Without the reassuring tether of the gangplank, I was suddenly very aware of how small the yacht was, compared to the vast ocean that surrounded it.

'Where's Mags?' I asked. I didn't really care where or how Leon was after last night.

'I tried to wake them up but they're both really out of it,' Harry explained. 'I'm guessing they maybe took something to get some sleep.'

'Great.' I sighed. Maybe it was for the best though. At least with Leon out for the count there'd be less to worry about. Or so I thought until I looked at the horizon again. 'Are we . . . getting further away?'

Harry looked as well. The coastline seemed fuzzier than before and I couldn't see individual elements anymore, just a sort of grey-green blur.

'Olly, mate, can you get up to the cockpit or whatever?' Harry asked in a slightly strangled voice. I could tell he was keeping a lid on his panic for the moment, like I was trying to do.

'The bridge.'

'What?' Harry said.

'The bridge,' Olly repeated snippily. 'It's not a cockpit. It's the bridge.'

I watched Harry's face contort as panic mixed with fury. In the end he pressed his lips together and gestured at me to speak as if he physically couldn't bring himself to do so.

'Olly, can you go up to the bridge and get us back to shore . . . please?' I threw the please in because I'd started to feel a tiny bit like we were being held hostage. As if getting back to land relied on Olly being willing to allow us to go. Which, I realised as he turned to look at me, was actually the case. As far as I knew he was the only person who knew how to drive a boat. And every minute that he waited saw us moving further away from the coast, further out to sea.

'I've literally just woken up.' Olly sighed. 'Can you not just phone somebody if you want to run back home so badly? The coastguard or something?'

I gritted my teeth against the urge to yell. 'I already tried that. There's no signal on my phone or Harry's and we can't find any Wi-Fi networks on the boat.'

'There's not?' Libby looked to her husband. 'We paid for—'

'There's probably just a mistake with it,' Olly cut her off. 'Just . . . find the router and reset it.'

'What, so we can call a fucking sea Uber and take that?' Harry exploded, his face flushing angrily. 'Just take us back to shore.'

'I will!' Olly shot back, pale cheeks turning shell-pink with irritation. 'How about you do something useful like making me a coffee?' he shot in my direction, before storming off towards the stairs to the middle deck.

Libby rubbed a hand over her mascara-smudged face. 'Make that a pot of coffee, Han. I feel like death.'

I wanted to scream. We were adrift in the ocean and my best friend – former best friend, though she didn't know that yet – was ordering coffee from me like I was her paid help.

'I'm going upstairs to try and find the router,' I told Harry.

'You should probably make the coffee first,' Libby said, her face crinkling with concern. 'You look dreadful.'

'Well, once I find the router you can google how to make me one, can't you?' I snapped.

I left Libby with her mouth open and Harry standing there looking like he wanted to cheer and laugh at the same time. I went after Olly, determined to find a way off the yacht as soon as possible. I was done.

CHAPTER EIGHT

I picked my way up the glass-shielded stairs to the middle deck. The destruction in the lobby was mirrored up there. The hot tub was still steaming away like a pot of soup, only now it had a pair of Burberry boxers floating in it. I guessed from the size that they were Leon's. They weren't exactly clean either. There was also a mirror on the edge of the tub with a half-unfurled fifty pound note on it, flopping limply in the breeze. The canopy was heavy with dew and all the cushions and rugs under it were wet with it too, left to sit out and get ruined overnight.

In the viewing room there were more spilled drinks and it almost looked like someone had started a food fight with the hors d'oeuvres. They were all over the table, picked apart and left out overnight. Some had fallen on the floor and been trodden on, and there were smears of something pinkish-brown on the wall – pâté, at a guess. A dish of some sticky dipping sauce was upside-down on an antique fainting couch. I wasn't surprised at the level of disorder; I was more annoyed that they had the nerve to pretend that I was the classless one.

I found Olly in the adjoining control room, or 'the bridge', apparently. The controls were in a teak veneer console and the first thing to jump out at me were the two steering wheels. What on earth did you do with a second steering wheel? I suppose I'd always thought that boats were a bit like cars inside. They had engines and you steered them over water, instead of a road, but the controls were probably similar. Looking at them I realised how wrong I was. This was like the difference between my hatchback and a fighter jet.

Olly was lounging in the captain's chair, flipping switches. He twisted round to look at me as I came in.

'There's nothing for you to do in here.'

I held my tongue and hoped we'd be back to shore soon so I could get started on never seeing him again. 'I'm looking for the router?'

'Oh . . . I don't know where that is. Probably somewhere below.'

'Right. Any idea where below? Or should I just check every room?'

Olly theatrically rubbed his temple as if just hearing my voice had caused a crippling migraine. 'Why would I know where it is? Can you not do one thing for yourself?'

I decided to keep a lid on my irritation and go looking elsewhere. If nothing else, it would give me an excuse not to be around anyone for the time being. The less time I spent in the company of Olly and the rest of them, the better I'd feel.

I cast a quick look out of the window. The coast was a faint smear on the horizon now. Trying to focus on it against the white sky and shifting water made my eyes hurt and my heart clench tight with worry. Despite knowing that Olly was at the wheel, and we'd be turned around soon, I didn't like the idea of not being able to see where we'd come from. I knew logically that the boat had all kinds of map software and fancy tech, but I couldn't shake the feeling thaat we were getting more and more lost with every second we spent at sea.

Harry and Libby were coming up the stairs as I went back down. They moved quickly, more purposefully than they had before, though I wasn't sure they were actively aware of it. A sense of urgency was getting to us all. A shared desire to be doing something, anything, because just contemplating our situation was too nerve-wracking. I shared a look with Harry and he rolled his eyes behind Libby's back. Clearly we were both having a nightmare of a morning. I tried to hide how anxious I was. I didn't want to make things worse.

Back in the cabin area below the lower deck I went room to room looking for a router. Nervous energy had me clicking my fingers, chewing my lip as I went. As I shut the linen cupboard I nearly bumped into Mags and let out a tiny yelp.

Mags looked at me like I was nuts. She alone seemed unaffected by the stress of our situation. She hadn't even gotten fully dressed, just thrown on a kimono. For the first time I noticed how skinny she was looking. Not just model thin – deathly thin. I could see the tendons in her neck and shoulders, the top part of her chest was corrugated, the skin tight as a drum as she breathed. It was so jarring that for a moment I struggled to look away. When Mags had come to uni she'd brought with her a framed quote, gifted by her mother, saying 'You can never be too rich or too thin'. She was really pushing that maxim to its limits.

'What're you doing in there?' She asked, eyeing the shelves of towels, fancy cosmetics and premium cleaning products. What did she think, that I was loading up on freebies? Actually, that was probably it.

'I'm looking for a Wi-Fi router. Have you seen one anywhere?'

'How would I know?' She blinked, her face a mask of confusion so perfect that it had to be put on. Perhaps she was so used to playing the idiot for Leon that she'd forgotten it was an act.

'Why wouldn't you? You helped me set ours up in our uni house, remember?' I said, not up for a game of 'I don't remember how normal people live' at that particular moment.

'Oh, that was a thousand years ago. I don't really remember. Anyway, why do you need it?'

Right, Harry said they were still asleep. Maggie and Leon didn't know what had happened. No wonder she looked so much calmer than I felt.

'We've drifted out of the harbour in the night and Olly's going to take us back, but because there's no phone signal, I wanted to make sure we could still reach someone in case something happens.'

'Oh,' Maggie said, sounding bored, though I noticed a line form between her perfectly pencilled brows. 'OK, well, good luck with that.' She yawned and padded off towards the stairs. 'Do you know how to make a Bloody Mary?'

'Ask Libby,' I said. Between my anxiety and my temper I was hanging on by a thread and I didn't know how much more of this I could take before I blew up., I had never felt this close to losing it before. It was like now that I'd finally had my eyes opened to how they all treated me, I just couldn't handle it anymore. Especially not now, with everything else going on.

I heard movement in Mags' room and realised Leon was probably about to surface. I didn't want to see him, especially whilst I was alone, so I ducked into Libby and Olly's room., There was no sign of a router in there either. Still, I hung around long enough for Leon's footsteps to recede and then headed into his room to check there.

It looked like a wardrobe had exploded. Empty and half full suitcases took up most of the floor space, and the rest was covered in discarded clothing. A velvet case on the dressing table was stuffed with enough gemstones and gold to give the Tower of London a run for its money, and when something crunched under my foot, I looked down to find it was one of Mags' earrings from the night before. I'd just stood on diamonds. Diamonds Maggie had left on the floor. I'd once taken a hoover apart to rescue an Accessorize bracelet because it was fifteen quid. I wanted to laugh and cry at the same time. How had I managed to convince myself that these people saw me as their equal, as a friend? Our shared history was nothing compared to the glittering world they lived in every day.

Now fully in a mood, I left the cabins and went back upstairs. Doing something wasn't making me feel any better than doing nothing. In fact, it was actually making me feel worse, what with the fact that no one was helping me. Worse, I was starting to think there wasn't a router on board at all and that sent my anxiety spiralling all over again. I just wanted to get back to the harbour and go home. I wiped my damp palms on my top and told myself that I'd been downstairs for long enough that we were probably heading back now and there was no point in scrambling around after a router that probably didn't exist. That made me feel a little better, but didn't calm me down entirely. The words 'what if something else goes wrong?' would not stop circling my brain.

When I reached the lower deck and realised we weren't moving, I felt my panic rising again. A quick, nausea-inducing look out to sea showed me that only a shadow of land was still visible. What was taking so long? Was something wrong with the boat? I could feel cold sweat beading my lip, soaking into my clothes. I tried telling myself that this was just Olly enjoying the feeling of being our captain and wanting to prolong it as much as possible. Still though, I quickened my pace and almost jogged up the stairs to the second floor, my hangover and dread weighing on me equally.

Mags was the only person in the viewing room. She looked as cool as I felt frazzled. She was sipping from a giant tumbler of lemon water and looked completely unaffected by the mess around her, or the shouting coming from the bridge. What was going on in there? With my heartbeat lodged somewhere in my throat, I went to investigate.

Inside, Libby was filming the view with her phone. From the sounds of things she was making a video for her social media. Leon, clad only in his boxers, was on the opposite side of the control panel to Olly. He and Harry were leaning over and pointing at controls, talking in raised voices as Olly acidly attempted to shout them down and wave them away.

'What's going on?' I asked, my voice coming out a little more strangled than I'd intended.

'He's not bloody doing anything,' Harry said.

'I told you, she needs time to warm up. The water temperature is lower than optimal and it'll ruin the engine to overwork it before it's ready.'

'You wouldn't get it,' Leon put in. 'It'd be like using E10 in the Lambo. You can't run these things like some old beater.'

'I'm not asking him to pilot us around Antarctica. It's a few miles of calm sea. Just get us back to port and bill me for any "damage",' Harry snapped, his wiry frame tense with barely suppressed anger as he loomed over Olly's chair. He smacked one tattooed hand on the console, a hair away from striking Olly's fingers. 'You've had it "warming up" for nearly twenty minutes now. Just fucking go!'

'Who do you think you are?' Olly retorted, stiffening in his seat as he attempted to gain a height advantage. He wouldn't look Harry in the eye. 'You're a guest here, have some gratitude.'

Harry was practically pinning Olly down with his chest at this point, leaning over him and glaring at him. He grabbed his shoulder. 'Oh, yeah. I'm really grateful to be lost at sea because you can't tie a rope properly.'

'I didn't tie it, so I fail to see how this is my fault.' Olly couldn't get up but wriggled in Harry's grip. Leon tried to get hold of Harry's arm, but he threw up a hand to force him away.

'But you know how to drive the boat, right?' he said, shaking Olly by the shirt.

'Of course I do!'

But Olly had left it a second too long and we all felt it. That second of uncertainty, of embarrassment, hanging in the air like a bad smell. My stomach turned over. Harry stared at him, letting the silence stretch on and on until Olly's cheeks were burning and he looked like he wanted to hit him.

'You don't know how, do you?' Harry finally said, letting

go of Olly in shock and taking a step back. There was a weird mix of disbelief, triumph and disgust in his voice. 'You bought a yacht . . . and you don't know how to drive it?'

'Oh be serious,' Leon said, rolling his eyes and taking a step closer, getting between Olly and Harry like a bouncer. 'Obviously he knows how to sail. You're just insecure because the only boat you've ever owned was inflatable.'

'Can you both just shut up!' Libby finally exploded. 'You've ruined my video like five times now.'

'No one gives a fuck. S'cuse my French,' Leon said, then sniffed thickly. Libby shot him a dirty look, then glanced at Olly as if expecting him to say something. When he didn't, she folded her arms, phone dangling from her talon-like nails. Olly didn't even seem to notice; he was frozen in his chair like a china doll, as if too scared or too furious to move. His pale eyes were fixed on the view ahead of us, scanning the empty horizon.

I watched all this and felt a bubble of hysteria rising inside me. I was stuck on a boat owned by a man who didn't know how to work it. We were drifting further out to sea with every passing minute. Land was a faint memory in the distance. I had no phone signal and no one could tell me if there even was a Wi-Fi router, let alone where it was so that I could try and get it working.

It was that last thought that stopped me short. An insane idea bubbled to the surface of my brain, and I stood there looking between Libby and Olly before I could bring myself to say it aloud.

'Is this even your boat?'

Libby gave me a look that even a few hours ago would have reduced me to tears. It was so full of hatred and disgust.

Now, though, I just matched it with a similar look of my own. Harry, leaning against the console, let out a shocked little laugh.

'Do you ever shut up?' Olly snapped.

'It's true, isn't it?' I said. 'This isn't your yacht. That's why you can't sail it and you don't even know if there's a router on board – like Libby said you 'paid for' there to be. You've borrowed it – rented it or something. You were never going anywhere on it, were you? It's just for the party. You made it all up.'

Olly was out of his seat before I'd finished, avoiding Harry's attempt to grab him and stopping only an inch from me. He inhaled harshly, taking up as much space as he could, like a threatened animal. Harry got him by the shoulder but Olly shrugged him off.

'I never said it was mine. Obviously I chartered it. Can *you* afford to do that? No. I didn't think so. You can't even afford to lease a car,' Olly shot out, voice barely rising above a hiss.

'At least she would know how to drive it if she did,' Harry muttered, shoving Olly so he staggered to one side, allowing me to get some distance between us.

Olly turned on him, whip fast. 'I am working it out. What's your contribution here? Hmm?'

'I'm not sure you can just "work out" how to sail a boat like this,' Harry said, eyes crinkling in scorn.

'Of course he can,' Libby said. 'He actually finished university, unlike some people.'

'Yeah, like you'd know anything about it. How many boats were you on growing up?' Leon asked Harry. 'Aside from the Channel ferry when your parents went to stock up on cheap fags.'

'There it is!' Now that Olly was standing, I could see the shape of a router under the console. I snatched it and found that it was still fresh from the box. All the cables were wound up and tied neatly with wire twists. It was probably new and the real owners of the boat hadn't installed it yet. I quickly undid the wires and plugged it into one of the sockets set into the cabin floor. Several lights flashed on immediately and I let out a sigh of relief. Finally we had a way to call for help.

I got my phone out at the same time as Harry and went into my settings again. After a few seconds of enduring everyone else's hopeful silence, I looked up at Harry and he shook his head.

'Come on!' I snapped, flipping the router off and on again. I checked my phone. 'Work, you stupid thing.'

'It's no good, Han,' Harry said. 'It must be something to do with being this far out at sea. I mean, that's just a normal router like you'd have at home. Don't those use the phone lines?'

'When you rented this thing, was it always going to stay in port, because if not . . .'

'Chartered,' Olly said, aiming a stern finger at me, his cut-glass accent becoming sharper by the minute. 'Not "rented". It is a yacht, not a pedalo. And you can stop trying to rub that in my face, because as I already said—'

'She's not making fun of you, you prat,' Harry said, batting Olly's accusing finger out of my face. 'She's saying that if this thing was never meant to leave the harbour, they probably didn't bother fitting it with some kind of satellite internet or phone. Because you'd be in range of all the phone towers on the land, right, Han?' Harry said, slowly and loudly.

I nodded. Olly paced away from us, trying and failing to hide the fact that he was deliberately getting Leon between himself and Harry. Harry watched him go with barely concealed disgust and a sliver of grim amusement. I placed a warning hand on Harry's arm.

'OK, fine, yes,' Olly said, secure behind Leon's bulk. 'Are you happy now? I never intended to use this as anything more than a venue. We planned to leave after the party, the same as you ingrates.'

Harry's arm muscles tensed under my hand, but he didn't move, just glared. Olly refused to look at either of us but it was clear he was keeping Harry in the corner of his eye. Wary of attack.

'If that's the case for everyone who rents this thing, they wouldn't need the Wi-Fi to work at sea . . . that means we're out of range. We can't contact anyone,' I said. 'Does anyone have a satellite phone or . . .' I trailed off when they all just looked at me blankly.

'What are we going to do?' Libby said, in a small voice. 'We just lost sight of land.'

I whipped around to stare at Mags. She was standing in the doorway, glassy eyed and fragile looking. She took a shaky sip of her 'lemon water' and a waft of neat vodka hit me. That wasn't the reason I had tears in my eyes though. I was, for the first time, completely and totally terrified.

CHAPTER NINE

Libby started to cry. No one moved to comfort her. I felt bad for her, for all of us, but I couldn't do that for her just then. I didn't have it in me, not with everything she'd said and done since my arrival still playing on a loop in my head. Olly was just ignoring her entirely. I looked to Harry for support and he shrugged helplessly.

'I guess . . . we need to try and work out how to get back,' Harry said, clearly embarrassed by Libby's tears, or at least his own role in causing them.

'I'll have a look, mate, all right?' Leon motioned Olly away from the console and to my surprise he actually went, sidling over to Libby and slouching against the wall, watching like he couldn't care less if Leon managed to get the thing going or not.

'Right, so . . .' Leon started flipping switches at random and several things began to beep, flash and whir.

Harry stepped in and reached over. 'There's two ignitions. Let's get both of them on for a start.'

'This is probably gears?' Leon pushed part of a divided

lever up and the light next to it went green. He did the same with the second half and that light went green too. Green was the universal sign for 'Go', right? Maybe we were actually going to manage this. All we had to do was get the thing going and then turn around. Frankly, I didn't care if we crashed it into the harbour. Olly could foot the bill for that. I just wanted to reach dry land and escape this horribly tense atmosphere.

'Feels like she's in neutral? Let's try . . .' Leon pushed a few more buttons and several coloured levels started to appear on the LCD screens in the console. Green bar, yellow bar, green, yellow . . . red.

'What does that mean?' I leaned over and squinted at the tiny display, then turned to Harry, my insides plummeting. 'Fuel level . . . below minimum.'

'Are you kidding me?' Harry rounded on our hosts. 'Did you know this thing was empty?'

'And I suppose you'd fuel up a boat you weren't planning to take anywhere?' Olly bit out. 'Use some common sense.'

Harry looked ready to beat that sense into him. I placed a warning hand on his arm.

'What about a radio?' Libby asked, wiping tears from her cheeks with her hands.

'That's a good point, thank you, Libs,' I said, when no one else did. I cringed at myself for slipping into my old role again. Cheerleader and support system for Libby and Mags. So much for my new backbone.

I hunted on the console for anything that looked promising and grabbed what looked like a TV remote connected to the controls by a spiral phone cord. I pressed a few buttons but nothing happened. The tiny screen on it, like the one on a calculator, stayed empty. 'It's not working,' I said, feeling like a failure despite myself. As if anyone else might have been able to will the thing to work, but I'd had to step in and screw everything up first.

Leon snatched the radio out of my hand and pressed every button again. Nothing happened. He smacked it against the console and Harry jumped in to wrestle it away from him.

'Hey! I can maybe fix it but not if you make it worse.'

'Oh right, I forget you were a welder,' Olly said, rolling his eyes.

'Electrician,' both Libby and I corrected him. Which surprised me. I looked up and found that she was giving Olly a look bordering on hatred. Her face was blotchy with tears and her lip trembled as if she was fighting to contain another outburst.

'I'd need to find some tools first.' Harry put the radio back and glanced out of the window towards the lower deck. 'Wait a minute – what the hell are we standing here for, there's a bloody helicopter!'

I'd been through so many cycles of panic and relief that I was starting to worry my heart might never recover. My adrenaline-charged brain unclenched at the reminder that we had a means of getting back to land without having to move the boat an inch. It was fairly small, yes, but we only needed to get one or two people back to shore so that they could raise the alarm and get help to us.

We all turned to Olly expectantly. Libby was still glaring at him. The sight of his tense face made my hopeful smile falter. He looked like a child furious at being caught in the act. His whole body radiated anger and discomfort.

'Don't tell me that's got no fuel either?' Harry asked. 'You must have put enough in it to get back home?'

An awkward silence held us all in its spell until Libby burst out, 'Will you just be a man and tell them?'

'Hey – steady on,' Leon said. 'That's your husband.'

Both Libby and Olly ignored him.

'If it's so important, why didn't you tell everyone already?' Olly sneered, his cool tone undermined somewhat by how red his ears had become. 'Obviously you're dying to.'

'I thought you could sail!' Libby wailed. 'There was no point telling everyone about the boat situation if we were going to get back to port anyway. But you're just stalling for nothing now. You need to do something and just standing there isn't accomplishing anything.'

Olly glared at her, pale hands flexing. For a panicked second I actually thought he might hit her. Instead he took hold of the back of the captain's chair and squeezed until his knuckles turned white.

'The helicopter doesn't have any fuel in it,' Libby spat, 'because it's not real. It's a fake. Oliver hired it with the yacht as part of a package.'

'A . . . fake helicopter?' Harry said, the concept so strange that he was clearly struggling, as I was, to comprehend it. 'Are you being serious? That's a thing that you can get? Why? Oh . . .' Harry sighed as if finally putting something together. 'Of course – gotta keep up appearances, right? Is it just decommissioned? Does it at least have a radio in it?'

Libby shook her head, fresh tears gathering in her eyes. 'I think it's just a shell. Nothing works.'

'That's enough, Libby,' Olly said.

She turned on him with a look that could have melted glass. 'You're pathetic, Oliver.'

'There's nothing to be gained by engaging with him,' Olly snapped, gesturing at Harry.

'Nothing to be gained? Other than the truth, you mean.' The words were out of my mouth before I had time to pull them back. Frankly, I didn't really want to. This had been the morning from Hell, following the party of my nightmares. I was so done with holding my tongue for the benefit of these people. 'You've had us waiting like idiots thinking we were going to get out of this and now you tell us even the helicopter's fake?'

'You wouldn't understand,' Leon said, apparently fully behind Olly and his idiotic game of pretend. 'It's about branding. Is there any point buying a real helicopter to impress the likes of you? No, it just has to be there and be shiny and you'll lap it up.'

'It's kind of important that it can fly now though, isn't it?' I retorted. 'What with us being stuck out here with no working phones or Wi-Fi or any fucking fuel to get back to the shore. Or are you going to whip out your wad of cash again and chuck that in the engine?'

Leon went red. 'Fuck you.'

'I think we already covered that I wouldn't even if you paid me.' To my surprise I didn't feel at all anxious or upset. My body was cold all the way through. As if all that fear and anxiety and shock had short-circuited my brain and I couldn't feel it anymore. Anger was the only thing getting through to me and I welcomed the focus it brought with it. I glanced at Maggie to see if she'd put two and two together from my comment to Leon, but she was looking at the floor. If she'd realised that Leon had tried it on with me, she wasn't going to say anything. Still, I wasn't done yet.

'And as for you.' I pointed at Olly. 'If you're done flexing on the rest of us with your rented boat and your cardboard helicopter, you can get off your high horse and do something

86

useful because Libby's right – you're not helping. You've been trying to save face and all it's done is waste our time. So, tell me what you do know about this boat and then, if you can't think of anything helpful to do, stay out of our way.'

'Who the hell do you—'

I held up my hand and shouted over whatever Olly was trying to say. 'I am the person who is stuck on this idiotic boat because of your incompetence. And whilst I might just be Libby's "povo mate", right now your money's about as much use as your fake fucking helicopter. So what else do you have to offer? Because it's certainly not sailing expertise.'

I looked between him and Leon. Both of them were flushed, angry and embarrassed, but neither seemed willing to speak up and be shouted down again. A quick glance at Libby told me she hadn't picked up on my word choice – the same name that Olly had called me the night before. She was standing there with her eyes shut and her mouth twisted like she was about to have a breakdown. I wanted to shake her, make her pay attention, but I was also aware that if she went to pieces the others would quickly follow. We all needed to stay calm, or panic and hostility would spread through us and screw any chance we had of thinking our way out of this mess. Everyone needed something to occupy them.

'Maggie, can you get everyone's phones and try sending a text to emergency services?' I vaguely remembered seeing something once that said a text would keep trying to send instead of being immediately dropped like a call. I was praying that was true. 'If you keep messaging every half hour or so we might drift close enough to get some kind of help. Harry, if you work on finding some tools to use on the radio, I'll go and check for anything else we can use on this thing. Libby . . . you're coming with me,' I said, mostly to remove her from the powder keg in the bridge. It would only take her aggravating Leon or Olly for another screaming match to break out. Or worse.

'Aye aye, Captain,' Harry said, sounding a little shocked but pleased. He performed an ironic salute.

I offered him a weak smile and then led Libby out of the bridge and downstairs to the lower deck. I was hoping that somewhere down there I'd be able to find a lifeboat, a means of contacting the mainland or anything else I could cling to in my growing helplessness. With every minute we were stuck on the boat my fear was rising in waves. Stronger and stronger, threatening to pull me under.

CHAPTER TEN

On the lower deck I had Libby show me where she and Olly were keeping the paperwork about the yacht rental. There wasn't much of use in there. I'd been hoping for a map of the boat, including all the emergency features, but it was more of a brochure and only covered the more luxurious talking points. Gold-plated taps weren't high on my list of priorities just then. The paperwork also didn't mention if there was a satellite phone, so I assumed there wasn't one. Aside from the radio we were out of contact, at least until we got closer to land. *If* we got closer to land.

With no idea where to start looking, I figured we'd go for something easy first – lifeboats. Surely there had to be some? That sounded like it should be a legal requirement, especially if this was a rented yacht.

'Did they show you round when you picked up this thing? Any idea where the lifeboats might be?' I asked Libby as she trailed behind me, sniffling.

'They're . . . um . . . they're back at the dock.'

I turned around to stare at her. 'Why?'

'I told you. We had the caterers move stuff around before the party. The boats took up most of the deck in these big pod things. There wasn't really any space for . . . dancing.' Libby looked away as she said it, like she'd just realised what she was saying.

'You moved the lifeboats to make space for the dance floor,' I said. Even as I heard it aloud, I couldn't quite believe it.

'I didn't move them.' Libby sighed. 'I asked for them to be moved. They're in storage. One of the lockups by the dock. Olly rented one so we could offload the things we didn't need. Obviously we had no idea this would happen,' She said, crossing her arms.

'Right . . . because usually people plan to need lifeboats.' I sighed. 'Anything similar that you managed to save room for?'

'I don't know. Maybe somewhere near the engine room.'

'Which is where?'

'I don't know,' Libby repeated through gritted teeth.

'All right. We'll check every cabin then – there must be an entrance down here somewhere.' I strode off without waiting for her. I might have taken her with me to avoid causing conflict with Olly and Leon, but now I was liable to start yelling at her instead.

It took a while to find the engine room, mostly because the yacht's designers had opted for a hidden door rather than just putting one in that said 'Engine Room' in huge, unmissable letters. I only spotted it because of the handle, one of those ring ones that fold flush into a little groove. The sort of thing you sometimes saw on caravans, which I had some limited experience of as a kid, when Dad was alive and we still went on holidays. The door was in the wall of the master bathroom, to one side of the toilet. Unfortunately, it didn't want to open.

'It must be locked to keep guests out.' I sighed, giving up my attempts to prise the door open. 'There must be a key somewhere. Look, there's a hole under the handle.'

'The company probably has it,' Libby said.

'Hopefully not, or else we're a bit screwed,' I said vaguely, only half listening to her. I was running my fingers up and around the top of the sink unit. It extended almost to the ceiling and had a mirror and shelves moulded into it.

'What are you doing?'

'Looking for a spare key. Can you check around the door frame?'

'They're not just going to have a key hidden here,' Libby sneered. 'The cleaners would end up throwing it away. It's a luxury yacht; there are standards.'

I swept a hand over the top of a sconce and a tiny, hot key tinkled to the floor.

'Yes! OK, let's hope the router's in here.' I unlocked the door, ignoring Libby's mutter of 'smug cow' as I did so. If she wanted to be petty, I wasn't going to waste time telling her off. We were all on the same team and I was hoping that eventually she'd get that.

The difference between the engine room and the rest of the boat was pretty stark. Nothing in there was aesthetic or glamorous in the least, which was actually quite reassuring. At least one part of the boat was designed for practicality. On either side of a thin walkway were two identical but mirrored engines. Each one about the size of my car. They looked in good repair, at least to me. All the cables were neatly gathered and pinned in place, there were no signs of rust or leaking water and everything was spotlessly clean.

I'd imagined the bowels of a boat to be a bit sinister and dungeon-like, but it felt more like being on a space station than in the belly of a ship.

Right at the back was a larger space with a tool cabinet, as well as a logbook for the servicing of the lifeboats. I flicked through until I came across a picture of what looked like an orange tipi on an inflatable raft. An arrow showed it being folded away into a large white cylinder the size of my boiler at home.

'These were on deck?' I showed Libby. She nodded.

'This says they have food and water, flares . . .' I looked down the list and sighed. 'Other stuff that would have been really useful.'

'Can you stop going on about it? They're gone, OK?' Libby said.

On the one hand, she had a point; it probably wasn't helpful for me to keep harping on about the rafts we no longer had. On the other, though, it at least helped me to get some of my irritation out without just shaking her by the shoulders.

At the bottom of the cabinet I found a large yellow pack about the size of a pillow. It was dense and wrapped in clear plastic. Printed down one side were the words 'Compact Life Raft'. My heart soared. Finally, some good luck. I dragged it out and turned it over. The back had some serial numbers and instructions for deploying it.

'You found a lifeboat?' Libby asked.

'It's not like the ones you . . . the other ones,' I corrected myself. 'No supplies either.'

'But it's something, right?'

'Yeah . . . can you see any oars?'

Libby looked around. 'No. Are they packed with it?'

I eyed the small pack doubtfully. It was only just over a foot long. At best it would contain a short paddle and even that seemed unlikely. There was nothing mentioning one on the pack itself. The only way to be sure would be to open it up and that was impossible in the engine room.

'We'll have to take it up and see. I'm not sure we'll be able to fold it up again once it's deployed though, and it only has space for four.'

Though since there wasn't some means of propelling or even steering the thing it would be suicide to attempt to reach land in it. I tucked it under my arm and raided the tool cabinet, dumping screwdrivers and a few other things into a bag I found under some boxes of solder. Hopefully Harry could use them to work on the radio.

'What's the deal with the fake helicopter anyway?' I asked, because I couldn't not. It had seemed like Libby was just as annoyed with Olly as anyone else over it so I didn't think it would piss her off any more than she already was.

'Ugh.' Libby rolled her eyes. 'That. It was Olly's idea. You know Mags and Leon went to New York over the summer?'

I did, because I'd seen it on social media. I'd last seen Mags in person about four months ago, when she passed through Bath to visit the spa and scheduled me in for a quick cocktail afterwards.

'They hired a helicopter for a tour around the city – see the monuments and the buildings, all that stuff.' Libby waved a hand as if we were both intimately familiar with all the sights and attractions of New York. 'I showed it to Olly and he was angry about it because when we went last year we had a limo and I'd told Mags how annoying it was being sat in one traffic jam after another.' She rolled her eyes and imitated Olly's nasal RP accent. 'I can't believe you would tell that social-climbing witch about that. Are you that desperate to undermine me?' She snorted and returned to her regular voice. 'As if he was any happier being stuck in that limo.'

'So, what's one better than hiring a helicopter – owning one?' I said, sarcastically, eager to move this story along towards a point.

'Exactly.' Libby seemed pleased that I appeared to be on her wavelength. 'Same deal with the yacht, only that was because Harry just bought a boat.'

'Harry owns a boat?' I said, surprised and genuinely interested for the first time. Why hadn't he mentioned it to me?

'Yeah, one of those river ones that homeless yuppies live in,' Libby said breezily. She rubbed her lips together and frowned. 'Do you have any lip balm? I'm parched here.'

'A narrowboat?' I said, trying to translate 'Libby' into regular English.

'Yes.' She sighed, exasperated. 'God knows he could just buy a house like the rest of us, but no, he's got to be different. I was sort of hoping he'd know how to drive this thing, but I suppose that's different.'

'I guess. Must be like the difference between driving my car and a Formula One car.'

'Mmmhmm, so . . . do you have any?'

'What? Oh, no, I don't have lip balm.'

'Ugh!' Libby shook her head. 'I'm not sure how much more of this I can take.'

I ignored her and carried on with a search of the smaller compartments in the cabinet. I quite liked the idea of Harry on a narrowboat, actually. It sort of suited him. I could imagine him emerging onto the deck in the morning, coffee in one hand, cigarette in the other. He'd never been one for breakfast, but when I'd stayed at his – the night it was just us – he'd made me toast in bed. I ought to have made my move on him then, in that moment when it was just the two of us. Before I had a chance to get in my head about it and get insecure about going after one of Libby's 'castoffs'. Not that she'd ever have let me forget that she got there first.

'We should probably grab some food and stuff from the kitchen,' I said, as my stomach rumbled threateningly. The nausea stage of my hangover was passing and I was ready for some breakfast. The last thing I wanted was to have to deal with a hangry Leon.

Being back in the kitchen made me feel tense, even with Libby at my side. I tried to shake it off and just keep moving forward. I had things to do, things to focus on to keep the panic at bay. Ignoring the fancy cookware that had hypnotised me the previous evening, I started opening cupboards.

I uncovered shelf after shelf of serving platters, spare glasses of all shapes and sizes, napkins, cutlery, crockery and all the equipment for making cocktails, ice-cream and rotisserie. What I didn't find, anywhere, was any actual food.

'Libs, did you guys stock any more food? Or were the nibbles last night all of it?' I asked, looking up to find her perched on the kitchen island.

'The caterers brought the hors d'oeuvres,' she stressed the words, 'and the drinks. Then they left. Olly thinks they judge you – the staff, I mean – if you let them hang around. He's old fashioned – likes everything done out of sight.' She heaved a sigh and kicked her feet, looking like the old 'chain smoking behind the bike sheds' Libby. 'It's super annoying. He's always telling me these "rules", like I'll care.'

Yup. That tracked. Olly probably thought the goings on of *Downton Abbey* were too liberal. Though to be fair, his staff probably *were* judging him. If I'd had to serve nibbles and drinks to Olly and Leon, I'd have probably been arrested before the end of the night for trying to stab one of them with a corkscrew.

'I think we ordered some smoked salmon and blinis for a champagne breakfast,' Libby said, her voice softening as if she was seeking a truce, having done one thing right at least.

'That'd be in the fridge then.' I went to the oversized fridge and threw open the double doors. A waft of chilly air rose to greet me from the pristine interior. I could see the water reservoir for the dispenser on one side and the rest of the fridge was packed with bottles of BLVD mineral water, except for one shelf, which held a single covered platter with an invoice taped to the lid. I lifted it out and stared at it in disbelief.

'You paid . . . twenty quid per bottle for this water?'

'It's Tasmanian,' Libby said, like that explained everything.

'It's like two grand's worth of water and one tray of food!' I said, pulling the invoice off the lid. Underneath it was a plastic pod of hardboiled eggs, some smoked salmon, a log of carefully shaped butter and a pot of caviar with some blinis arranged around it.

'There's more over there.' Libby pointed triumphantly to a Fortnum's bag I'd missed, tucked in beside the fridge. Inside I found a single sourdough loaf, a pot of jam and another of honey and several bags of gourmet ground coffee. *At least, thanks to the oranges in the juicer, we don't have to worry about scurvy,* I thought. But even that weak little internal joke didn't help my dire mood.

'Great,' I muttered.

'How much were you planning to eat, Hannah?' Libby snapped.

My temper flared. 'I don't know Libs, how long do you think we'll be stuck out here?'

Libby's irritation melted into shock as she considered the possibility that we might be out here for longer than a few hours, apparently for the first time. There were six of us and we'd found about enough food for one, maybe two meals, if we really pushed it.

'There has to be something else in here,' she said, and starting checking cupboards I'd already gone through. I knew she wouldn't find anything. The boat had clearly been cleaned and prepared for its next rental. Unlike every holiday home I'd ever stayed in, we weren't about to find some forgotten pasta or cooking oil lurking in a cupboard. This place only held what Libby had asked her staff to provide.

'Stop looking at me like that,' Libby snapped, and I blinked, refocusing to find her glaring at me, eyes gleaming with furious tears.

'Like what?'

'Like I'm some kind of idiot. I didn't know this was going to happen. I wasn't planning a survival weekend; I was hosting a party.'

'I know that. I'm just worried that we aren't going to have anything to eat whilst we wait for someone to notice we're missing. I'm not blaming you.'

'Bullshit. Of course you are. That's all you've been doing since we came down here. The lifeboats, the water . . . and now this. All you've done is made me feel like crap and blame me for this whole situation.' A tear, blackened with eyeliner, slid down her face and dripped off of her chin. Libby let out a shaky breath and I found myself wondering how much of this was genuine and how much of it was a performance. She's always been good at getting her own way with the waterworks.

'There is a big difference,' I said, trying to retain some composure, 'between me thinking what you did is stupid, and thinking that this whole mess is your fault. I'm sorry that I can't pretend that offloading all the lifeboats was a good decision, or that twenty pounds a litre is a reasonable price for water, but that doesn't mean I am blaming you for the fact that we are out in the ocean.'

The tears evaporated as quickly as she'd summoned them. Libby narrowed her eyes but pressed her lips together and didn't respond. I sighed.

'I'm going to go search the linen cupboard for anything we can use.'

She didn't respond and I left without looking back. If Libby wanted to sulk, she was welcome to it. I didn't want to waste time arguing. Though, as I crouched down to go through the cupboard, I did feel a little guilty. I *had* been getting at her over the lifeboats and all the rest of it. It was true that I didn't blame her for our situation, but I also didn't think she was entirely blameless. Even if we'd drifted off into the sea by accident – something that I still couldn't quite believe had happened – Libby and Olly had definitely made things worse than they might otherwise have been with their lies, attitude and bad decisions.

'There you are.'

It was Olly, but he wasn't talking to me. It sounded like he was in the kitchen. I kept searching the cupboard. I had nothing to say to him at that precise moment and I was hoping to find some complimentary biscuits or an emergency phone that had escaped Libby's purge of the boat.

'Where's your unpleasant little friend?' Olly asked.

'Sulking somewhere because I dared buy water.'

I bristled. How had I ever managed to convince myself that Libby would defend me to him? The longer I spent on the yacht the harder it was to remember why I'd ever considered her a friend. I was seeing all our history together in a new light and I hated how it made me look; spineless, grateful and desperate. She'd dared me to walk across a frozen lake, for God's sake, and I'd done it! I could have died, and all she had to do was pick up a band member who she probably wanted to get with anyway. I'd been a total idiot.

'I can't believe she spoke to me like that,' Olly was saying. 'At our party, in front of our guests. Who does she think she is?'

A flash of me crying in the powder room sent a wave of anger at myself and at them crashing through me. I was done hiding myself away and letting them tear me down without worrying I might catch them at it. Slowly, I got up and walked back to the kitchen door.

'I'm never inviting her to anything, ever again,' Libby said. 'She so ungrateful.'

'My thank you card's in the post.'

Both of them jerked around at the sound of my voice. Libby at least still had enough shame to look away. Olly just gave me a haughty look that said he was glad I'd heard, and that my reaction was already boring him.

'You don't have to worry about not inviting me. I'm uninviting myself, for good. As soon as we manage to get off this boat, I never want to see you again. You'll have to find another "povo friend" to help you appreciate all you've got.'

Libby's eyes darted about and her mouth moved, but she seemed at a loss for words. This time my jab had landed. Now she knew I'd heard. Good. I headed for the stairs back up to deck level. Time to get the tools to Harry and see about fixing the radio.

'Pathetic,' I heard Olly spit behind me.

I couldn't agree more – they both were.

CHAPTER ELEVEN

'Tools for the handyman,' I said, probably too brightly, as I dumped the bag beside Harry. He was on his own in the bridge. God only knew what Leon and Maggie were doing. In my absence, Harry had taken the front off of the control panel and there were wires and bits of circuit board dangling out. He'd managed to find a pair of pliers somewhere. I'd brought him screwdrivers, some snips and a soldering iron; surely something in that lot had to get us out of this mess.

'Cheers. Any chance of a brew?' he said, by way of greeting, winking at me to let me know he was just playing the part and not actually expecting me to cater for him.

I collapsed into the captain's chair. 'Not even slightly. There's no milk and basically no food.'

'You're joking me.' Harry looked as appalled as I'd felt looking into that fridge. 'What, like, none? I thought this place would be kitted out with oysters and black truffles up the waz.'

'I found some oranges, enough ground coffee to keep a

whole office buzzing and enough breakfast food for a generous two-person brunch.'

'Shit.' He kicked the base of the panel in disgust. 'Do I want to ask about lifeboats?'

'Probably not. They're in a lockup back at the dock. Took up too much space. I did find this' – I showed him the yellow raft – 'but it'll only take four people and I don't think we have anything to steer it with. No oars or anything. Unless we try and improvise something from the furniture?'

'Jesus. I suppose we'll have to try, though I must've missed all the lessons on oar carving at school. What the hell were they thinking? Olly I expect this from, but Libs wasn't born with a silver spoon up her— Well, maybe half of one. How did she lose all her common sense?' His face was screwed up in disgust. Maybe, like me, he was only just starting to see how much Libby had changed.

'I don't know, and she's too pissed for me to ask. I might have slightly let her have it after I overheard her talking to Olly about me – twice, actually. Last night and just now.'

Harry pulled a face somewhere between commiseration and expectant grimace. 'Nothing good, I take it?'

'Oh, you know – I'm jealous and ungrateful and having me here is like keeping your first cheque to remind you where you came from.'

Harry's eyebrows launched themselves upwards. 'He didn't.'

'No, *she* did.'

'Jeee-sus.' He shook his head in disbelief.

I was embarrassed to find myself tearing up, despite my carefully light-hearted tone. Of all the things to be worried about, some comment of Libby's shouldn't have even made the list. Yet it hurt me, deep down in a place that no amount of fear or anger could touch. Maybe because I knew it was the truth – to her, at least. It was how she really saw me.

Harry set down the pliers and squeezed my shoulder, making my thoughts falter. 'I'm sorry, Han. Look, we're going to get home soon and then you have my full support in never having to come to one of these things again.'

'Thanks.' I sniffed, though a part of me wondered if he meant he'd steer clear too. Or maybe he fully intended to keep coming to these parties with Libby and all the rest of them. They were his people now. I was the only odd one out.

'Hey, I didn't know you owned a boat,' I said, trying to slap a brave face on and change the subject. 'I suppose it's not much like this one?'

'Nah, this is like a whole different league. But yeah, I bought one and I'm happy with her. Just enough space and it's out of the city but still close enough to the studio. You should come and see it some time.'

A genuine smile curled the corners of my mouth. 'I'd like that.'

'I promise we'll stay moored up and that I'll have milk in for tea.'

Harry's hand was still on my shoulder, the heat of it creating goose bumps up my neck. He moved it as someone's footsteps disturbed the quiet moment, and the sudden chill in its place made me flinch.

'How's the radio?' Maggie asked from the doorway. She was still wrapped up in her little satin robe and negligee, painfully thin and gaunt. She floated over to us and peered at the radio's exposed guts.

'I'm trying to fix it. Some kind of short must've fried these wires and I'm not convinced this circuit board is salvageable. We'll see,' Harry said, clearly trying to sound optimistic, but not quite succeeding.

The pit of despair in my stomach only grew. For him to sound so unsure was worrying. I'd been convinced that Harry could fix the radio. He could fix mostly anything. He'd unstuck my car window when it refused to roll back up, repaired every appliance and faulty socket I'd called him round to have a look at.

'How's the texting going?' I asked Maggie.

She wafted away and returned with the phones she'd collected from everyone else. They were in a decorative basket, which had been down in the lobby bathroom, I was sure of it. It struck me as inappropriately funny that even in a situation like this, she had effectively applied aesthetic to the cause.

'No answer and I'm still getting bounce-back messages,' Mags said, setting the basket on the control panel like it was an unexploded bomb. 'I've stopped trying for a while. When we can see land, I'll start again.'

She had a point. *If* we saw land, that was. I wasn't a hundred per cent sure what direction we were floating in now and how fast we were moving. Logically, I knew that we were probably still fairly near the Italian coast, but were we now drifting along it or away from it? Would the tide take us south towards Northern Africa or would we drift between Spain and Morocco, out into the vast Atlantic? The idea that we might be as close to land now as we would ever be again filled me with soaring panic.

'Is there anything else we can do?' I asked Harry, trying to sound calm and capable.

Harry only shrugged, as at a loss as I felt. 'I sent Leon off looking for small electronics I could scavenge from, and he hasn't come back so . . . you could find him, or find something I can take apart and use the bits of.'

'OK,' I said, seizing on this task. 'Mags? Can you help me?'

I'd only asked because she looked so lost. She nodded numbly. I glanced at Harry and he just shrugged. He had no idea what was up with her either. To me she looked exhausted and stressed. I wondered for the first time how much work she actually did as part of her fashion empire. I'd assumed she just let the money roll in like Olly, who had other people managing his investment portfolio, but I guessed that Mags was probably a bit more involved. She'd worked hard at uni, both at her course and at maintaining her weight, then had a bit of a breakdown in our third year. She'd collapsed behind the scenes at the end-of-year fashion show – dehydration and exhaustion. Maybe Maggie was suffering from a bit of burnout, working her business as hard as possible to keep up with Libs and Olly? Not that she stood a chance of that. That, or it was the effects of the cocaine. Perhaps that wasn't just something they brought out for the party.

'Are you feeling OK?' I asked, as we rounded up lamps and a smart clock from the lobby and viewing room.

'Hmm? Yeah, fine. Well, not fine because' – she gestured to take in our entire situation – 'but nothing's specifically wrong with me. Why?'

'You just seem a bit . . . down. Is it work?'

'No, no. Work's the same as it ever was. The market's down everywhere but going high end and low end have kept us going.' Her voice rattled out like stones thrown at a window – hard, fast and sharp. It definitely sounded like she was on something.

'There'll always be a market for couture,' she continued. 'The very best, you know? Set your own price and it's never too much. Someone always pays. And Elliott – Elliott my right-hand man, my ideas guy – he talked me into doing this line for that awful website – Lilypad?'

'The fast-fashion one?' I'd been seeing their ads for ages. Dungarees for thirty-eight pence, a full prom gown for under a fiver. God knows what the stuff looked like when it got delivered. Or how much the people making it were being paid. I knew from bitter experience that those websites thought nothing of exploiting both their employees and small creators. Lilypad's predecessor – ShopSmile! – had duplicated my viral sausage dog design only days after I'd first posted it. My version cost £28 on a hand-dyed cotton t-shirt, whilst theirs was just £5.80, both the design and the tie-dye background printed on viscose. Guess which one everyone flocked to? That was the week I packed my design ambitions in. Even when I managed to make something everyone wanted, someone else just took it for themselves.

'Them, yes. You've probably bought from there. I know those places mostly steal their ideas but we've got the funds to sue them into the ground, so they cut a deal instead. It's going to be huge. Massive.'

I nodded, bitterness swimming in my veins. I wished I'd had the money to take ShopSmile! to court. Instead I'd only been able to bleat about it to two hundred or so TikTok followers.

I looked around to avoid the topic and spotted a telescope in the viewing room. It was an antique, or a reproduction of one; polished copper and brass on wooden legs. Would it be useful for spotting any nearby boats that could help us? I folded it up to take it to the bridge.

'So, if it's not work, what is it?' I asked, letting the tiny barb about Lilypad pass me by. I screwed up my courage and went for it. 'Is it . . . Leon? Does he . . . I mean, is he making any money of his own or do you feel like he's kind of . . . taking you for granted?'

'It's nothing you need to worry about,' Mags said, sniffing. 'I'd say Libby has bigger problems with Olly. At least my relationship isn't built on lies. Can you believe they rented a fake helicopter? I mean, God.' She tutted.

Was that all she had to say? Her relationship was fine, even if Leon was taking advantage of her, because Libby's was worse? Was 'Is this better than what Libby has?' the one metric Mags cared about, still? The thought both saddened and repulsed me.

'Are you sure you're all right? It just sounds like—'

'We're fine,' Maggie said, turning sharp. She cast her eyes over me and sniffed again. 'You should worry about finding a man of your own. You're not getting any younger.'

With that frosty end to the conversation she took her armful of electronics to Harry, slick ponytail swishing in her wake. I was left watching her go, astonished and hurt. Maggie had hit closer to the truth than she probably realised. I wasn't getting any younger and I hadn't even dated casually in three years. My string of casual flings had ended with Jimmy – a fellow artist I'd met through my last job at a craft supplies shop. He'd been everything I wanted – kind, funny, easy going and adventurous – but within weeks of him inviting me on that America trip I was picking stupid fights and ignoring his messages, pushing him away. Maggie was right, I wasn't getting any younger, and unfortunately, I wasn't getting any less broken either.

I'd also clearly touched a nerve by mentioning her fiancé.

God knows how she would have reacted if I'd tried to tell her about last night. Still, I was worried for her. Maggie came from a family with unsteady fortunes, their celebrity status already questionable before she was born. It was obvious she felt she needed Leon around to shore up her credentials, just as Libby used Olly's name and status, but was that really worth what Maggie was putting up with? She was the one with the money, as far as I could see, yet he was the one calling the shots.

As if I'd summoned him, Leon wandered into the viewing room. He'd put a robe on over his boxers and popped his sunglasses on top of his head. As though we were still on a pleasure trip and not stranded at sea. He didn't look at me as he went past, puffing on a vape pen. Clearly he'd decided I wasn't worth the trouble.

'Did you seriously bring me nothing?' I heard Harry say.

'What? Oh right. No, I couldn't find anything,' Leon said.

I took a rallying breath and headed into the bridge. I handed over my finds to Harry, who was in the middle of dissecting a Bluetooth speaker. Maggie was leaning against the cold glass of the window, looking out to sea.

'Do you think we'll be back to shore by five?' Leon said. 'I've got plans to meet for dinner.'

I checked Maggie's reaction, noting Leon's use of the singular. She remained impassive, like a model trained to ignore the sticks of pins as she was dressed and discussed.

I felt suddenly exhausted. I'd hardly slept and had spent the last few hours being dealt blow after blow to my nerves. To top it off, I was dealing with people who refused to grasp the kind of mess we were in. Thankfully, Harry spoke up.

'Do I think we'll be back by five . . .' He twisted his face in a pantomime of deep consideration. 'Umm . . . no. No,

I don't. I think there's a good chance we might still be out here by next bloody year if I can't get this radio fixed. Especially if you keep asking me stupid questions instead of doing something useful,' he said, voice climbing until he stopped just short of shouting.

'Like what?' Leon said. His tone held a little of the rage he'd displayed last night, just on a colder setting. I inched forward, ready to get between the two of them – for what good that would do.

'Like whatever Hannah says you should be doing,' Harry said, turning back to his work on the radio, effectively dismissing Leon as not worth his attention. 'She's the only other person actually trying to get us out of this mess.'

I felt myself flush. Thanks, Harry, just put the spotlight of Leon's anger on me, why don't you? Besides which, Maggie had been doing something to help. I swallowed and tried to summon some of the confidence that had filled me when I told Libby we were done.

'Why don't we get the broken glass cleaned up before someone gets hurt, get some food down us and then . . . then we need to set up some kind of watch for tonight. It's going to get dark sooner than we'd like, and someone needs to be awake to signal in case another boat passes or we drift closer to land.'

I didn't say 'because that's our only hope if the radio can't be fixed', but I thought it and it was as if that thought infected everyone else in the room. I saw Leon glance at Harry and for the first time he looked a little worried. Maggie folded her arms around herself and nodded.

It had taken several hours of me and Harry running around like Chicken Little, but it looked like they were starting to grasp that we were all equally trapped now. There were no special perks or options available to Leon and Mags that I just hadn't thought of or couldn't afford. In this one, horrible situation, we were all on the same level. At any other time I might have dreamed of being able to bring them down to earth so sharply. Just then, though, I really would have bitten my tongue and played the poor little mouse girl, if any of them could have bought our way out of that mess.

CHAPTER TWELVE

Despite Harry directing everyone to me for instructions, no one seemed that interested in actually helping me out with cleaning. Which was fair enough, I supposed. It wasn't urgent, just a matter of making things a little safer. So I left Leon and Mags to watch as Harry worked on the radio and did my best to clean up the more dangerous mess.

I swept up the worst of the broken glass from the lobby and stairs, then dumped it in the kitchen bin. The vomit-covered bathroom on the lower deck was a lost cause and instead of tackling it I just moved a sofa in front of it to stop anyone going in. I left the smears on the wall, the sticky dried-on drink puddles and Leon's stained boxers in the hot tub. I was doing this to avoid cutting myself on broken glass, not to return the boat to its former glory. I hoped Olly would lose his deposit.

I then attempted to salvage some of the party food. Between the broken glass, the power of the heaters and the picky fingers of the other guests, a lot of it was completely irrecoverable. What wasn't dangerous, off or smashed to bits, I transferred to the fridge.

I didn't run into Libby or Olly once. I guessed they were in their room. I didn't have the energy to confront them and try to force them into helping. It was easier to just get on with things. I took some water bottles upstairs to the bridge and then went back to the kitchen to make some coffee – because I needed some and didn't mind making extra whilst I was at it.

By the time I was finished with everything and brought food and a pot of black coffee up to the bridge, the sun was slipping beneath the sea. The winter-shortened days weren't ideal for us. I wanted us to be seen, to be saved, but we hadn't spotted a single boat all day. Harry had been keeping an eye out from the bridge and grimly reported that he had yet to spot a sign of land or another boat, even in the far distance.

None of us understood the yacht's readouts enough to understand where we had drifted to. I was praying we weren't going out into the Atlantic. Though we'd know eventually. The further we went the colder it would get. Not that it was particularly balmy on deck to start with.

'Finally.' Libby breezed into the viewing room and immediately went to pour herself a cup of coffee. 'Is there any milk? I'll take whatever – though non-dairy, obviously.'

There was of course no milk of any kind whatsoever, a fact which had probably already sailed right out of her mind, but I wasn't her personal barista, so I ignored her. She huffed and sat down, sipping the coffee and screwing up her face in exaggerated disgust.

I'd put together a tray of food, since we hadn't actually eaten since last night. Or at least . . . I hadn't. For all I knew, when the others had disappeared to their own rooms or God knows where else, they had been eating whatever they could find.

'Thanks, Han,' Harry said, squeezing my shoulder as he passed. 'Gonna find a loo.'

'Steer clear of the one in the lobby.'

I felt bad, watching him go. He'd been working on the radio for hours and the air smelled of solder and singed plastic. Still no progress though, or he'd have said something. No one asked about the radio. I don't think it was entirely obliviousness. I think we were all too scared to face what it meant to have no way of contacting help.

Instead we sat around on the stained, crumb-strewn furniture and ate wilted salad, stale bread and dried-out lumps of meat and fish. The coffee at least was very good, and even though I normally drowned mine in syrup or dumped sugar in it, the bitter brew felt appropriate. It paired well with the sour lump in the back of my throat, where everything I wanted to say but couldn't was rotting on my tongue. I wasn't just keeping quiet to prevent a panic, I was also still trying to keep the peace. Despite my outburst earlier I didn't want to get into yet another argument. I was already dead on my feet and didn't have the energy to waste.

Then Olly started talking.

'I see you're still happy to eat the food I paid for, despite your contempt for me and my success,' he said lightly, spreading some crusty-looking pâté on a piece of hardened bread as if he was having afternoon tea at The Savoy.

A quick look in the direction of Maggie and Leon told me they were watching and waiting for my response. I was apparently the on-board entertainment for the evening. Again. Libby was sitting slightly apart from the rest of us, looking out to sea. Ignoring me in particular, or just everyone in general, I had no idea. Possibly both.

'Thanks. It's nice of you to come up and sit with us. Finally,' I said.

'Hannah, maybe don't start drama?' Libby put in, without turning round.

'I didn't start anything,' I said, hurt despite myself that she would say something like that, even though she'd already shown her true colours.

'That's rubbish,' Olly said. 'You're the one who attacked Libby.'

'Attacked?' I scoffed.

'You launched into a diatribe against my wife, unprovoked. When we are all at our lowest right now and should be banding together . . .'

'Unprovoked?' I repeated in disbelief. 'I think hearing the pair of you talk about me like I'm a cross between a Victorian orphan and a tatty souvenir you're not sure if you want anymore was provocation enough.'

Olly glared at me, not a trace of shame anywhere in his expression. 'Were we wrong? You *are* being ungrateful.'

I looked at Maggie for support, but she just rolled her eyes and waved her hands limply as if to shoo us all out of sight and hearing. I could see from the corner of my eye that Leon was smirking. With Harry still somewhere down in the cabins, I didn't have a single ally on deck and Olly knew it.

'He's right,' Leon drawled, looking critically over the food rather than at me. 'The way you were last night? So fucking uppity.'

'Why, because I stopped you slobbering over me?' I glanced at Maggie again, hoping this might jolt her into action, but she only looked once at Leon and then away again. So it wasn't news to her that he did things like this. She just put up with it. A weird mixture of pity and disgust filled me. How little did she think of herself?

'There you go again. Bitch, bitch, bitch. It's like you don't want anyone to like you. You should be grateful I'd even touch someone like you.' He looked to Olly. 'I'd have double-wrapped it. You should hear Mags' stories about her. Is it any surprise you're alone – like, really?' Leon said, focusing on me again. 'No one stuck around once you shut your legs and opened your mouth. It's obvious that you're jealous of Mags and Libby. They're hot, they've got successful men to take care of them and you're this close to hitting the wall. Every guy can smell it on you.' He inhaled. 'Desperation and old minge.'

I was so tired and so wrung out from a whole day spent navigating these people and the shock of being set adrift. There was a ringing in my ears and I felt like I had in middle school, when one of the cool girls pulled my shirt up whilst I was hanging from a tree branch and everyone saw my too-small greying bra. Everyone was watching me be humiliated and no one wanted it to stop. I wanted to scream.

'Olly's right, you should be grateful, because you don't belong here. You belong in a council flat, being smacked about by whatever loser'll still have you. It'd do you good. Teach you to mind your fucking manners.'

'Oi!'

Harry was on him before Leon's smirk had time to fade. The pair of them hit the floor in a flurry of grasping hands and gritted teeth. I was still reeling from the vicious words but a tiny part of me was elated that Harry had knocked them right out of Leon's mouth.

'Harry, stop it!' Libby cried, finding her tongue now that it wasn't me who was in danger of being hurt. 'Leon!'

Leon and Harry separated as quickly as they'd collided. Leon's sunglasses were bent and bloody saliva was running down his chin. Harry had a red eye, which was sure to turn black soon, and his nose was bleeding. He was fixated on Leon, ready to attack again at a moment's notice.

'Another word out of you,' he panted, 'I'll put you down for good – you got that? Hannah has done everything she can for you today, you fuck.'

Leon slunk over to Maggie, one eye still on Harry. Maggie dutifully examined his face, though I didn't think she knew what she was looking for. She was just playing a role in this little scene; the damsel to his barbarian.

'Sit down and stop acting like a thug,' Olly sneered at Harry. 'God, you really can't buy class, can you?'

'Yeah, apparently you can't rent it either,' Harry retorted, genuine anger hidden under sarcasm.

Olly's cheeks pinkened. 'I swear if either of you two ingrates mentions that again, I'll—'

'What? You'll what?' Harry advanced on him slowly, but with the eyes of someone you'd avoid on the way home from a night out. The kind of expression that screamed 'what you lookin' at?'. Olly shifted backwards slightly, then looked annoyed with himself for doing so. He stood up straighter, trying for a height advantage over Harry's steel-cable frame, built on pints of Guinness and hammering scrap metal into works of art.

'I'm getting really sick of this big "I am" act of yours,' Harry said, voice all the more dangerous for becoming quiet. 'I kept it to myself today, mostly, because I was busy trying to get us out of this mess. *Your* mess. But you are taking the piss if you think you can just hide away in your cabin and come out to play lord of the manor once the work's done. As of right now, you're pulling your weight. Both of you,' he said, glancing at Libby, who looked down, as if finally feeling just a bit ashamed.

'Oh, shut up,' Leon barked from the safety of the opposite side of the room. 'Who put you in charge? This is Olly's yacht, Olly's party . . .'

'Party's over, and the boat's a rental, so . . .' Harry gave an exaggerated shrug. 'As for who put me in charge—' He seemed to swell with anger, even as his face showed a trace of indecision. It was like he was holding back, though what and why I had no idea.

'Don't,' Libby said, quietly.

'Don't what?' Olly snapped. But she wasn't talking to him, and we all knew it.

'I'm not letting this go on,' Harry said. 'Olly, either you drop this lord and master shit right now, or I'm not giving you a penny when we get back to land.'

Silence has its own sound at sea. The waves rush in to fill even the most awkward, loaded pauses. The ocean breathes in and out, marking the time and making it drag on and on, building until you can't take it anymore.

'What have you done?' Olly said, finally breaking. For the first time he appeared truly rattled, sweat gleaming on his upper lip as he looked at his wife, his eyes almost bugging out of his fine-boned skull.

'What you wouldn't,' Libby spat back, turning to play to the rest of us, her captive audience. 'And I'm sick of trying to hold you up. Guess what, everyone – Olly went "hands off" with our portfolio and the management firm he brought in scammed us. He didn't even realise until a few months ago. There's been almost nothing coming in and everything going out. So, I asked Harry for a loan.' She laughed again, humourless and sharp. 'I should have used it to get a divorce lawyer.'

'You traitorous bitch,' Olly murmured.

'Gold-digging slut.' Leon's eyes strayed to Maggie as if reassuring himself that she was still beside him. Maggie hadn't moved but she was watching Libby, the corner of her mouth twitched in what might almost have been a smile.

'You're one to talk,' Harry laughed at Leon.

'Hey, I'm a man – I provide!' Leon snapped.

'I thought you were a podcaster?' Harry said. 'What are you providing? Commentary?'

Leon looked ready to go for him again.

Things were finally clicking into place for me. The lack of staff, the rented yacht and the fake helicopter. The pared-down guest list, which somehow still had me on it – because I was the person best placed to stroke their egos. This party was about saving face, playing through the pain. Olly and Libby had invited us because we were the ones who were in awe of them. Even Leon and Mags aspired to be them. We were the ones who'd be fooled by all this. I wondered if Libby had been planning on using this party on her socials to give the impression that everything was fine. To try and fool business partners and potential investors alike that she and Olly were still winning at life.

'If you want to go – go!' Olly suddenly thundered. He and Libby were face to face, both practically vibrating with anger. I was worried, though for whom I didn't know. Libby looked ready to give as good as she got, and Olly had a murderous expression on his face.

'Gladly!' Libby retorted. 'Oh and babe? I hope you realise

that the properties bought with my money won't be taken in your bankruptcy. And thanks to your weaselly little pre-nup, I might not get half of your . . . nothing, but you're also not seeing a penny of my portfolio either.' She smiled a sweet, glossy smile. 'I'm sure your mother will be more than happy to have you back home though. I can send your things on.'

Olly stood there like a well-bred statue, unblinking and stiff as if his rage had fossilised him. Only his eyes moved, flicking between all of us and back to Libby as if he was trying to calculate a way out of this trap.

'Anyway.' Libby faked a yawn. 'I'm off to bed and hopefully tomorrow we'll spot a boat or whatever and get home, because I have a lot of phone calls to make.' She tossed her hair over her shoulder and headed for the stairs.

'You think I honestly believe you're willing to lose my name, my reputation? Not a chance. You're nothing without me, babe,' Olly called after her, finally finding his tongue and trotting out the pet name in a mocking tone. 'That money's not going to keep you warm at night either.'

'Someone else has been doing that for the last six months . . . babe,' Libby called back, not bothering to turn around as she disappeared onto the lower deck.

I glanced at Leon and found him watching Libby with an odd expression. A mixture of disgust and blatant desire. Was there something going on there? He'd tried it on with me, why not another of Mags' friends? Though I wasn't sure if Libby would be into him. Then again, I could see her using Leon to get one over on her husband. That was a very Libby move. Olly and Leon might have been from the same posh tree, but I knew Olly considered himself a true aristocrat and barely tolerated Leon's overly boisterous

119

'rah' demeanour. If Libby wanted to drive Olly crazy, Leon would be the perfect person to use against him. Especially if she wanted to keep moving in higher social circles.

In the silence that followed Libby's departure I locked eyes with Harry. He raised his eyebrows as if to say 'hey, don't blame me'. Ever since he'd gone for Leon mid-rant I'd been trying to pull myself together. I'd let myself get beaten into a corner and my pride was dented, my nerves a wreck. I swallowed the bitter taste in my mouth and told myself not to let them see me cry.

'If we're going to turn in, we should sort out a watch. Make sure someone's awake in case we pass a boat or spot land.'

Harry picked up several discarded cocktail sticks and snapped the end off of one, closing them all in his fist.

'Short straw takes first watch.'

For once, nobody disagreed. I think for the first time, we'd had enough of arguing.

CHAPTER THIRTEEN

Harry got the first short stick, followed by Leon, who picked the other half. I wasn't too thrilled that Leon would be the only one of us awake once Harry went to sleep but I knew at some point we had to start delegating. Harry and I couldn't do everything, and we'd burn out fast if we tried. Leon was an adult and even if I didn't trust him, I at least trusted that he wanted off this boat as much as the rest of us did. Even he couldn't be blasé about it as we went into our first full night out at sea.

To make matters worse, as Harry set up the telescope and some lamps to use for signalling, the weather began to change. I'd hardly noticed the cold outside. In fact, aside from when I'd tried to leave the boat that morning, I hadn't really been outside at all. The route from the cabins to the bridge was all enclosed – aside from the window Leon had partially shattered – and the heaters were still blazing, as they had been all night.

As everyone headed below, however, I paused in the viewing room and looked out into the night. It was impossible to see anything further than a metre or so from the boat. Out there it was all black, a darkness that moved and sighed and churned around us. On the boat, spotlights lit everything up and so it was easy to see that there was a storm brewing. The bower on the middle deck swayed dangerously, and the floaty fabric of the canopy thrashed in the growing gale. The boat was rocking as it crested each wave and I stumbled as I headed for the stairs, feeling drunk as I eased myself down them to the lower deck.

The wind had knocked some of the shattered glass out of the cracked window and was howling at the gap. The injection of icy air was breath-taking, as if someone had opened the door of a plane mid-flight. The furious roar of the sea and the blasts of freezing air sent me shivering to the cabins below. Down there, the sound of the sea was masked somewhat by the sounds of Libby and Olly yelling at each other. I heard my name once or twice and rolled my eyes. However the pair of them felt about one another, apparently they were of one mind when it came to me. Perhaps it was a good thing they had at least that in common.

I went to my room and collapsed on the bed. It felt like an eternity had passed since I'd crawled out of it that morning, hungover but determined to leave this boat and everyone on it behind me. I so badly wanted to wake up again and find that this was all just a nightmare. A champagne-addled imagining of how awful it would be to be trapped with my former 'friends' and their awful partners. I just wanted to open my eyes and see my bag unpacked on the floor, my dress from last night still damp. The past twelve hours just a horrible memory.

Lying there I tried to calculate how long it would take until someone came to look for us. I wasn't scheduled to work for the next three days, and even if I was, I doubted my manager would do more than try to phone me. If there was no answer, Rin might send a snide email, but that would be it. No one at work would be ringing the police to raise the alarm about my disappearance. They'd just process my termination and send the letter to my flat, where my landlord would bin it as he cleared the place out.

It was more likely someone would notice the others were missing first. Libby's assistant might try and call her to find out what flavour smoothie she'd like on her return. Or perhaps Harry had an art show booked and his agent would be trying to reach him? Maggie probably had meetings she would be missed at and Leon . . . well, his dealer might miss him, and perhaps his podcast 'fans'. But did any of those people know the exact details of where we were? Maybe Libby's assistant, or someone who worked for Olly. But what if they'd lied to them, too, about taking the yacht on a cruise around France? How badly had they wanted to keep up appearances? Enough to lie to the people they were employing as well? I wanted to ask but it was unlikely they'd tell me the truth, not without a fight anyway.

Then there were the people who actually owned the yacht. If Olly had only rented it for a few days, there was a chance they'd notice pretty quickly that we'd gone adrift. Or they might even have a tracker on board and have realised already. They'd probably go right to the police and send them and the coastguard after us – but only if there was some way to track us, which, given the state of the radio and the lack of fuel, I wasn't sure there was. Otherwise they'd have to get Italian search and rescue out looking for us and that was a lot of ground, or water, to cover.

What if they didn't check on the yacht? What if, like Olly,

they were rich enough to delegate the work of maintaining the ship to a company somewhere? Would they be closed for the bank holiday? Maybe for a few days after that as well, as a thank you to their staff, who probably worked over Christmas so that all of the Ollys of the world could get the yacht of their dreams for the festive season. What if it took a week for someone to realise what had happened to us? Or longer?

How long would it be before someone knew we were gone and started looking?

How long until they actually managed to find us?

That question, and all the infuriating, unknowable variables inherent in trying to answer it, kept me awake even after I decided it was useless trying to work it out. I couldn't turn my brain off. Couldn't stop trying to find an answer that would set my nerves to rest for even a minute before the doubts crept back in. The storm outside rocked the boat and the wind roaring overhead added to my unease.

I was still awake when a door slammed and someone marched past my door on their way to the stairs. Had Olly finally had enough of arguing? Or was that Leon heading up early to have a row with Harry? I listened but couldn't hear any shouting. I debated going to see what was up but knew Harry could handle himself. If it really was Leon, my appearance would be like a red flag to a bull. He hated Harry but he loathed me. I wasn't just the only poor person on board – by their standards, at least – I also had the nerve to be a woman. One who'd rejected both him and his money. It probably would have pleased him to know how scared of him I'd been that first night. How worried I now was about a repeat performance.

I was awake when Harry came down to wake Leon for

his turn on watch. I heard him knocking on the bedroom door and calling out, then Leon shouting groggily through it that he was 'coming now, so shut up'. Either Leon hadn't been the one to leave or he'd come back whilst I was dozing. I listened as Leon thudded down the corridor and up the stairs, stumbling as the boat rolled on the waves. I heard him swear as he encountered the cold draught and the howling wind.

I felt sick lying in bed, and not only because of the uncertainty and fear. The boat wasn't just rocking now, but pitching from side to side. I could feel the force of the waves, even through the layers of engineering and décor that stood between me and the sea itself. The whole boat seemed to be caught between the hands of something enormous that kept shaking us as it pressed in on all sides, harder and harder until it seemed the walls around me would crumple. I kept thinking about the hollow books and the weight limit Libby had talked about. Was that just a story she'd concocted to sell the idea that this was their yacht, or had she been repeating something she'd been told when they rented it?

Sleep finally idled into my brain. It was fractured and shallow, but I didn't care about feeling fresh in the morning. I just wanted to escape the confines of the boat and the other people on it, however temporarily.

I was ripped out of this downtime by a frantic bellow so loud and deformed that it took me a moment to realise that it was a word, still longer to realise that it was Olly shouting it.

'Libby!'

I rolled out of bed as soon as the fog in my brain cleared, still fully dressed from the day before, and tore open the door to my room. The motion of the boat swung the door back at me, and it hurt my arm as I tried to push past it. Down the hallway Harry's matted head appeared, and moments later I saw Mags as her door cracked open and swung on its hinges. She'd finally taken down her ponytail and her long black hair hung to her waist, tangled like seaweed. Olly came stumbling down the stairs and gaped at us. He looked terrible – his skin greyish with lack of sleep and his eyes red and puffy from drinking.

'Where's Libby?' He demanded.

Harry stepped into the hall, immediately alert. 'What's happened?'

'I don't know! She's just . . . gone. I've been looking everywhere and she's not here.' Olly normally looked like a disgraced MP being tailed by the press when he got angry; all tight lips and flushed cheekbones, stiff and unapologetic. Right then, though, he looked like the schoolboy he must have been once. He was sweaty and shaking, eyes darting around as if he was expecting Libby to appear from behind one of us.

'There's nowhere to go,' I said. 'She has to be here somewhere.'

Olly's head jerked towards me and for a moment he looked unsure of who I even was. How much had he had to drink? And where had he got it from? I remembered the bar upstairs and grimaced. I should have hidden the booze before, knowing how volatile things were.

'You! You've done something to her,' He yelled, pointing at me.

'Me?' I looked to Harry for help, but he seemed just as off-kilter as I felt in that moment. The idea that something had been done to Libby hit me like a stone to the chest.

'You've been desperate to bring her down since you arrived.

126

Libby told you she wasn't going to let you parasite off of her anymore and you couldn't take it, could you?' Olly attempted to stalk towards me, but the boat shifted and he stumbled into the wall. He clung there and glared at me.

'That is not what happened, and you know it. You think I'd seriously hurt Libby? Over her not inviting me to any more of these parties? You're insane. She's probably sleeping it off somewhere away from you after last night!'

'You as good as assaulted me,' Leon said. He was behind Mags, like she was a fragile climbing flower and he was the brick wall that held her up. 'In the kitchen.'

'I threw water on you because you were being disgusting. That is not an "assault". If you start flinging that word around it'll stick to you – not me.'

Leon paled slightly and then nudged Maggie. She swayed slightly at the touch, flinching from it.

'Don't talk to my fiancé that way,' Maggie said flatly, as if she was a doll and he'd pulled her string. 'My solicitors could destroy you before you got two words out to anyone.'

I looked at her, pity mixing with anger. How could she be so wilfully blind? So stupid? Apparently it was fine for her to know what he'd done, but she'd rather sue to hide the truth than face up to it herself.

'He was meant to be on watch,' I said, jabbing a finger at Leon.

'Yeah, why are you down here? Did you just wake up?' Harry demanded.

It was pretty obvious that he had. Leon was once again shirtless and wearing just boxers. There were pillow creases on his face and arm.

'Only just.' He shrugged. 'There was nothing to watch for and I was tired. It's a good thing I was down here otherwise maybe Mags would be "missing", too.' He gave me a 'so there' look as he threw the blame back my way.

'Or maybe you tried to do to Libby what you tried on with me and it got out of hand.' My nails bit into my palms and I realised how hard I was clenching my fists. Despite Harry's presence I felt like I was being attacked from all sides.

'Fuck you, you little bitch. How dare you accuse me of something like that. If you repeat that anywhere else, I swear to God we will sue you into oblivion – won't we, babe?' Leon wrapped a meaty hand around Maggie's bird-like elbow and squeezed.

'Yes,' Maggie replied tightly. 'Watch yourself, Hannah.'

'Take a look at yourself, Maggie,' I snapped. 'Your friend is missing and all you care about is threatening me because your fiancé's a creep.'

'Stop it, all of you,' Harry said, stepping between me and Mags. I felt immediately ashamed, but a tiny part of me was angry he hadn't spoken up for me when the accusations started flying. Angry and hurt. I uncurled my fists and jammed my hands under my arms to hide the fact that they were trembling.

'When did you last see Libby?' Harry demanded of Olly, turning to face him. 'You two were in your room, last I knew.'

'She was still there when I . . . when I fell asleep,' Olly said, rubbing a hand over his drink-bloated face, the other still braced against the wall.

'Or when you passed out,' Harry said, folding his arms. 'I can smell the booze from here.'

'I was trying to unwind. It had been a stressful day,' Olly hissed through clenched teeth.

I rolled my eyes. Like the rest of us didn't know that. Still, beneath my annoyance I was starting to panic. There were only so many places Libby could be, and if Olly had already searched them, that meant she was somewhere we wouldn't expect. Which meant she was hiding. Or hidden. Two very different states but neither of which boded well.

'Where have you looked?' Harry asked, glancing down the corridor behind Olly. 'Obviously she's not in anyone's room, so that leaves the upper decks or your room.'

'She wasn't in our room or the bathroom. I went upstairs to see if she was with anyone . . . but she wasn't there. Not on the lower deck or up by the bridge.'

Was it my imagination or had Olly's eyes flicked towards Leon then? Quick as a whip. Did he know, or at least suspect, as I did, that the affair she'd claimed to be having was with him? A cold dread settled in the pit of my stomach. What had he done to her? Libby might not have been my favourite person just then, or have ever been a real friend, but that didn't mean I wasn't worried. She was still a person. She was still someone I'd cared about for a long time and like a phantom limb those feelings were still there – even after the traumatic amputation that had occurred yesterday.

Olly's long fingers twitched, nails digging at his cuticles. 'I called for her and I looked but . . . where the fuck is she?'

'We should search the boat,' Harry said, turning from Olly to the rest of us, ready to take control of the situation. 'Leon and Maggie, you do the cabins down here. Olly, we'll cover the upper and middle decks. Han—'

'Not on her own,' Olly said, stumbling away from the wall. 'She can't be trusted.'

'I'm not the one she said she was cheating on and then threatened to ruin,' I couldn't resist retorting, though my voice was shaking. 'If she isn't just getting some space and something has happened to her, you're the one with the massive motive. Not me.'

'Hannah . . . you look with Mags and Leon,' Harry said, throwing up an arm to cut Olly off. 'We'll find her. We have to. There are only so many places she can be.'

I didn't argue, just went over to Maggie and Leon. He immediately started to shut the door on me, probably so he could get dressed but also to make a point, but Maggie stepped out as he did so, and he gave her a look before slamming the door behind her. I watched as Olly and Harry climbed the stairs to deck level.

'Do you really think he did something to her?' Maggie asked, so softly I almost didn't hear her.

'I hope not. But it's nice to know you give a damn.'

'Of course I do. Like you said, she's my friend.' Maggie clutched her arms around herself, swaying with the boat's motion. It was as if now that everyone else was out of sight she felt able to treat me like a person. Which was probably exactly what was going on. Libby had at least been a fairly consistent level of bitchy. With Maggie it was harder to predict what she'd do or say. Two-faced didn't quite cover it though. Mags seemed to have a limitless supply of them.

'Come on. We'll start in the engine room and work back up.'

We went down the corridor and I chewed my lip as we went into Libby and Olly's room. The place had been reasonably tidy yesterday but now the bed was a tangled mess and there was broken glass on the vanity. I jumped as the boat rocked and a bottle of perfume slid across the vanity, stopping just short of falling off. Libby's gold party dress was half draped over the mirror, weeping beads from unravelling threads. Something, or someone, had torn the shoulder strap and it hung down limply.

'Do you think he did that?' Maggie asked.

'I don't know,' I said, not looking at the dress but at the wall behind it. 'But that mark there . . . It looks like blood.'

CHAPTER FOURTEEN

It wasn't a lot of blood, but it was smeared as if someone had steadied themselves against the white panelling. Someone with blood on their hands. Maggie and I both stared at it for a long time, neither of us wanting to say what we were both probably thinking. Something had happened to Libby in that room. Something bad.

'We should search the rest of this level,' I said finally. I didn't say for what. I wasn't really sure by then if we were looking for Libby herself, or more evidence of what had happened to her. Olly was a bastard – Leon, too, come to that – but what was I accusing them of here? Murder? Were either of them capable of killing Libby and covering it up? Olly had seemed genuinely anxious but was that because his wife was missing and we were still drifting at sea, or did he have something to hide?

I could hear Harry and Olly calling Libby's name in the distance, shouts half stolen by the storm. My heart felt caught in a fist, squeezing every few seconds. When I called her name my voice came out slightly mangled, tearing at the edges.

There was no sign of Libby in the engine room. I'd been hoping she'd be there as it was one of the only places Olly probably hadn't already checked. Of course there was no reason for her to be in there, but then again, there was no reason for her to be missing at all. We checked the bedrooms again, despite all of us having been in them when Olly was searching. Or when he claimed to be searching. There was no sign of Libby, not so much as a loose bead from her dress. We even checked the built-in wardrobes and tiny wet rooms, as if she might have decided to play a solo game of hide-and-seek just to fuck with us. Which I was sort of hoping she had. Because what was the alternative?

In the kitchen the racks of cooking utensils swung, chiming together as the boat crested tall waves outside. I found my eyes straying to the magnetic rack of expensive chef knives, winking under the fluorescents. None of them were missing. I told myself I was being stupid, but it was still a relief to see them all there. There was, however, an empty bottle of gin and two of premium tonic water, left out to sweat condensation onto the counter. They must have been from Olly's late-night binge. No wonder he looked so terrible. And if he'd drunk that bottle by himself, it wouldn't have been hard for Libby to leave their room without him noticing.

As we checked the larger kitchen cabinets I ran through all the other places on board that she could be. Places Olly wouldn't have looked already. There weren't many options; the vomit-covered bathroom seemed unlikely, at least in terms of places she'd go willingly. The helicopter? It was a possibility, but the outside was glass, so surely Olly had taken a peek when he searched the deck? Unless he hadn't bothered to go outside into the storm. The gin bottle slid

133

across the counter and exploded on contact with the floor. Maggie and I both jumped in surprise, then exchanged embarrassed glances.

We finished our fruitless search with the powder room and the linen cupboard. I'd been listening out for the others, hoping Olly or Harry would come running to tell us they'd found her. They hadn't and I also couldn't hear them calling for her anymore. Had they finished looking already? Or, like me, were they starting to feel like there was no point in shouting? The longer the search went on the less hopeful I was of hearing a sudden shout from above, or Libby giggling and calling out that she'd managed to get one over on Olly, on all of us. Something – anything – but the reality that seemed to be looming out of every dark, Libby-less space: that she was no longer on board the yacht.

It was the only thing I could think of, the answer that was all around us but which nobody had dared to mention. We were trapped on a boat. If one of us had vanished, as it seemed Libby had, there was only one real possibility. The question was how it had happened. Either she'd jumped in herself, or someone had thrown her in. And Libby hadn't seemed the least bit suicidal the night before.

Mags trailed after me as I climbed up the stairs to the viewing room, struggling to keep my footing as the yacht heaved to and fro. I was hoping that Libby would be there when we arrived. After all, it wasn't exactly beyond imagining that the others had just neglected to come and get us after finding her. Though I thought Harry would probably remember that we were still looking.

Harry was in the viewing room with Olly and Leon, who must've left his room whilst we were in the engine room and decided to follow the guys upstairs. Through the floor-to-ceiling windows I watched the bruised sea thrash in the wind. The sky was as dark as the waves, smothered in cloud. Not a single speck of white signalled the presence of another boat, and no wonder. No one was going to come out in this.

There was also no sign of Libby. All three of the guys looked up as Mags and I came in. I just shook my head. Harry was pale and uncharacteristically silent, working a stainless steel skull ring around and around on his thumb. He sat down heavily on a sofa and shook his head as if by copying my gesture he could somehow understand this situation better. Olly was already seated, a white-knuckled hand on either arm of the chair. Leon stood near him like a bodyguard . . . or an arresting officer.

'This can't be happening,' Olly finally said, quietly, like he was scared someone might hear. 'She was here. She was . . . Where could she have gone? Did you look everywhere? Everywhere she might have been?'

Of course we all knew where she could have gone, where she had to be if she wasn't on the boat. But none of us said anything.

Then Leon snapped, thumping a hand down on the back of Olly's chair for attention. 'She's doing this to us on purpose. Hiding. Making everyone worry. Making Olly look bad because of what happened yesterday. This is textbook manipulation. She didn't get what she wanted so now it's tears and the silent treatment and making a scene to get her way.'

'Hiding where, exactly?' Harry asked, jaw twitching with irritation. 'We've searched the entire boat.'

'Wait, no, we haven't,' I said, realising with a sudden dart of hope that, with the discovery of the blood, I'd forgotten about the significance of the extra door downstairs. 'There's a fifth cabin – Libby told me it was locked and off-limits so I didn't even think to check it.'

Relief was as contagious as panic and everyone seemed to succumb to it at once. Harry raised both hands to his forehead as if pained by the fact that this hadn't occurred to him before. Olly sagged in his chair as if I'd just issued a stay of execution that he couldn't quite believe.

'There you go, see? Idiot,' Leon sneered at me, his face losing some its hardness. 'She's in there having a little nap and waiting for us all to lose our minds looking for her.'

'Let's go and check then.' Harry was out of the room a moment later, jogging down the stairs. I followed after him with the others on my tail. I felt slightly drunk with hope, despite the raging storm outside. I wanted so badly for Leon to be right, for once. I think we all did. As angry as I'd be to find Libby having a laugh at our expense, it would be worth it to not have to feel that awful sense of loss and fear again.

When we reached the door at the end of the corridor Harry tried the handle. It was definitely locked. Libby hadn't been making that up. Though of course the bedrooms could be locked from the inside anyway, so that didn't really prove anything. Harry knocked but there was no answer.

'Libs!' He called, rapping his skull ring harder on the door. 'Come on, this isn't funny anymore.'

'She obviously doesn't want to come out,' Mags said, reclining against the wall behind me.

'I don't really care what she wants,' I said, looking at her in disbelief. 'We need to see that she's OK.'

Mags just sighed, like she was done trying to explain something incredibly complex to me.

Leon shoved past me and hammered on the door. 'Libby! Come out here and stop acting like a brat.'

I shared a glance with Harry when no answer came. If Libby was in there she couldn't have slept through that noise. Maybe she was in some kind of trouble? I had visions of her shutting the door and passing out on the bed, choking on her own vomit or accidentally overdosing on some of the party drugs she'd been offering around.

'We need to get this door open – is there a key?' Harry demanded of Olly, still shaking the handle.

'I don't have any keys,' Olly said, like every word was made of piano wire. 'If I had keys, I'd be using them, you half-wit.'

'Check above the door,' I said.

Harry ran his hands over the frame but came up empty.

'All right then . . .' He looked up at the door and pushed it on either side with his hands, as if contemplating a DIY job. 'The hard way it is.'

Harry took a step back and Olly reached out to try and grab him.

'What do you think you're—' Olly began, before the sound of Harry's foot meeting the door drowned him out. The mirrored surface immediately cracked, but the wood underneath was solid. It took a few more hefty kicks before Harry managed to bust the latch. Olly had stopped shouting and was watching the door, completely still and tense, waiting for it to come down so we could see inside.

The lock finally fell off the splintered door, which swung open on its own. All five of us looked into the pristine bedroom. It was the mirror image of my own cabin and the bed had obviously not been slept in since being made up. Harry went in and looked behind the bed, then under it.

Finally he turned back to us, bewildered and pale with shock, still sweating from beating the door down.

'This is ridiculous!' Olly strode into the room, threw the covers off the bed and started opening the wardrobe and cupboards. 'Libby!'

Harry came back to us where we stood clustered around the door.

'If she's not here then . . .' His helpless expression hardened once again. 'The raft.'

I blinked at him and he repeated himself, grabbing my arms in his panic. 'The raft, Han.'

It took a second for me to realise what he was suggesting. My stomach dropped. 'You don't think . . . there's no way she'd be that stupid.'

'You just can't help yourself, can you?' Olly exploded, standing in the midst of the rifled bedroom. 'My wife is missing and you're still insulting her.'

'I'm saying she *wouldn't* be stupid enough to get in our only life raft and try to reach land, in this storm, with no paddle,' I said.

What I did not say was that Libby was certainly selfish enough to take our one life raft. Possibly even angry enough after the set-to last night. Which was why I immediately rushed back up to check the bridge, where I'd left it on the console.

The solid yellow brick of compressed plastic was gone.

My heart stopped for a half second before I spotted it on the floor. It had slid off the console and across the floor with the motion of the boat. I was both relieved and disappointed to have found it. Libby hadn't taken the raft and gone on a suicide mission, but we were no closer to finding out what had happened to her, to proving that she was OK still, but somewhere else.

I brought the raft back with me and met the others in the lobby, where I dumped it on the table. Harry sank into himself when he saw it. Even Olly deflated, dropping into a chair like his strings were cut. It was a slim hope but at least with the raft she'd have had a tiny chance of survival if she went into the stormy sea. Without it? We all knew what that meant.

'This is bullshit,' Leon said. 'You said it – she's not stupid enough to jump in the ocean. Not in winter and not in a storm. She's probably hiding somewhere, if not that bedroom, then somewhere else.'

We all stared at him but Leon only nodded, angrily agreeing with himself. I realised he was talking fast again, his movements jerky. Clearly he still had some coke on board.

'She's doing this on purpose,' Leon said, massaging his fist with a cupped palm. 'When she comes back I'm going to make her pay for causing all this panic, just you wait—'

'Don't!'

Harry's mouth was open, but Maggie got there first. It was the first time I'd seen her contradict Leon and possibly the first time he'd seen it either. His eyes were wide and he looked at her like he was trying to decide if he ought to hit her or just keep talking.

'This isn't Libby! Tell them, Hannah.' She turned to me and I couldn't decide if she was supporting me or deflecting fire in my direction. 'Tell them about the blood.'

Olly's head, which had been hanging down, snapped up. His cool eyes flicked between me and Maggie and I watched his fingers curl on the arms of the chair. What was he thinking? Was he afraid we'd found him out, or just overcome at the idea that his wife was possibly injured?

'Blood?' Harry's whole body stiffened. 'Blood where?'

'There was blood on the wall in Olly and Libby's bedroom,' I said, trying to keep my voice level because it looked like Harry might be about to flip out. 'Just a smear, by the vanity, but . . . Libby's dress was hanging off the mirror next to it and it was ripped.'

I heard Olly finally exhale, a tiny choked little sound.

'You fucking piece of shit.' Harry was on Olly before I could move to stop him.

Olly's armchair tipped backwards as Harry dived at him, then started to punch him, over and over again. This wasn't some brawl either; there was a set to Harry's face that I'd never seen before. He just kept hitting Olly; mechanically, purposefully. He was going to kill him, I realised.

'Harry!' I tried to grab his arm but he twisted away from me. 'Harry, please!'

Leon grabbed Harry's throat from behind, got his forearm around it. Harry left off punching Olly to claw at the arm pressing into his windpipe. His hands were bloody. Olly moaned and rolled to one side on the floor, dribbling blood. Mags looked frozen in place, so I darted forward and tried to put him in the recovery position. He struggled a bit, but I managed to get him shifted and hissed at him to 'Please, just stay still.' I felt a tear roll down my face. I looked up at Harry where he was still struggling against Leon's hold.

'Harry, please stop,' I cried out, voice cracking. 'Leon, don't hurt him.'

'Stop it, now!' Leon said, shaking Harry like a disobedient puppy. 'I hope you enjoyed playing at being one of us – because I'm going to help Olly sue you for every last penny you've made on your trash.'

140

'I . . . don't . . . care,' Harry managed to get out, along with a lot of frothy spit. 'He . . . killed . . . her.'

'Based on what? A smear of blood?' Leon choked Harry harder. It was clear he was enjoying this; his revenge for Harry going at him yesterday. 'All that might prove is that he hit her. Which, given what she did, she had coming. If I were him, I'd have done it in front of all of you. Not that I'd have to. Maggie knows her fucking place.'

I heard Maggie's sharp intake of breath. Her face twitched and a tear slid down her nose as she glanced around. So, Leon wasn't just a creep, but an abusive one, too, and now we all knew. My insides twisted to see Maggie so vulnerable. She opened her mouth but didn't get a chance to say anything before Harry did something that made Leon howl in pain. Leon let him go and cupped his own crotch, then reached out and tried to grab Harry again. He got hold of his leg and pulled him down, then dived on top of him, only just missing me where I was still kneeling beside Olly.

'Stop it!' Maggie screamed. She flew at the pair of them – I wasn't sure who she was trying to protect – and grabbed Leon's beefy arm and tried to hold it back. He hit out in a blind rage, and before I could blink, Maggie was on her back, having hit the table and rolled to the floor.

'Mags!' I struggled to my feet and went to her. She looked stunned and there was a sharp red groove on her temple where her head had made impact.

'For God's sake, stop it!' I ran to the bar and grabbed the first thing that came to hand – a cocktail shaker. I threw it at the pair of them and it hit Leon on the back of the head. He shook it off but the distraction was enough for Harry to flip them over and pin Leon down beside Olly, who was either unconscious or just stunned.

141

I ran to help Harry hold Leon down and we stayed like that until Leon stopped spitting abuse at us and finally sagged to the floor. Harry was gasping for breath, I was shaking and I could hear Maggie quietly sobbing in pain. I got Harry's attention and as one we both, slowly, released our grip on Leon and backed away.

Leon rolled over and sat on the floor, glaring at us like a toddler after a tantrum. His eyes were black dots in a face swollen with fury. Outside the wind screamed, cheated of a fight to the death.

I almost jumped when Olly sat upright. He'd apparently recovered his senses. Looking at him I couldn't help but wince. His cut-glass features were obscured by blood and the beginnings of bruising. One of his eyes wouldn't open. He coughed and spat blood onto the floor, then raised a trembling hand and pointed at Harry, his one good eye glaring at him.

'You're through,' he growled, chest heaving with the pain of speaking. 'Finished.'

I glanced at Harry's hands and saw how badly his knuckles were torn. He'd gone full-force at Olly and I couldn't really blame him. Not when Libby was missing and Olly was the one with the best reason to make her disappear – to protect his money and his pride. Still, the sight of him injured like that made me feel sick. Harry had done that to him.

My gaze moved to Leon. If Leon was the one Libby was having the affair with, why wasn't he worried about her? Perhaps because he cared about as much for Libby as he did for Mags. Maybe, I thought with a shiver of dread, he was the one we ought to be questioning about Libby's disappearance. If he beat his fiancée, why not his mistress?

Mags whimpered, dragging herself to her feet using a chair. 'I'm bleeding.'

'You shouldn't have interfered.' Leon spat the words. 'You never know when to shut up. Don't make me tell you twice.'

Maggie's face crumpled and she fled past all of us, up to the bridge, slamming the door behind her. I would have followed her but there was no way I was leaving the three guys alone. The air was still charged with too much testosterone.

'You all need to calm down,' I said, trying to keep my voice steady. 'Now.'

'Tell him that,' Olly said, probing his damaged face with hesitant fingers.

'You said it yourself – there's blood,' Harry insisted, tensed as if to go for Olly again. 'He killed Libby. Or if not, he at least hurt her and now she's missing,' Harry said. 'She wouldn't . . . there's no way she'd try to top herself. We'd have noticed something was off. She was pissed but not fucking suicidal – so someone did this to her. He did it.'

'I know what I said. But we can't do anything for Libby whilst we're stuck out at sea. If he did do something, we'll take it to the police and they will deal with it.'

'And with you,' Olly muttered, glaring at Harry.

Harry laughed bitterly and spat a mouthful of bloody saliva onto the floor an inch or so away from Olly. 'Yeah, because the rich usually get brought to justice.'

'I don't care what happens to him, so long as everyone knows what he did. I care about what happens to you.' I grabbed Harry's hand. 'You are not getting put away for assault or murder because of this . . . piece of shit.'

'He is,' Leon said. 'I'll be Olly's witness. I'll press charges myself. Look at me. Look what he's done.'

'If you do, I'll be first in line to tell them that you have been snuffling coke like a truffle pig since we boarded, that you hit Maggie, and that you were having it off with Libby behind Olly's back.'

'What?' Olly stopped mopping his face with his sleeve and gaped at Leon, his face a mask of anger and disgust.

'That's not true!' Leon had gone spanked-arse red and looked even more like a scolded child about to have a howling tantrum. 'Ols, I would never!'

'You've been sniffing around my wife?' Olly's voice was a bit indistinct, his lips already swelling, but the outrage in his tone was obvious.

'Sort it out later,' I snapped, really regretting having let that suspicion slip out in front of Olly. 'The point is . . . we need to get off this boat and that's not going to happen if we start ripping chunks off of each other. We won't be able to get to the police, or get a search out for Libby, if we're stuck here.'

'You think she might be alive? Even if she went into the water?' Harry asked.

'I . . . I hope so,' I said. Because the truth – that I knew very well what water that cold felt like and that no one could survive even an hour in it – wouldn't help matters right now. I had to keep everyone focused on getting us to safety. We wouldn't make it if we fell apart. So, I couldn't think about Libby, about all the things we'd said to one another and what her last moments might have been like. I couldn't help her. I could only try to make sure the rest of us made it home.

I was about to ask Harry if he was any closer to fixing the radio when the spotlights in the room died, all at once. The last glow of their elements faded into the gloom of the storm. Across the room, the TV, with its reassuring video of birch logs crackling, went blank. The heater in the corner clicked off and began to tick, cooling down and marking time as we all just stood there, helpless.

CHAPTER FIFTEEN

'What the . . .' Harry looked up at the dark bulbs and then across at me. 'Did we just . . . blow a fuse?'

'The storm, maybe?' I said, though I hadn't heard any lightning. Perhaps the rain beating down on us had gotten into the electrics somehow?

The door to the bridge opened and Maggie came out. She looked a wreck; the red mark on her head matched her red eyes and her nose was running.

'The lights went off. Oh . . .' She looked around, taking in the dead TV and the silent heater. 'What's happened?'

I felt sick. How had I not thought of this. 'I think we're out of power. We must've been running off a battery . . .'

'And now it's dead,' Harry finished, clearly thinking along the same lines as I was. 'Jesus, why didn't we notice that? We should have turned everything off yesterday!'

I thought of all the heaters chugging away both inside and on deck. Belching heat into the freezing air even though no one was out there. All the energy it took to keep the fridge cold and the hot tub bubbling, three decks of spotlights and who knew what else all sucking up power for the last twenty-four hours. We'd been distracted, running around looking for a way to contact the outside world. We hadn't thought to conserve the power. Hadn't even realised we needed to.

'We must've been connected to the mains when we were docked,' Harry said. 'Probably had mains water too. Fuck! Why didn't I think of that?'

'We were all distracted,' I said, trying to make him feel better. 'At least we've got bottled water,' I added, though it wasn't much of a consolation.

'Who cares about water?' Leon said. 'We're going to freeze.'

He was right. The temperature in the room was already falling, thanks to the glass walls and the staircase down to the lobby, where the hole in the window was leaking heat into the storm. It was January and we were way out at sea now, with nothing to shelter us from the elements. Yesterday would look like a party compared to what tonight was going to be like.

'The radio,' Harry said. 'It's not going to work. Even if I fix it we'd still need to run it off something and we don't have any electric left.'

We digested this in silence. Finally, Harry snapped his fingers and pointed at me, suddenly becoming animated. 'My boat, the narrow boat – it's got a leisure battery and a starter battery. If this thing's the same then the starter one might still have some juice. I might be able to connect that to the radio. That's if it can maintain a charge until I get the radio fixed.'

If he got it fixed. He didn't say it, but I heard it in his tone.

'It'll be in the engine room, if it's anywhere,' I said. 'Right? I'll go look.'

'I'll come, too,' Maggie said.

I was surprised but nodded and she followed me down the stairs to the lobby. There was already a pronounced chill down there, despite the boat no longer rocking so violently, indicating that the storm was dying off a bit. I shivered in the cold air. My sweatshirt and leggings would have been perfect for the quick march back to my car, not so much for braving the sea air indefinitely. I shuddered as that word crossed my mind.

Indefinitely.

Only that wasn't accurate, was it? We couldn't survive forever on a few leftover hors d'oeuvres with no heating and what had to be a finite amount of drinking water. No, there was an end in sight and it was very definite indeed. I didn't feel brave enough to look directly at it just then.

In the engine room for the third time, I finally realised that the floor was made up of removable panels – access hatches, labelled and snapped shut.

'Here.' Maggie unclipped a cover and pointed down at a black box that looked almost exactly like a car battery. Or at least, how I remembered one looking from the few times my dad had brought the one from our dying Volvo inside to charge. I'd never gotten up close and personal with the innards of my own car. I'd have only done more harm than good.

Between us we attempted to get it disconnected and out of the small space, huddling over the hatch and trying to worm our fingers in around the battery's casing. There wasn't much room to get leverage. The little compartment had probably been designed to hold just the battery and if there was a tool that would make removing it easier, we didn't have it.

'Are you feeling OK?' I asked, after several minutes of us

trying to get a grip on the battery and failing. Both us sat back to catch our breath and rub our bruised fingers. 'You know, since the—' I gestured to her head.

'I was dizzy. I feel better now,' Maggie said tightly.

'Sorry. I shouldn't have let it get that crazy,' I said, not sure how to broach the topic of Leon's abuse, or even if I ought to.

'I don't think there was much you could have done to stop them. Harry looked insane,' Maggie said, picking at a loose cuticle.

I bristled slightly. Harry wasn't the only one in that fight. 'Well, Leon wasn't exactly being reasonable, was he? I thought he was going to break Harry's neck. And what he said to you – that wasn't OK. And he hit you.'

I wanted to ask if it was the first time but didn't know how. I'd never really experienced a serious relationship other than my parents, and they'd been completely devoted to one another. I was only eight when Dad died and Mum didn't go out with anyone more than once or twice afterwards. And even that wasn't until years later. Dad was her first and only love, had been since they were teenagers. No, I couldn't see myself ever letting myself fall for someone. Not completely. It would only lead to pain one way or the other. Mum's death had only solidified for me that love meant inevitable pain.

'He isn't like that with me, not normally,' Mags said, reaching out to pat my knee, showing that she could still read me perfectly. When she wanted to. 'I mean the whole "know your place", alpha male thing. It's part of his brand identity, you know? All those guys who pay to stream his podcast and buy his book . . .'

'Leon has a book?' I was genuinely surprised.

'Yeah, obviously. He outsourced it though, no one cares who wrote the thing.' She waved that notion away with a flick of her wrist. 'But those guys would never buy that stuff if he didn't tell them what they wanted to hear,' She continued. 'It's different.'

'To what?'

'To Olly.' Maggie's normally carefully expressionless face creased with worry. 'Leon might say that stuff but he'd never act on it. Olly's different. He would. He could. He's who we need to be worried about. He's the one who . . . He's the person who'd hurt Libby.'

'Leon hit you,' I pointed out, as gently as I could.

'Accidentally. Like he said, I shouldn't have interfered. I know he probably scared you, when he "made a move",' she said, making air quotes with her painted talons.

'He did do that, Mags. It's not just me making something out of nothing, or a simple mistake. He cornered me in the kitchen and he wouldn't let me leave. He licked my fucking neck, Maggie.'

She shrugged, batting my accusation away. 'I told you, it's just an act.'

'It was real to me though, wasn't it?' I said, not willing to let it go. 'And I was the only one there. He wasn't "acting" for anyone.'

'You wouldn't understand,' Maggie said, brushing me off. 'It's just something he has to do, so much so that it's become second nature. It's like how Harry pretends he doesn't care about money,' Maggie continued. 'He probably even convinces himself sometimes.'

'Harry *doesn't* care about money,' I said, distracted from my disgust over being a pawn in Leon's game by this sudden shift to Harry.

'Oh, Han. Everyone cares about money. Even you. Especially you,' Maggie said, giving me a look that was almost pitying.

'What is that supposed to mean?' I laughed, honestly confused, I went back to trying to prise the battery free. Any excuse to avoid Maggie's gaze.

'You care because you don't have any. We don't care because it's just whatever at this point. You know? You see a glass of wine fall over and you're like, that's fifty pounds wasted. We see it and we're like, fuck, now I need another glass of wine.'

'The wine was fifty quid a glass?'

Maggie spread out her fingers. 'See? I don't even know how much it was, I was just guessing. I don't need to know. But you, you always have to know.'

The battery came free then and I pulled it up to floor level. I glanced at Maggie and wondered if she was right. Well, obviously she was right, in some ways. I did care about money and yes, it infuriated me when I saw it being wasted. But I didn't believe for one moment that none of them cared about the money. All right, so they could waste fifty-pound-a-glass wine without turning a hair, but they had to have that wine in the first place. They wanted it because of how much it was, not how good it was. That's what I saw when I spent time with them. I cared about the money wasted, they cared about the money spent.

'I'm worried about Olly,' Maggie said as I carried the battery out of the engine room. 'Maybe we should keep watch on him tonight?'

'Hmmm,' I said, not wanting to agree or disagree just then. Of course I was worried that Olly had something to do with Libby's disappearance. I'd only become more certain

151

that someone had done something to her and dumped her into the sea to drown. Or just to dispose of her body. The idea made me flinch. A body. This whole thing was getting out of hand. Yesterday we'd only had the elements and technology to contend with. Now there was probably a killer in our midst. Only I wasn't as sure as Maggie was that Olly was the only person we had to worry about. If Leon had been high last night he might have lashed out at Libby in a rage. Maybe he was angry that she as good as outed their affair to Olly? Either way, I was going to keep my guard up around both of them.

Something else was bothering me, too. I wasn't entirely sure what it was until we reached the top of the stairs and crossed the lobby. The temperature there had dropped further and I could only imagine how cold it would get by the time the weak sun set. The storm had broken and the heavy cloud cover had begun to drift away. Soon there'd be nothing to hold in what little heat the day had brought.

I glanced through the broken window as we passed and froze. That was it. I'd seen it yesterday morning, when I was alone on deck, but I'd been so hungover and so shocked that the land had just vanished that I hadn't really considered what I was seeing.

'The rope's gone.'

'What?' Maggie turned back to me. She was already halfway to the next flight of stairs.

'The mooring rope. It's not on the boat.'

'Right . . . so that townie who untied it probably took it away,' Maggie said. 'Or the storm blew it into the sea.'

That didn't alter my theory though. I put the battery down and opened the door. The blast of cold air shredded straight through my clothes and for a moment I couldn't breathe. Still, I managed to cross the deck and looked over the side, thinking that perhaps the rope was fastened lower down, floating in the water.

'What is it? Come on, Hannah, it's freezing!' Maggie whined.

'It's not here,' I called back. 'It's not tied on.'

'So? Like I said, it probably blew away. Oh my God, will you get back in here and shut the door!'

I did and Maggie seemed placated, but I was still thinking about that rope as we went up to the middle deck. I'd sort of put it out of my mind, the question of how we came to be adrift in the first place. If anyone had asked me, I'd have probably said it was an accident. That Olly didn't know how to tie ropes. Only it wasn't his boat and it had probably been moored there for a while. Too long to have not drifted off already if the ropes were tied badly.

One thing I was sure of though was that the wind couldn't have untied the rope. Which meant someone had done it, purposefully. What if Mags was right and it had been that pissed-off local guy? But why would he untie it from the boat and not from the dock? And even if he had untied it from the dock, the rope would still be attached, floating behind us like an umbilical cord. Besides which, he was a local, someone who knew how dangerous the sea was. Especially in winter. Would he really risk our lives over some loud music?

Either he was angrier than I'd thought and had decided to go above and beyond to screw with us . . . or someone on board had untied the rope from our end and set us adrift. I didn't want to believe it but, I had to wonder: if one of us was responsible, what possible reason did that person have for doing this? In light of Libby's disappearance, I wasn't sure I felt safe with any of them anymore.

CHAPTER SIXTEEN

When I returned to the viewing room Harry rushed out of the bridge and swooped me off my feet, whirling me around. My chest immediately felt lighter – Harry was ecstatic and that could only mean one thing. I caught a glimpse of Olly, who was draped on the sofa, holding a cloth full of melting ice to his bruised face. Leon was across the room, pacing in front of the window.

'I fixed it!' I could feel Harry's grin against my cheek as he planted a kiss on me, two days' worth of stubble raking my skin as he confirmed my hopes. He took the battery from me and almost danced back to the console. 'Civilisation – here we come!'

I glanced at Olly and Leon, glad to see that in our absence they hadn't ripped each other apart. Either I'd managed to convince them of the need to work together, or they were too tired and injured to kick off again. Maggie collapsed into a chair, apparently boneless with relief. Her pale fingers crept to her temple, as if chasing away a headache. The sooner we got to land, the better. Both she and Olly needed to see a doctor – and we needed to call the police.

'How much power do we think it'll use?' I asked, chasing after Harry. I was hoping we had enough. Leon followed us, as eager as I was to get confirmation that this nightmare would soon be over, and the two of us stood over Harry as he connected the radio to the battery.

'Nothing major. Question is how much is in this thing.' Harry tapped the side of the battery. 'If it's like a car battery, it charges when the engine's going. But if this boat's been tied up at dock for however many months, the engine's been off. No engine, no alternator, no charge going into the battery. It slowly starts to . . .'

He didn't say the word 'die' and I wondered if it was being on the boat that was making us so superstitious, or whether it was out of respect for Libby who, by then, I think we all believed was dead. I was trying to keep that thought locked up tight so I wouldn't cut myself on its sharp edges.

'Don't waste it then,' Leon said, butting up against my back like a bouncer.

Harry rolled his eyes but didn't say anything. A fight was the last thing we needed now that we were so close.

Filled with nervous energy, I had to do something. I couldn't just stand there waiting for the radio to work in case that somehow made it fail. So I headed over to the bar and found the ice machine – powerless like everything else, but still stocked. We'd been wasting energy making ice. In January. Jesus. I loaded up another cloth with melting ice and handed it to Maggie on my way back to the bridge. She took it, surprised, then pressed it to her head.

'We'll be out of here soon,' I said, my face breaking into my first smile in days.

Maggie nodded. 'My inbox is going to be packed.'

We shared a look and both sputtered into borderline hysterical giggles. The idea of returning to a life of emails and work deadlines felt unreal and tantalisingly close.

The air abruptly filled with crackling as the radio came to life, spitting like an angry cat. My heart leapt. Oh thank God. This was really happening.

'Yes!' Harry yelled.

'Do something!' Leon prompted.

I left Maggie's side and returned to the bridge, leaning in the doorway to watch Harry, who was pressing down the red button on the radio handset. 'Uh . . . Mayday, mayday? We're on a yacht that's drifted out from Ventimiglia harbour with no fuel. Anyone there?'

He released the button and the crackling returned, even more furiously. Was that someone speaking, distorted by static? Or was that just my imagination letting hope play tricks on me? All the nervous energy of relief gathered together to form a tight ball in my chest. A ball that reverberated with one word: please. Please please please.

Leon elbowed Harry and snatched the handset. 'This is Leon Astor-Radcliffe demanding immediate rescue from—'

Every light on the radio died. Leon released the button with a sad 'click' but no hissing burst from the speakers. It was out of juice. He just stood there, holding the handset as if he were still hoping for it to crackle back to life.

I felt sick, as hollowed out as one of the books in the next room. Leon leaned against the wall and slid down it, head in his hands. I'd been expecting him to kick off again, but he just sat there, crushed.

'Do you think anyone heard us?' Maggie asked in a small voice, hovering just behind me.

'Do you think they could find us, if they did?' Olly called from the viewing room, voice slurred by swelling. 'No coordinates, no bearing.'

'There's no electricity to use the console,' Harry snapped, still fiddling with the wires on the battery, trying to squeeze a little life out of them.

'There's a magnetic compass on the far right,' Olly retorted. 'Fucking amateur.'

'Then why didn't you tell us that before!' Harry tried to rush back through to the viewing room but I grabbed him before he could start another scuffle with Olly. Harry pulled away from me, all the fight going out of him as he returned to the radio. My heart ached for him; he'd tried so hard and worked himself ragged. In the end it had only given us seconds of airtime with no guarantee that we'd been heard.

'All that work for ten seconds. Ten seconds nobody might have heard.' He punched the console. 'Why couldn't it have worked yesterday!'

'What about the phones?' I asked, trying to buoy him up. 'We haven't tried those for a while. Maybe we'll get something now?'

We'd left them in the ornamental basket in the bridge. I realised I'd forgotten to fetch the chargers last night, distracted by all the arguing. We had not way of charging them now anyway. Harry picked the basket up and went through it. 'There's only four here.'

'Libby's is missing?' I guessed, a chill creeping over me. 'Maybe she took it back to record something . . . or . . .' I looked at Harry and realised we were both thinking the same thing. What if the same person that had apparently made her disappear had also taken her phone?

'Leon, where's yours?' I asked, noticing that the mono-grammed leather case was gone. It was impossible to forget.

'It's out of battery,' Leon said into his knees.

'Why? What did you do with it?' Harry asked, gripping the edge of the console beside Leon's head.

'I wanted to get something down, for the podcast.' Leon looked up, daring Harry to have a go. His eyes looked wet, like he was on the edge of tears.

'Are you actually serious?'

I jumped, not having heard Olly come up behind me. He shouldered Mags and me out of the way to take a stand in the centre of the bridge.

'What does that mean?' Leon demanded, hauling himself upright.

'It means that if I die out here because you had to pretend to have something noteworthy to contribute to humanity, that will be the final irony of a life that has made us peers.'

Leon didn't look angry, he looked completely done. 'Oh shut up, Oliver, for once in your life.'

'I don't answer to you,' Olly said, sneering down at Leon from his two-inch height advantage.

'Oh, right, I forgot. You're better than me because your great-great-great-grandfather held a flag for Charles the First or some shit.' Leon's tongue pushed out over his bottom lip, a playground insult that almost made me want to laugh.

'That'd be around the time your family were presumably having a wonderful time marrying their own cousins to guarantee your single-digit IQ!' Olly folded his arms, drawing himself up – the headmaster chastising an impudent child.

I tuned out their bickering and turned to Harry. 'What about the four phones we have left?'

158

'Two dead – that's yours and mine. Old models, old batteries. Mags' is just over a quarter and Olly's is still at fifty-eight per cent.'

'Any power banks?' I asked, desperate for something to cling on to.

Harry's thousand-yard stare hardly wavered as he shook his head. 'I don't have one. Do either of you?'

Mags and I both made noises in the negative. We'd all expected to charge our phones on board.

'Not sure if Libby had one – she was filming a lot, so you never know – so maybe we should search their room?' I said, feeling crushed under the burden of being the one optimist on board. I only hoped someone was buying my performance. I certainly wasn't.

'I don't want to go back in there,' Mags muttered.

'All right . . . Harry, can you come with me?' I didn't want to be on my own, not when one of the others might find an excuse to follow me downstairs.

He nodded. 'Mags, are you going to be all right up here?'

'Yes. Leon's here,' she said, like it was obvious that that meant she'd be perfectly safe.

I exchanged a glance with Harry but neither of us was about to touch that one. It was obvious by then that she wasn't budging on her belief in him. No matter what he did or what anyone else said.

'Oh, did you guys find any sign of a water tank?' Harry asked, as we skirted Leon and Olly's argument and headed downstairs. 'I tried to get a glass of water from the bar tap and after a bit of spluttering nothing happened.'

'You'll have to get a bottle from the kitchen. Do you think the pipes are frozen, already? It's getting colder outside.'

'Not sure. But it's more likely to be the pump. Off the

mains there needs to be an electrical pump to cycle the water – I've done something similar with water features. Without it, there's no pressure. The water'll just sit in the tank.'

Crap. Another thing I'd taken for granted yesterday – running water and flush toilets. Things were going to get even more unpleasant on board if we didn't find a workaround for that. 'I saw the runoff tanks from the toilets and drains down by the battery hatch. No fresh water though. I was wondering if it was under the deck? I mean, we've got bottled water, but what're we going to do about the loos, or washing, come to that? I already feel disgusting.'

'We'll have to look. Glad to be out of there anyway.' He nodded back towards the stairs as we reached the lobby. 'The pair of them are doing my head in. Kind of glad they're picking on each other for a change.' He tucked his hands under his armpits; the cold air had become biting without the heaters to take the edge off.

'Mags is blaming Olly for Libby . . . being missing.'

'Too right. What else are we meant to think? She's not stupid enough to try and swim for it. And we know she didn't jump in to do herself in – even if she was going to do that, it's not really her scene, is it? She'd be worried about her hair for the open casket.' He barely managed a half smile at his own joke. 'Only other option is he did something to her. Threw her in.'

'What about Leon?'

'You think he's in on it, too? That maybe he helped Olly . . . dispose of her?' he said, with a wince.

'I'm not sure. But if he walked in on something he probably would have taken Olly's side. Unless . . .'

'Unless what?'

160

'Well, she said she was seeing someone else and then sort of looked at him, so . . . maybe she was cheating with Leon.'

Harry pulled a face. 'God, I hope not. Olly was bad enough. You'd hope she'd at least have traded up. Shit, it's freezing in here.' He rubbed his hands together furiously and then grabbed mine, chafing them together until my fingers tingled.

'That's better. Wish we had gloves.'

I cleared my throat. 'Only going to get colder too with that window broken and no doors between levels. Maybe we should try and get a fire going and patch the window up? We could all sleep in here.'

'All the better to keep an eye on Olly,' Harry agreed. 'If that fireplace works.'

'God, I hope so. If that's fake as well I say we mutiny and lock Olly up in a cupboard.' My lame attempt at a joke raised more of a facial twitch than a smile, but at least it meant that for a second the idea that we were probably harbouring a murderer was pushed aside.

Outside the weather was blowing up again, hard pellets of icy rain ricocheting across the gleaming wet deck. Harry and I braced ourselves and went out in it. I immediately had to bend my head and squint to keep the rain out of my face. It stung whatever bare skin it could get at. My feet were bare in the stolen slippers and I began to lose feeling in my toes within seconds.

'You check that side!' Harry called over the rolling of the waves and the rattling of ice. 'I'll go this way.'

I circled around from my side, eyes fixed on the planks for any sign of a hatch or inlet. The wind plucked at my clothes, buffeting me around. When I reached the narrow end of the deck a wave crashed against the side, soaking me with sub-zero water that was cold enough but too restless to freeze. I cried out as it drenched me to the skin, the cold burn a visceral reminder of my plunge into the frozen lake.

'Over here!' Harry called.

I shivered my way over and crouched down next to him. He'd managed to open a shoebox-sized panel in the deck. Inside was a capped-off pipe – almost like the ones tankers deposit fuel into at petrol stations. Beside it a gauge showed water level – or it would have, if there'd been any power.

'Help me get this open.'

Between us, Harry and I managed to loosen the cap and unscrew it. The opening was just about big enough for him to get his arm into. Lying almost flat to the deck he pushed his hand in as far as he could, until the width of his upper arm stopped him going further. I watched his face crease with effort.

'I can't feel anything,' he said, finally, with a grunt. 'I've got my hand right out as far as it'll go and I can't reach the water.'

'Maybe it's a really big tank?' I offered. 'Hang on.'

I rolled my sweatshirt up and pulled at the drawstring on my leggings. It came free in a series of rips. I rolled it up as I went and passed it to Olly.

'Dip that down and see if it reaches.'

Harry fed the end of the drawstring into the pipe mouth and let out the slack. Buffeted by wind and rain we crouched there like ice fishers around that small hole. Hoping and praying for a bite.

'I can feel something.' Harry fed out more cord. 'I think it's hit water and . . . yep, that's the bottom.' He pulled the cord back. The bottom foot came up wet.

'Is that it?' Not knowing how wide the tank was, it was

162

hard to tell how much water that foot of damp string equated to. That was if it had even measured accurately and not folded at the bottom. Still, it didn't look like much.

'I'm more worried about how we're going to get at it.'

He was right. With no electric pump and no opening large enough for us to reach down to the water, our options were limited.

'We'll deal with that later. The bottles should last us until . . .' I wanted to say 'until help gets here', but that meant thinking about how long that might take. If it ever came. There were a lot of water bottles but there were also five of us and at least three of us weren't exactly built for sharing or conservation.

'Let's get to the cabins, out of this weather. If we find a power bank we can get out of here before we need to resort to tap water,' Harry said, in an attempt at a joke.

It was only slightly less cold inside the boat than out on deck, but at least it was dry. I grimaced as my soaking wet leggings clung to me, the slippers squelching. I didn't have anything else to change into, aside from my thin pyjamas, or one of two party dresses, which were probably worse than wearing wet clothes in terms of insulation.

'We should bring anything we can burn back up with us,' I said. 'Get a fire going.'

'Yup,' Harry said, his teeth actually chattering. 'Solid plan.'

Down in the cabins we made straight for Libby and Olly's room. Inside Harry froze at the sight of the chaos – the broken glass and the ripped dress. Then he turned away and went to the bedside tables. That left it to me to check the vanity. I went through all the drawers and even got down on the plush carpet to stick my hand under the unit, just in case anything had rolled under there.

'Nothing here,' Harry called, making me look up. 'Well, no power bank or anything like that. Got some magazines though and those makeup removal cotton pad things. Those'll burn, right?'

'Yeah . . .' I said, no longer listening to him as I stared at the wall above. I slowly brought my arm out from under the vanity and sat up.

'Got some acetone too,' Harry was saying.

'Harry?'

'Yup?'

'The blood's gone.'

CHAPTER SEVENTEEN

'You're sure it was here?' Harry asked, pacing past me as I sat on the bed, staring at the wall.

'Yes,' I said for the tenth time. We were going around in circles, neither of us able to believe what we were seeing. Harry followed my gaze, then pivoted on his heel and started to pace again.

'And you're sure it was blood? Not, I don't know' – he waved his hands in the direction of the vanity – 'lipstick or nail polish?'

I closed my eyes so I didn't have to watch him stalk around the room. It was making me feel more anxious by the minute.

'Even if it wasn't blood, that still wouldn't explain why it was there earlier and now it's gone, would it? Someone obviously cleaned it off and they wouldn't have done that if it was just an innocent little lipstick smear, would they? I mean, there's definitely bigger messes they could have tackled if they felt the urge to clean.' I realised I was rambling and bit the end of my sentence off. I opened my eyes and took a deep breath, trying to steady myself.

Harry came to a stop and nodded, conceding the point. He was still bobbing on his toes but at least the pacing had stopped. We both needed to hang onto this fragile calm. Going to pieces wasn't going to solve anything, and I knew that.

I got up and went to check the wall, close up. The panelling was slightly shiny and showed no sign of being stained or cleaned. If someone had removed the mark there'd been plenty of time for it to dry. A quick check of the gold bin under the vanity revealed several soiled cotton pads and a sheet mask. Nothing that was obviously bloodstained.

There were two options. First, Mags and I had both mistaken a shadow or something for a stain on the wall. Not very likely. Second, someone had cleaned the mark up – already pretty incredible considering the kind of people on board – and, for some probably not very innocent reason, had disposed of what they'd used to clean it with elsewhere.

'Who could've done it?' I asked Harry. 'Think. Who had a chance to, whilst we were looking for Libby? I don't think I lost sight of Mags. We were together the whole time.'

Harry looked slightly sick. 'Olly and I split up to do the lower and middle deck. Do you think he could've . . .'

'He might have come in here whilst Mags and I were in the kitchen or the engine room. But we hadn't told anyone about the blood yet so how would he know it was there?' I chewed my lip, certain that I was missing something.

'I don't know, maybe he noticed it, or heard you talking about it through the wall?' Harry rubbed a hand over his face. We were both too tired for this kind of theorising.

'What about Leon – you said you and Maggie were together. Where was he?'

'In his room. I didn't see him come out, he was just upstairs when we joined you guys.'

Harry clicked his tongue, slowly circling around the bed towards me, lost in thought. 'I was pretty busy with the radio when he caught up to us, so I can't swear he and Olly were with me the entire time you were looking for the battery. But isn't there the same problem – how would he know about the blood before you pointed it out?'

'And why clean it after we found it, which looks incredibly suspicious?'

Harry pointed at me, face clearing as he leapt to a conclusion. 'Which means whoever cleaned up the blood didn't know you'd found it until after they'd wiped it off. So, they must've come back to check for any evidence.'

I wasn't convinced. 'And they left Libby's torn dress here because . . .'

'I don't know! Because they're either stupid or they think that can be explained away. Or they didn't notice it was torn. I'm not a mind reader!' Harry threw his hands up in frustration.' Fuck, this is . . . I can't believe we're talking about one of us murdering Libby. Olly and Leon are shitheads, but do you really think either of them could kill someone?'

'On purpose? No idea. By accident . . . You saw what Leon was like that night. And Olly, well, he had a lot to lose. Libby threatened to ruin him. Which reminds me.' I lowered my voice further, worried that someone might have crept down behind us to listen in. 'Earlier, I noticed that the mooring rope isn't on the boat. Which it should be if it was untied from the dock.'

'So someone undid the rope where it was attached to the boat?' Harry said slowly. 'You think that local did it when he was leaving?'

'Maybe. Mags seemed to think so. But what if it was someone already on the boat? What if Olly knew Libby was planning to leave him and he arranged all this, somehow?'

Harry looked at me in appalled silence, then hissed, 'You're telling me he could be the reason we're stuck out here? The reason Libby was ever in danger to begin with?'

'We can't know, can we? He's not going to admit it. It could even have been Leon.'

'But why would he do it?' Harry asked, eyes crinkling as he tried to follow my train of thought.

'No idea. Could be Leon's excuse for a joke. You know what the rugby lads were like at uni – the alcohol-poisoning pub crawls, climbing on the roof of halls, breaking into the union. They do stupid, dangerous shit without thinking it through. And Leon was drunk and high enough to do it.'

Harry tipped his head back and groaned. 'I don't like this. I hate being stuck here and not being able to do anything! Libby's gone. Where, we don't know. This ship could have dozens of hiding spots to put her in and we wouldn't know it. Or else she's out in the ocean, never to be seen again. We've no power and no way to communicate unless we get a phone signal before the last battery dies. And now we've got to share a room with those two when one of them might be the reason we're stuck here.' He stopped, breathing heavily, looking at me as if hoping for a thin ray of hope.

Unfortunately, I was out of hope and out of answers. I desperately wanted to offer some comfort but I had no idea what to say. I put my hand on his arm and tried to sound as calm as possible. 'I don't think there's anything we can do about it. Not until we make it ashore.'

'You mean *if* we make it ashore,' Harry said stonily, shrugging my hand off. He rubbed a hand over his face. 'I don't know how much longer I can take this.'

'As long as possible and then maybe a bit more,' I said, trying to lighten his mood. 'Come on, you're the only other sane one here. You can't lose it now.'

'OK. You're right.' He sighed. 'Let's . . . find something to burn and get set up by the fireplace. I'm freezing, and I'll probably have to stay up again to signal if any boats pass in the night. We can't trust Olly or Leon to do it.'

We rounded up what we could from the cabins and the kitchen; magazines, acetone to start a fire, cotton pads, kitchen roll, wooden chopping boards and a sort of bone saw from the utensil drawer, which Harry though we could use on the antique furniture if it came to that. We loaded everything into our empty weekend bags, along with several bottles of mineral water and the last of the food. Seeing all the water bottles laid some of my worries about thirst to rest. At twenty quid a pop, two grand's worth of water gave us a hundred one-litre bottles. Twenty each. If we only drank one litre a day we had a twenty-day supply. We were more likely to starve first. Terrific.

Harry piled things into the fireplace and got a fire going with a cheap Pac-Man lighter. I watched him as I fiddled with some tit-tape from Libby's vanity – it was the only thing I'd found to close up the hole in the window, and though it wasn't perfect, it would keep some of the draught out. I wondered how much foil there was in the kitchen, if any, and whether it would be worth covering the windows.

Would it keep heat in or just be a waste of time? Either way, I wasn't sure we had enough tape to do it.

'Do we say something?'

I turned to find Harry behind me, clicking the lighter restlessly, just short of sparking a flame. I didn't need to ask what he was talking about. We both had serious suspicions about Leon and Olly. The question was, would saying something to them help or hurt our chances of survival? I shivered, thinking of what they might do if they thought for a moment that we knew what they'd done. How easy would it be to silence us, one after the other?

'No . . . we keep it to ourselves. It's safer that way.'

Harry nodded, but still seemed to be wrestling with something. 'What about Maggie? Shouldn't we warn her? I mean, her fiancé might be a murderer. But then, she might just tell him what we suspect so . . .' He looked at me, waiting for me to decide what we ought to do.

I thought for a second, then slowly shook my head. 'We can't risk it, can we? You're right, she might tell him or cause a scene if we try and convince her otherwise. She doesn't think Leon's a threat.'

'Just you and me then,' Harry said, nudging my arm with his knuckles.

'Looks like it.' I offered him a tight smile. 'Let's get everyone to bring up their bedding. It's going to be a cold night.'

Unfortunately, we hit a snag with that plan almost immediately.

The others were still where we'd left them, mooning about in the gloomy viewing room. Leon had cracked open a bottle of beer – his third since Harry and I had left, judging from the empties. Maggie was perched beside him on the arm of his chair, bird-like and nervy. Olly was looking out at the sea, his expression equally stormy.

'We've got a fire going. We'll all have to stay in the lobby downstairs to keep warm,' I said. 'Can you help bring up the duvets and maybe something to block the draught from these stairs?'

'I'm not staying in a room with him,' Maggie said, pointing at Olly.

Leon shook her bony knee. 'Don't be stupid, of course you will.'

Apparently the class system had been re-established in our absence. Leon was back on Olly's side and it looked like Maggie wasn't too happy about that. Her shoulders were taut as a coat hanger and she flinched away from Leon's touch, jumping up and coming over to me, her eyes huge and pleading.

'Hannah, you can't seriously think we'll be safe sleeping in the same room as him. Not after what happened to Libby.'

'We don't know what happened, if anything,' Leon said. 'Like I said, she probably stormed off in a sulk and had an accident.'

'I don't want him in there with us,' Maggie insisted.

'I'm not sleeping in the cold because you're paranoid,' Olly drawled. 'If you don't want to stay there, you can freeze outside for all I care.'

Harry sighed. 'Nice, Olly.'

'It's my boat,' Olly snapped. 'I'll sleep where I like.'

'Fine. I'll sleep in my room.' Maggie made as if to leave but Leon crossed the room in a few quick strides and caught her by the arm. Not roughly, but I winced nonetheless.

'You have to stay with me, Maggie. Otherwise I won't be able to protect you.'

'Then come with me,' she pleaded.

'I'm not going to freeze my bollocks off below deck because you've got it into your little head that Olly's some kind of common killer. We're staying where it's warm and that's final.'

'Let her go, Leon. Now,' I said. I'd meant it to come out as a request, but it sounded more like a threat. I cleared my throat and tried for a more neutral approach. 'Maggie, you should stay with us. We're safer together. There's going to be someone on watch all night anyway – in case we pass another boat.'

'See, even the feminist agrees you're safer with me to protect you, provide for you. That's my job. I'm the man and I'm putting my foot down.'

Maggie's eyes flashed with a tiny spark of defiance. 'And what is it that you provide?'

Leon let go of her and she stumbled, as was probably his intention. Maggie scuttled behind Harry and me, tossing a barb over her shoulder as she went. 'Unless you want to be cut off when we get out of here, you'll sleep where I want.'

Leon turned an ugly purplish-red and seemed to swell like a pissed-off toad. 'You listen to me, you bitch, I'll—'

'No, you listen!' Maggie cried, turning shrill with either panic or fury. 'I have been quiet and I have been respectful. I have done everything you wanted and let you pretend you've got it all figured out – but this is it. I've had enough. So, here it is, everyone, the truth about Leon Astor-Radcliffe, who hasn't had his own money in five years.'

'Shut. Up. Maggie,' Leon snarled, eyes darting to Olly.

'No. No I won't. Everyone deserves to know how you blew through your trust fund on lads' weekends and paying off damage to hotels and party buses – not to mention the three abortions you used my money to hush up. Did you think I didn't know about that? Do you really think women don't talk to one another? You should see my DMs, every slut you picked up practically sprinted to me with the details, wanting a payday.'

Leon's face mottled to a luncheon meat texture, splotches of white and pink glazed with unappetising sweat. A glance in Olly's direction told me he was enjoying this, that he loved seeing someone else squirm. I couldn't deny that witnessing Leon humiliated didn't appeal to me, but any enjoyment was tempered by anxiety over what he might do now that he was cornered. To Mags or to me. To any of us.

'I said shut your mouth!' Leon hissed, shifting almost imperceptibly towards us, tensed to spring at Maggie.

'Why should I when yours is never shut? Always talking about "bitches" this and "gold-diggers" that. You've been relying on my money since your parents cut you off. You call me a "shallow bimbo" who only cares about fashion? My fashion brand supports you, Leon! I bought you the microphone and the cameras that you use to call women freeloaders with nothing to offer except their "loose pussies",' Maggie spat. 'You record that shit in *my* home and maybe your "fans" deserve to know it.'

Leon got past me and Harry in seconds.

'Don't!' I shouted automatically, stepping forwards to try and intercept him, but it was too late. He hit Maggie, right across the face, and she staggered back into the wall, clutching her jaw. This wasn't some grazing blow in a fight – I heard his knuckles glance off her bones. Felt the whoosh of her hot breath as it was forced out of her, droplets of blood or spittle flecking my cheek.

Harry and I grappled with Leon as he tried to grab hold of Maggie by her hair, each of us wrestling with one of his arms until we had them behind his back. Still he tried to charge at her, lowering his head like he was about to ram her. I managed to get one leg wrapped around his, hobbling him enough that Harry and I could fold him to his knees on the floor. Maggie staggered backwards, knocking over empty beer bottles as she steadied herself against a side table.

'Let go of me!' Leon threw himself against our grip. 'You think she's your friend? She can't stand you,' he hissed at me.

Maggie cupped a hand to her bloody nose and then looked at her red-streaked palm as if trying to decide on a lipstick shade. She'd defaulted to that blank expression I'd seen on her before. Distancing herself from all of us.

'Enough!' Olly came up behind me and pushed Leon hard. He was already off balance and fell forwards onto the floor, nearly taking Harry and me with him. Harry quickly transferred his weight to Leon's back to keep him down.

'I'm cold and hungry and I want to go to bed,' Olly said, as if we were the stragglers at an impromptu house party and he was the host's annoyed parent. 'I'm not sleeping anywhere but downstairs by the fire. Anyone who has a problem with me is free to go to another part of my boat.'

I realised we couldn't fight both of them. How would we keep Olly and Leon from getting into the lobby when it had no doors? Even Harry couldn't take them both on at once. I glanced at Maggie who seemed to wilt even further with each passing moment.

'I'll be in my room, then,' she whispered, turning to go.

'I'll go with you,' I said. As much as I wanted to sleep in the warm, I didn't trust Olly or Leon enough to let my guard down around them. I also didn't want Maggie to go off on her own, defenceless. I'd already lost Libby. I wouldn't lose her, too. Even if she wasn't my friend, not really. That didn't mean I wasn't going to show her the same loyalty I'd show any other woman in this situation.

'There, that's settled then,' Olly said, with a condescending smile. 'Bring up my things whilst you're down there, will you?'

'Get them yourself,' Harry said, then turned to me. 'Here – you'd better take some of the food. I'll keep watch – properly, OK? Make sure they stay put and keep an eye out for land or ships.'

'Thanks,' I said, wondering how he could possibly do both without missing something. 'But come and get me to take over from you at midnight so you can get some sleep. Can Harry come stay with you then?' I asked Maggie.

She nodded reluctantly and I took her gently by the elbow and walked her out of the room. The boat was freezing now, every inch of it, and my wet clothes were leaching my own body heat from me. It was going to be a long, cold night.

CHAPTER EIGHTEEN

Once downstairs, I brought my duvet into Maggie's room and folded it in half to make a sort of sleeping bag on the floor. Maggie still had the damp cloth with ice in it that I'd given her earlier, and lay down with it over her face. She didn't ask if I wanted to use the bed and I didn't expect her to offer.

'Do you have anything warm I could wear whilst my clothes dry?' I asked, after a moment's hesitant hovering.

'You can look.' She waved a hand towards the heap of suitcases and discarded outfits. 'I'm not sure anything will fit.'

I rolled my eyes. To be fair, it probably wouldn't. Maggie was tiny and most of her clothes were tailored and made of fabrics with no stretch whatsoever. Half of it was stuff you couldn't even wash – beads, feathers, plastic and leather. Nothing warm. I settled on an 'oversized' jumper that just about fitted me, with a cashmere shawl knotted over it for added warmth. In terms of bottoms, there was nothing I could get past my knees. I raided Leon's suitcases instead and put on a pair of Jack Wills joggers that still had the tags on them. If he said anything about them I'd just have to deal with it. Maggie had the same slippers under her bed as I'd had so I pinched those as well as a scarf, which I tied gratefully around my neck, and one of her dressing gowns to use as a blanket.

'Here's your half of the food and some water,' I said as I set the things down on her bedside table. Maggie didn't respond. I decided to let her process in her own time whilst I got some sleep on the floor. She'd had a horrible altercation with Leon and she was probably thinking through some stuff. If she wanted to talk later, I'd be there.

I ate my portion of near-expired salmon and stale sourdough. Tomorrow I'd have a hunt around behind the bar for some jars of olives or cherries or anything else we could live on. Otherwise we'd have to start getting our daily calories from beer and wine, which would be throwing fuel on the discontented fire.

Thinking of the fire just annoyed me more. Olly, Leon and Harry were upstairs right then, enjoying the warmth, whilst I was freezing on the floor between Maggie and the door. Like a guard dog. When it was my turn to keep watch I'd definitely be making trips down to the lobby to warm myself up.

Unlike the previous night, I didn't lie there calculating our odds. In fact, I did everything I could to avoid thinking about them. I knew that the longer we were out here, drifting, the more dire our situation was becoming. Our odds of encountering another ship were remote and we had no way of knowing if we'd ever drift towards land again. No, I didn't want to think about any of that, just like I didn't want to think about Libby. Unfortunately, I could only distance myself from one nightmare at a time and by not dwelling on our odds of survival, I ended up thinking about her instead. Or rather, about what might have happened to her.

I was certain she was gone. Dead. As much as I didn't want that to be the case, we hadn't found any sign of her. Her phone was missing, too. That sent a chill through me that had nothing to do with the temperature. Someone was hiding something. Someone who was still on the yacht.

I could picture Libby going into the water. Had she drowned right by the ship? Had whoever chucked her overboard stayed to watch her die? The idea filled me with fear. Was I trapped with someone so heartless that they could watch a woman drown and do nothing to save her? That they could pretend to search for her with the rest of us? My breathing became shallow and I felt my pulse rising, my body aware of the threat that lurked close by.

I was sharing a boat with a killer. Maybe more than one.

It hadn't escaped me that Olly and Leon had each other's backs in most things, despite Olly's obvious dislike of Leon, and so I wouldn't put it past Olly to use Leon to help him get rid of Libby, or to help cover up her death, if it meant he got to keep his dwindling fortune to himself. Perhaps He had even bribed Leon. After all, Maggie had as good as said Leon had nothing to his name.

If Olly could kill his own wife, what could he do to someone he barely knew? Someone he hated? Someone like me or Harry?

I just couldn't shake the feeling that this was all part of someone's plan, a plan which wasn't finished yet. The boat going adrift, Libby disappearing, the vanishing bloodstain. It all felt deliberate and cunning. Which was the only thing that made me think it was Olly's plan. Was this why the guest list had been so 'exclusive'? Had he planned this from the start, with me an unwanted complication at his murder party?

With all that floating around in my head and the cold sinking its teeth into my extremities, I couldn't get to sleep. Like the sea outside, my mind refused to stop moving. I was so tired I wanted to scream, to yell at my own thoughts to just shut up. Then suddenly I really did hear shouting, from above me.

I sat up, automatically looking around for a clock that wasn't there, because they were all 'smart alarm clocks' that were useless with no power. Maggie was snoring and I could see my breath in the dark, billowing with each ragged exhale as adrenaline flooded my body. The shouting upstairs grew louder, a mixture of voices as multiple people yelled over one another. I strained to hear what was going on. Was the shouting something to be concerned about or was it just Leon popping off without any real heat, just because he felt like being an arse?

Although it was muffled by the deck between us, the noise carried enough that I caught the words 'my wife' ricocheting down the hallway like bullets. That had to be Olly. He was yelling about Libby, which meant this was serious.

With one last glance at Mags' sleeping form, to convince myself that she'd be all right, I let myself out and ran for the stairs. If it really was all kicking off again between Olly and Leon, or even those two and Harry, someone needed to intervene.

Harry was nowhere to be seen when I reached the lobby. None of them were. Their discarded duvets and blankets were on the sofas and the floor, the fire was almost burned out and the room was empty, at least as far as I could tell in the pitch dark. I stumbled over a pillow and spread my arms out, feeling with my fingers and hesitant feet as I tried to find my way across the room. The clear, icy air outside had probably allowed the sound to travel further than I'd thought. They were somewhere else on the boat.

'She got what she deserved!' That was Leon and it sounded like he was on the deck above me, his voice ringing out over the endless water stretching in all directions. I fumbled my way to the stairs and took them up to the viewing room as quickly as possible in my slippers.

Leon and Olly were outside on deck. I could see them clearly through the enormous viewing pane. Someone had started to stack the hollow books into a weekend bag – maybe one or both of them had come to get fuel for the fire. Now, though, they were having a shouting match and even in the darkness I could see that Olly had something in his hands – something large and heavy, from the way he was stooped. I was frozen between knowing I had to put a stop to their fight and fear that they'd turn on me if I got involved. It would only take seconds for one or both of them to wrestle me over the side and into the dark water.

Someone knocked into me from behind, jostling a small scream out of me. I whirled around and grabbed them, finding the familiar shape of Harry's hand in the dark. My fear faded a little, tinged with relief once I realised I wasn't alone.

'Jesus! I only left them for a minute to have a piss,' Harry said.

'I think Olly's got something out there. A weapon.'

Harry swore and broke away from me, though in my fear I tried to keep hold of him. Within seconds he was

180

scrambling across the room in the dark to reach the outer door. I followed him, scared he was going to get hurt, scared of being alone. We reached the door just in time to see Olly strike Leon on the head. Up close I could see what he was holding – a fire extinguisher from the bridge. Leon's hulking frame crumpled to the deck and Harry made a grab for the extinguisher as Olly swung it again. I clung to the doorframe, afraid to get closer in case Olly hit out at me.

'Enough! You'll have his skull open,' Harry shouted, wrestling with Olly over the extinguisher as Olly tried to prise Harry's fingers off of it.

Olly snarled. 'He killed my wife! You heard him! He deserves it!'

Harry faltered and Olly pulled the fire extinguisher away from him. That jerked me out of my frozen indecision. I threw myself away from the doorframe, getting between them and making a grab for the extinguisher. I managed to knock it off course, which put Olly off balance. I grabbed hold of the extinguisher and backed away, keeping it out of Olly's reach.

'He killed my wife,' Olly said again, his face locked in fury but streaked with tears. He was almost begging, desperate for Harry to let him get at Leon. 'Let go of me! He admitted it – he killed her.'

'That doesn't mean we're going to let you stove his head in,' I said, trying and failing to suppress my own tears. I didn't like Olly, but I felt his pain in that moment. His desperation to get to Leon. In his place, I'd have wanted to claw Leon's eyes out. But that didn't mean I would let Olly be the one to mete out bloody justice. Leon might be guilty but right then he was unconscious, helpless. As much as it sickened me, he needed my protection.

'If it was me you'd let him do it,' Olly said to me, whilst pointing at Harry. 'You'd help him do it.'

'I'm not letting anyone else get killed,' I said. 'That includes you.'

'You actually believe that, don't you?' Olly struggled away from Harry and me, backing up and glaring at us. 'You really think you're so much better than the rest of us. So good. So empathetic.'

I didn't say anything, just threw the extinguisher across the deck and picked up Leon's arm. Harry took the other one and we dragged his unconscious body into the viewing room.

'Leon!' Maggie had finally joined us upstairs and threw herself down beside her fiancé. She hadn't put anything on over her negligee and even from a distance I could see the goosebumps on her skin. She didn't seem to notice the cold though. 'Oh my God, there's blood! What did you do to him?'

Harry hauled Olly into the room and slammed the door to the deck. 'He did it. Not me.'

'Because he admitted to killing Libby,' Olly said doggedly, angrily dashing tears away with his hands. 'He as good as told me he was screwing my wife and that she deserved what happened to her.'

'Liar!' Maggie sobbed, stroking Leon's bloody face.

'We're not going to do this until we know for sure what happened to her,' Harry said.

I was thankful he agreed with me and that he was willing to say so. In all the chaos of the past few minutes I just wanted someone else to take charge.

'Rubbish. He obviously threw her overboard – where else could she be?' Olly demanded.

I hated to admit it, but he was right. That didn't mean,

however, that I believed Leon was to blame. But that was mostly because it was Olly doing the blaming.

'We need some light and something to stop the bleeding,' I said to Harry, when he had no response for Olly. It was Mags who answered.

'There are candles in the bedrooms. I'll get them, and a towel. Don't let Olly near him.' She dashed away, stumbling slightly as the boat swayed in the water.

'I want him locked up,' Olly spat, as Harry forced him down into a chair. His tear-swollen eyes were fixed on Leon's form even as his mouth wavered between a snarl and a crumpled mess, fingers locked into claws as if he wanted to rip him apart. 'He can't be trusted.'

'Shut it, or I'll lock you both up,' Harry said.

Olly refused to be silenced, however, flicking a burning glare towards Harry. 'If you try it, I'll have you arrested for false imprisonment and kidnapping.'

'That's if we get back to land though, isn't it?' Harry challenged, though his voice shook a little. I wasn't sure if Olly noticed but I did. Harry was trying to keep up his usual cool, but I could see how hard it was to do so in the face of Olly's raw emotion. 'There's a lot that could happen before then.'

Maggie returned with Jo Malone candles and a clean white towel. The awful tension that had settled over us subsided a little at the interruption. My hand shook a bit as I held it out towards Harry.

'Lighter,' was all I said, and he pressed his Pac-Man disposable into my hand. There was a time when all of us would've been carrying one. Once we got out of this mess I'd make sure I always had a lighter on me. It turned out you never knew when you were going to need one.

With the candles lit the blood oozing from Leon's head became visible. There was an air of black magic and sacrifices to the scene, what with all of us gathered around him, bathed in candlelight. I pressed the towel hard against his head wound and he moaned but didn't open his eyes.

'Is he going to be OK?' Maggie asked.

I had no idea – I was a call centre operative, not a nurse – but even I knew that being bashed in the head with the sharp edge of a heavy metal object wasn't good for you. I only hoped that Olly hadn't cracked his skull open or done serious damage.

'We should keep an eye on him, in case of concussion,' I said, realising as I did so that I wasn't sure how to tell if someone had a concussion. Without access to the internet, I couldn't check either.

'I won't say it again – either you transfer him to a locked room, right now, or I will not be responsible for my actions,' Olly said, clearly not just blustering but meaning every word of the threat.

'When have you ever?' Harry muttered to himself, but looked at me uncertainly. 'What should we do, Han?'

I wasn't sure. I felt like I'd never be sure of anything again, to be honest. It was all spinning out of control. Every time I let my guard down for even a second, someone else kicked off or went missing. I just wanted it all to stop so I could think. So we could plan. I was glad Harry was there with me because without him I doubted Olly would still be merely discussing revenge instead of actively seeking it.

'We have to separate them, or they'll just keep fighting,' I said. 'I'm not sure what options we have . . .'

'Option one,' Olly said, fixing me with a look that held none of his usual scathing insincerity, 'is you let me wring

184

that bastard's neck right now. Option two, you tell us to go to our rooms and the minute you turn your back, I wring his neck and then yours for trying to stop me.'

I glanced at Harry and found him already looking at me, hands still pinning Olly to the chair. 'Don't you threaten us,' he ground out, but I could tell he was rattled. Neither of us had seen Olly so bloody-minded before.

I went over to Harry so I could whisper in his ear. 'We don't seem to be able to keep them anywhere – not when we have to watch for boats and sleep too. And there's no way we can keep them apart, not if he's this set on getting to Leon.'

'There's a lock on the linen store downstairs,' Harry whispered back, surprising me. Was he seriously suggesting we lock Leon up?

'What if he actually has a concussion?'

'He only got hit once. It's just bleeding a lot. I don't like it but . . . what other choice do we have?' Harry said.

'We could lock Olly in there?'

'No bloody way!' Olly startled both of us, breaking Harry's hold on him. Within moments he'd kicked a sobbing Mags aside and fallen on Leon's unconscious form. Olly's hands were already around Leon's neck when Harry and I grabbed him under the arms and dragged him away. He managed to twist his head and bite Harry's hand as we got him back in the chair, and Harry pinned his neck with more force than I was comfortable with.

I knew what Harry was going to say before he opened his mouth.

'We can't,' I attempted to counter.

'There's no other way!' Harry snapped. 'I can barely keep him in this chair, let alone drag him all the way downstairs.

It has to be Leon. If he wakes up and goes for Olly, I won't be able to stop him.'

'No! It's too dangerous to just leave him in a cupboard,' I hissed.

'It's too dangerous for him not to be,' Harry said, ending the discussion with a glare in my direction. 'Right now, Olly's more dangerous than a bump on the head. I'll hold him here – you and Mags'll have to move Leon.'

I hovered, unsure and wanting to argue, to tell him there was no way I was going to do it. But I couldn't think of an alternative that he hadn't already shut down. Worse, I didn't want to see what would happen if I continued to obstruct Harry's plan. His voice had an edge that didn't seem open to reason. For the first time, I was scared of what he'd do.

'Mags?' I said at last, slowly crossing the room to her. 'Come on. We need to get Leon downstairs.'

CHAPTER NINETEEN

Maggie didn't let Leon go quietly. As soon as I gave in to Harry's plan she tried to claw her way back to him, apparently planning to pin him to the floor. I held firm and put myself between her and him.

'Maggie, listen – please listen to me. We need to do this to protect Leon as well as to protect the rest of us.' I felt vile saying it, and I didn't even really believe it. I just knew that with Olly and Harry on one side of the argument we didn't stand a chance on the other.

'That's bullshit, you're going to lock him up where I can't take care of him.' Maggie attempted to get past me but she was half my size and I caught hold of her, as gently as possible, and held her still.

'I will personally check on Leon to make sure he's OK,' I assured her, quietly. 'This is the only way to keep him and Olly apart and to make sure no one else gets hurt.' I knew Olly wouldn't hesitate to tear through any of us on his way to Leon, and if Harry and I were divided, restraining Leon as well, we wouldn't be able to stop him.

'But he needs me,' Maggie said in a small voice. 'He'll be so angry.'

'You need sleep – and he won't be able to get at you, all right? Just help me get him downstairs and let me watch him for the night, and tomorrow . . . We can talk about tomorrow when it comes, OK?'

Maggie sniffed but didn't answer. I hoped that was the end of it, at least for now.

Between the two of us we managed to get Leon's torso off the floor, and his legs slid over the polished boards as Maggie and I staggered to the stairs. We slid him down one by one, the way you'd do as a kid, bumping your arse on every step. Through it all he didn't wake up, though his eyes were moving under his lids. I was relieved to see that the wound on his head didn't look that bad up close. As Harry said, it had just bled a lot.

I was sweating and exhausted by the time we reached the linen cupboard. Maggie wasn't much help with the carrying and had mostly been clinging to Leon instead. I let her hold him whilst I removed the contents of the cupboard and slid the shelves out, stacking them in the hall. I was shaking and felt sick, not just from the exertion but from guilt and anxiety. I didn't want to do this, but what choice did we have?

After getting Leon into the cupboard, I sent Maggie for a blanket. She tucked it in around him and I wondered if when this was all over, she'd still stand by him. Maybe without Libby around to copy and impress, she'd finally drop Leon for good.

At the last moment I left Maggie with him and fetched a pot from the kitchen.

'For . . . you know,' I said, not meeting her eye.

It was the kind of thing you read about people doing to hostages or kidnapping victims. I didn't want to think of Leon as being our victim. We were trying to keep everyone safe – even him. Still, it didn't feel good, seeing him slumped on the floor of the cupboard.

I put Leon in the recovery position – the one bit of first aid I remembered from the 'don't die of alcohol poisoning, please' talk we'd had to sit through during Freshers' Week. Then we shut the door and locked it.

'I'll tell Harry it's . . . done. You should go back to bed.'

'I can't believe you let him do this,' Maggie said, bringing a hand up to her mouth to suppress fresh tears.

You helped, too, I nearly said, but didn't. She'd done it for the same reason I had – there wasn't much of a choice. I carefully threaded my hairband through the key and slipped it back onto my wrist. No matter what, I wouldn't let Olly get his hands on it.

I went back upstairs, my heart so heavy it dragged me down with every step. Harry and Olly were right where I'd left them and Harry seemed to sag a little in relief when I reappeared. Olly looked calmer, his cheeks dry and his eyes no longer red. Had it been an act, or was he just too exhausted to fight anymore? Was he acting now, trying to lower our guards?

'It's all done?' Harry asked.

I nodded, secure in the knowledge that the key was hidden under my sleeve. 'I've got next watch. In case . . . Just to make sure Leon's OK.'

'Give me a shout if anything else happens,' Harry said. He released Olly slowly, ready to grab him again if he moved to attack either of us. But Olly just stood from the chair, stretched and wandered towards the stairs, affecting an aura of complete indifference. If I hadn't seen him try to murder Leon with my own eyes, I'd have never thought him capable of it. Harry followed after him, but paused at the doorway.

'I'm sure we'll spot a boat tomorrow. The sea can't stay empty forever.'

'I hope so,' I said, thinking about how much distance we'd covered and how small boats were compared to the entirety of the ocean. Maybe the sea really could stay empty forever. Not that it needed to – we didn't have forever to wait.

Once they were gone, I went down to the kitchen and found an oven timer magnet in a drawer. I set it to twenty minutes. I was going to check on Leon three times an hour until he regained consciousness, if only to assuage my guilt. I sat down in the corridor with my back to the wall and the timer on my chest, I'd do my first check on him and then head upstairs to scan the horizon for lights.

I spent the hours between the fight and morning either checking on Leon or hauling my tired body up two flights of stairs to the viewing room. Harry and Olly both slept through as I tiptoed across the dark lobby. They were on opposite sides of the room, facing one another like warring armies. Maggie was between them, off to one side and curled against a wall. I saw her eyes glitter in the candlelight whenever I passed through. She was awake and watchful, alert for incursions.

Every time I unlocked the door to Leon I first listened for sounds of movement. Each time though he was in the same position. A towel was still wedged between his head and the floor and there were no signs that he'd woken up. I checked his pulse and then locked him in again. It didn't seem like anything was wrong with him; he was even snoring.

Finally, Harry woke up and came down to see me. He brought gifts in the form of a Red Bull from behind the bar. Probably something bought for Leon's benefit. But in the absence of any way to make coffee or tea, I wasn't going to turn down caffeine.

'This is the last of the bread,' he said, by way of 'good morning'. He presented me with a ragged lump of hard sourdough smeared with jam. I shoved it into my mouth whole and waited for it to soften.

Harry didn't even make a joke about my table manners, just slid down the wall and sat beside me. I chewed the bread down until it could safely be swallowed.

'How are Mags and Olly?'

'About the same. I think Mags was up most of the night, said she couldn't sleep whilst Olly was with us. Olly's still adamant that Leon confessed to killing Libby and Mags wants us to let him out.'

I shook my head, struggling to understand Maggie's actions. 'Do you believe him – that Leon admitted it?'

Harry stared at the door. 'I believe he's capable of it. But why?'

I wasn't sure and for the first time I was too exhausted to speculate.

'How's Leon?' he asked, after the silence grew heavy.

'No change. He's still breathing and hasn't puked. I think he went straight from unconscious to asleep.'

'He's not in a coma or anything though, right?'

I felt my heart constrict. 'Shit. I don't know. How do you know if someone's in a coma?'

'I think you try and wake them up and they . . . don't.'

191

We both eyed the door.

'Should we . . .' I began, but then we heard shuffling from behind it, followed by a moan.

I sighed in relief. Leon was at least moving around. A few moments later, however, he'd apparently made it to his feet and tried to get out. That was when the shouting started.

'What the fuck is this? Let me out!' He banged on the door and I saw the edges of it shiver, the gaps around it widening as he shoved it. Could he bring it down from in there?

'Leon, calm down for a second,' Harry called, jumping up and pushing back against the door.

'Calm down?' Leon snarled. 'First Olly tries to kill me, then you lock me up in here like some kind of . . . Is that a fucking saucepan for me to piss in? Are you totally mad?'

'We can't have you trying to get back at Olly over last night,' Harry said. 'Or him attacking you again. You're safe in there.'

'He attacked me! Lock him up!' Leon thundered. 'This was her idea, wasn't it? That bitch.'

Did he mean me or Maggie? Was there a difference to him or were we on the same team by default? I decided to keep my mouth shut. There was absolutely no chance that hearing my voice would calm this situation down. Even if I hadn't wanted him locked up to begin with, he was never going to believe me.

'Look, if you don't calm down we can't open the door and give you breakfast,' Harry said. 'So, can you just get it together for a minute? Otherwise we'll have to leave you in there.'

'I'll give you "calm down",' Leon said, rattling the door again.

'I don't think we're going to be able to let him out of

192

there any time soon,' Harry muttered to me. 'But at least he's not in a coma, eh?'

I thought for a moment, trying to weigh our options. We couldn't let Leon out whilst he was this angry, but it didn't seem likely he was going to calm down whilst he was locked up. So we were in a bit of a catch-22. We did need to feed him, however, and get him water. I also needed to be able to check on him and I couldn't do that through a locked door. I stared at the wood as it shook under Leon's fists. At the top, there was a ventilation grille, about the size of a letterbox. Four screws held it in, and I thought we could probably get them undone, even if someone had painted over them at some point.

I leaned close to Harry and whispered, hoping Leon wouldn't hear, 'I think that vent at the top might unscrew from this side.'

Harry looked up and his shoulders relaxed. He nodded, visibly relieved.

'Grab a knife from the kitchen,' Harry said.

I went and found a dinner knife, which Harry then used to unscrew the vent. As soon as it clattered to the floor the rectangle of darkness beyond was replaced by Leon's bloodshot eyes.

'I'm not playing around,' he said, sounding more controlled, but scarier for it. 'Let me out, now, or you won't like what happens.'

'Making threats isn't the best way to get us to trust you,' Harry said. 'Look, I'll bring you some food and we can talk about it, OK?'

Leon's only response was another attempt to batter the door off of its hinges.

'Maybe I should go get the food?' I said.

'Yeah . . . I'll watch him.'

I hurried upstairs to the lobby and found Olly and Maggie huddled on opposite sides of the fire. They looked older than I'd ever seen them, stooped and grey in the wintery morning light. The flickering glow of the small fire made their eyes and cut-glass, well-bred cheekbones appear gaunt and skeletal. When they turned to look at me I almost flinched. It was like being confronted by a pair of zombies.

The room itself was messy, crumpled duvets and stained monogrammed pillows on the floor, and discarded clothes thrown every which way. The air was thick with the musty smell of sleep and the odour of rancid sick leeching out of the quarantined toilet. The tables were still littered with empties from the party, joined since by jam-covered knives, empty water bottles and Harry's cigarette ends.

'Is Leon OK?' Maggie asked immediately.

'Yeah, he's awake. Doesn't seem to be anything wrong with him.' Aside from his attitude, of course. But if anything, that was more understandable now than it had ever been before.

She let out a sigh and nodded. It was hard to believe that only last night she'd been threatening to cut him off financially and that he'd hit her twice since we'd found ourselves stuck here. Whatever was going on between the pair of them it was toxic as Hell. I wanted to think that when this was all over I'd be there for her, but I didn't know if I could be that person for Maggie. I wasn't even sure she wanted me to be.

'Where's Leon's portion of breakfast?' I asked.

Olly looked at me as if I was the source of the sick smell. 'He doesn't deserve anything of mine.'

'I take that to mean you've eaten it?'

He rolled his eyes at me.

'Great. OK, I'm off upstairs to look for something he can eat.' I headed for the stairs because if I didn't leave immediately I was going to start a fight with Olly, and I didn't want to put myself or Harry through that. I was feeling increasingly as if we were the matriarch and patriarch of our own wayward tribe.

'Bring some more books down!' Maggie called after me.

I held my tongue and went upstairs to scavenge the bar. In daylight the distance around us was harder to ignore. The dark closed everything in, but now I could see to the horizon in all directions – the empty, barren horizon. Not a single boat or shadow of land to be seen. The cold pressed its fingers against the glass all round me, stealing away any hint of warmth rising from the fetid sleeping area below.

I shivered and ducked down behind the bar. There wasn't much alcohol left. Most of it had gone that first night, when we were actually having a party. Since then, I guessed Olly and Leon, even Mags, had been helping themselves. Most of what was left was the weird niche stuff for making cocktails – grenadine, bitters, soda water and syrups. In a cabinet under the optics I discovered a tray of shrivelled lemon and lime wedges, a jar of olives, one of cocktail onions and another of cherries. Not exactly a feast. I found one of the bags of hollow books that had been abandoned on the floor and added the food. There weren't that many books left; the cardboard covers obviously burned quickly. We'd have to start chopping up the furniture unless we wanted to freeze to death. After that, well, we'd have to get creative, maybe have the doors off the cabins.

I swung the bag over my shoulder and straightened. Then

I froze, not wanting to let myself believe what I was seeing. But no, it really was there, appearing out of the early morning mist on the horizon as we drifted onwards.

'Land!'

CHAPTER TWENTY

Olly and Maggie reached me first, followed shortly by Harry, who was breathless from running all the way up from the cabins. I heard him trying to suck in air as I attempted to get the ornamental telescope to focus. Though the lens was a bit scratched I could still see the distant shore. There were trees and what looked like it might be a telephone pole, just visible as part of a blurry, dark mass.

'How soon until we reach it?' Maggie asked, grabbing for the telescope and nearly poking me in the eye with it. I backed away and let her and Olly fight for it.

'I don't know. It looks quite far,' I said. 'I don't even know where "it" is. How far have we gone – and in which direction?'

'Doesn't matter. It's land,' Harry said. 'Thank God. We should try the phones.'

I hurried into the bridge and found the two remaining mobiles. Unfortunately it looked like Mags' had lost its last bit of battery during the night, but Olly's was hanging in there at fourteen per cent. I doubted the cold was doing them any favours and realised we should have kept them downstairs where it was warmer. Why did I have to think of everything too late? Why was no one else figuring this stuff out?

I quickly dialled the EU emergency services number. Nothing happened, the call didn't connect. Was that because we were too far from land, or too far from the EU? I went into the 'sent messages' folder and copy-pasted our SOS text into a new message, then sent that.

'Is it working?' Harry called.

'Maybe . . . No, it's not,' I said. The text showed as sent, but failed to change to 'delivered'. 'Maybe we need to be closer . . . but we're running out of battery.'

'I think that's the French coastline,' Olly was saying as I came back into the viewing room. 'I can tell by the shape of the trees.'

'Like hell you can,' Harry said.

'Can't we use the raft?' Maggie said, interrupting whatever Olly was about to say. 'We can't just sit here, waiting.'

I glanced at Harry and he shook his head. 'We don't know how the current would affect the raft – it might sweep it further out to sea. We're safer on the boat as it's heading right for the coast.'

'No, it's not.'

We all turned to stare at Olly, who was looking up from the telescope. He ducked back down and shifted it slightly, as if trying to find something.

'What?' I asked, the tiny spark of hope in my chest turning to ice at his words.

'We're not getting closer – I think we're moving parallel, or further away.' He looked up, face pinched and white. 'We're definitely not going to get any nearer.'

'That's bollocks, how can you know that?' Harry said. 'You don't know anything about boats, or sailing or—'

'You look then.' Olly stepped away from the telescope and pointed out of the viewing room window. 'You see that flag there?'

We all looked at the fluttering flag on deck. I hadn't really paid it much attention, even before we became stranded. There were a hundred other luxurious details to take in before the Union Jack registered.

'It's blowing away from land,' Harry said, numbly.

'Exactly. I don't need to know about sailing because any idiot can tell we're being blown away from that landmass. Well . . . almost any idiot.'

Harry looked as crushed as I felt. Even Olly didn't seem as pleased with himself as he might otherwise have been. His voice had risen in pitch, becoming more and more clipped until he sounded like he ought to be giving a press conference outside Downing Street. One that would end with his resignation.

Maggie collapsed onto a couch and put her head in her hands. I wanted to join her, to be honest. Everything felt suddenly so hopeless. We were right here, we could see the coastline, and it was about as much use to us as it had been when it was over the horizon. Still completely unreachable.

'What if they spot us?' I said, grasping at one last chance.

'They'd have to be looking, with a telescope or binoculars at that. And even then, what would they see? A boat in the water. It's not exactly noteworthy. There's nothing there that even suggests there are people around. It might be a deserted corner of some farmer's field,' Olly snapped.

'All right then, what if we . . .' I struggled, sorting through all the hopeless things we'd already tried. We could put up a banner or something to signal for help but by the time we'd made it we might be too late. Even now, as Olly said, it was unlikely we'd be seen.

'We use the raft,' Harry said. 'I use the raft.'

'What?' I couldn't believe what he was saying. 'You just told Mags—'

'I said it was safer to wait on the boat, when we thought the boat was going to make it to land. If it's not, this is our one chance to get help.'

'And what if it gets caught in the current, like you said? If we're drifting out, the raft will too.'

'I can paddle a raft.'

'Without oars?' I cried, trying and failing to get Harry to look me in the eye. He had to know this idea was insane.

'There might be one in the pack, we don't know,' He said, voice rising as we argued. 'If there isn't, I'll use something from in here – one of those stupid oil paintings, my hands, I don't care! One of us needs to get to the mainland and get help.'

'And why does that person need to be you, all of a sudden?' Maggie asked in a vicious, tearstained little voice.

'Because I'm the strongest person here.'

Olly scoffed.

'It's true,' Harry said, clearly trying his hardest to sound calmer. 'Mags has arms like breadsticks, Olly, you've never lifted anything heavier than a glass of Pimm's and Hannah . . . you're just not fit enough to make it.'

'I know,' I said, appreciating his gentle tone, though it wasn't necessary. Because it was true. I worked in an office and did crafts for fun. I liked to cook and eat. It was not news to me that I wasn't in the running for 'most athletic shipmate' in anyone's mind. 'That still doesn't mean you have to risk your life. That water is freezing. Going into it is suicidal.'

'Then I won't go in,' Harry said, aiming for bravado and falling short. 'I'll cling to that raft like my life depends on it.'

'This is insanity,' Olly said. 'How dare you stand there and tell us you're better than we are, because you hammer scrap metal all day like a navvy.'

'Do you want to go instead?'

Olly pursed his cat's-arse mouth until it vanished against his pallid skin.

'Thought not,' Harry said. 'I'm going. That's that.'

'Wait!' I tried to stop him but he was already snatching up the raft from where I'd left it the day before. He took the stairs to the lower level two at a time with me chasing after him, my heart in my throat. When he opened the door to the deck a blast of icy air tried to push me back inside. I struggled out after him, trying to grab his arms, to make him stop. Behind me I heard only silence. Neither Mags nor Olly were coming after me. They'd washed their hands of Harry already.

'Harry, please. Please don't go.' My voice broke as I said it, desperation clogging my throat. I couldn't lose him now, not like this.

'I'll be fine,' he insisted, though to me it seemed that he was looking out at the water with resignation more than hope. He knew how little chance he had of succeeding.

'No, you won't.' I grabbed his jacket, trying to pull him away as he flipped the raft over, looking for a way to deploy it. 'I mean it, Harry, it's too dangerous and . . . and you can't leave me alone here. Not with them.'

It was selfish and desperate, but I couldn't just let him leave. Not only would he be throwing his life away in a tiny dinghy, but he'd also be leaving me alone with two potential killers, with only Mags as an ally. This wasn't just dangerous for him. It would put the rest of us in danger, too. More than that, I didn't want to lose him. I couldn't bear the thought of it. I'd been stupid to think that I could spare myself pain by never telling him how I felt. If anything, that made it worse.

'I have to go, Han – give me the phone,' Harry said, clearly trying to be gentle. I was still holding it and he took it from my limp hand. 'I'll try and send the text as I get closer, in case . . . well, just in case.'

He finally found a rip cord and pulled it. The yellow plastic pack flew open and began to writhe as it filled with air and plumped up into a hexagonal dinghy. There were no oars, and no canopy either. It was just like one you'd buy to mess around with on a beach. Harry dragged the squeaking raft over to the side of the yacht and looked down at the sharp, steely waves.

'I'll climb down – you pass it to me.'

I didn't want to. I wanted to wrestle the raft away and fling it overboard so he couldn't leave me. Leave us. I knew we weren't safe on the boat but what he was trying to do was incredibly dangerous. Brave, maybe, but there were probably a lot of brave men lining the bottom of the sea. I'd have preferred for him to be a coward and try to survive with the rest of us.

Still, shamefully, there was a tiny part of me that was willing to gamble his life for our rescue. Despite my wild impulse to take the raft out of the equation, I didn't throw it away. Instead I leaned over the side and helped him get it into the water. Then I watched as he put one foot on it to hold it in place as he looked up at me.

'I can get something to row with,' I said, as a last desperate attempt to make him wait.

Harry's teeth chattered in the cold. He was pale as seafoam, mouth pinched with fear. 'We both know there's nothing we can use. Besides, there's no time. Look – it's already nearly disappeared.'

I looked up and saw that he was right. The coastline had dwindled to a smear on the horizon. A fading memory of land. I heard a splash and looked back, only to find that Harry had fully boarded the raft and was drifting away.

'Harry!' I gripped the side of the yacht as if by doing so I could keep him there. 'Harry, I . . . Good luck!'

'See you later!' he called back, barely sounding like himself at all.

The wind stung the tears off my face and I wiped them furiously with my sleeve. When he came back with help, the first thing I was going to do was pinch him, hard. Then I'd hug him. Stupid, idiotic, brave, selfless son-of-a-bitch.

I watched as Harry lay flat and hung his arms out, paddling himself along like a kid on a Lilo. I held my breath, but it actually seemed to be working and he moved away from the yacht and started heading in the direction of land.

Even with the wind flattening my clothes to my body and whipping my hair into my eyes, I couldn't bring myself to go back inside. I felt like if I looked away I'd be abandoning him, and that something awful would happen. As if by simply watching him I could protect him. The one time I glanced back I saw that Olly and Maggie were watching, too, from the viewing room window. Olly had helped himself to a bottle of water.

I followed Harry's progress with a tight ball of fear in my belly. Every time a wave got between us I held my breath and waited for him to reappear. When he did, I tensed up, waiting for the next one and the next one. He kept paddling until he was a child's toy in the distance – a little yellow raft with a tiny clockwork man on it. Only he wasn't a machine, and I could see he was getting tired.

'Come on, come on, Harry,' I muttered through chattering teeth, the cold searing into me. 'Please, please, please . . .'

The raft dipped behind a wave and I waited for it to reappear. The wave blended with the rest. My eyes burned and I had to blink. Which wave was it? Where was he?

I stared out at the unbroken sea, hoping for a flash of yellow. But there was only grey water and grey sky. The land had vanished over the horizon and Harry had vanished with it. Wherever he was I couldn't see him. Did that mean he was too far away, or that he'd been swept under?

'Harry!'

My breath caught in my throat and I clung to the side of the boat as my legs crumpled under me. The wind stole my shout and gave back only a thin, gravelly rain, which steadily beat down over the yacht as we washed further out to sea.

CHAPTER TWENTY-ONE

The cold and the rain drove me back inside. That and the sudden – not entirely irrational – fear that the others might simply lock me out on deck. Whether on purpose or because they'd simply forgotten about me. Either felt equally likely in that moment. I headed back upstairs in the vain hope that from higher up I'd be able to spot Harry.

Olly was the only one in the viewing room when I returned. Mags must have gone down to the cabins again. She hadn't even waited on the bottom deck to ask about Harry. I checked the window and felt my doubts rise when I couldn't spot even a flash of yellow in the sea. Please God, let Harry simply be too far away for me to see. Please don't let him be dead. Not now, not after everything.

I turned from the window and told myself that tearing myself up inside wouldn't solve anything. I had to regain some control. My bag from earlier was gone so I assumed Maggie had gone to feed Leon. I at least still had the key to the door, so she couldn't let him out – though I still wasn't certain he couldn't just batter his way out of the cupboard. I thought all this in a kind of fog as I stiffly made my way to a chair and collapsed on it. Despite the bright morning outside, it was dim and stale within the boat, even with all the glass walls.

Though Olly was still there, he wasn't looking out to sea. He was instead lying on the sofa and staring up at the ceiling, cradling a glass of amber liquid. I registered the bottle of whisky on the table, but it took a second for my frayed mind to recognise it as the one I'd brought with me as a host and hostess gift for Libby and Olly.

'You took that from my room,' I said, though my voice came out horribly slow and stilted, to my ears at least. It wasn't just my mind working slowly, I felt like I'd been knocked out of gear, and everything was struggling to keep going. Harry was gone and I couldn't reach him. Harry was gone and I didn't know if he was still alive.

'It's my boat; the rooms and their contents are mine. Besides, Libby told me you brought it as a gift. Those chocolates, too,' Olly said, without looking up. 'They were . . . fine, thank you.'

'A gift she didn't want,' I said. It was such a stupid thing to focus on, but I clung to it so as not to be swept away by grief. By despair.

'I can't say they were my first choice, but needs must. Anyway . . . how's the rescue voyage going? Do I need to start packing?'

I picked up the bottle and took a swig. I hated whisky, straight whisky especially. It burned through me and tasted like licking a petrol station forecourt, but it at least chased some of the cold out of my insides.

'Harry's . . . The raft's gone. It disappeared.'

'Great.' Olly rolled his eyes. 'What are we going to do now?'

206

Something inside me snapped back into place, completing a circuit that had shorted out as I watched the raft vanish. I was angry. So angry that I wanted to drag Olly outside and drown him myself in the same freezing waters that had claimed Libby and now Harry.

'That's all you have to say? Harry could be dead! He just risked everything trying to save us, to save you.'

Olly looked at me as though I were a child having a tantrum over something trivial. As if Harry's disappearance was just another box of chocolates he'd stolen, and he was sick of hearing about it already.

'If you'll recall, I never asked him to do anything for me.'

'You're fucking inhuman,' I said, unable to believe what he'd just said. 'Harry is out there . . . maybe, maybe drowning, and it's OK because he wasn't following your orders? I mean, God!' I threw up my hands and whisky splashed over my fingers as the bottle sloshed. My eyes blurred with tears. 'Do you care about anything except yourself? What about Libby? Have you already marked her down as an acceptable loss?'

Olly didn't blink when he got really angry, I was learning. He looked at you like a snake instead, unmoving, focused, waiting for you to break under the weight of his haughty stare and poisonous words.

'I'm sorry if I can't feign some overwrought display for your comfort,' he began, voice winding up like an air raid siren. 'But in case it had escaped your notice, I didn't like Harry. Point of fact, I don't like you, either, and unlike you bleeding hearts, I don't feel the need to perform outrage or empathy for the benefit of the rest of you.'

'Perform? How about feel?' I snapped back. 'I don't care if you hated his guts, he's still a person. A person who could be, who might be . . .' I felt my throat constrict and tears trickled onto my cheeks. 'Who might have died in one of the most awful ways that I can imagine, so—'

'Why is it your sort always have to prey on emotion?' Olly interrupted. 'Crying over everything, bleating on about life being precious when we all know the truth. If it were me out there, you'd be in here with Harry, secretly pleased that the horrible rich man was drowned at sea.'

'That's not true.' I sniffed.

'You know it is. You're just denying it because you want to believe you're better than me.'

'I'm saying it because I mean it. I can't believe that we're still trapped here and you're not doing a damn thing but trying to win some debate with me about my politics!' I shook my head. 'You do realise you're stuck here, too? That this all' – I waved a hand to encompass the dim, ravaged room – 'affects you, too? We're not talking about some issue that'll never impact your life – this is about how we're going to survive. How one of us just risked his life trying to get help. This is real!'

'I'm well aware. The only difference is I'm not going to be stupid enough to risk my life for the likes of you. Any of you. Harry's dead, by the way. Obviously. And he's dead because he wanted to play at being a hero, because he was a child, just like you. Naïve and selfish enough to think the world revolves around him – that his stupid risk would pay off because it was him making it.' Olly downed the last of his whisky. 'Well, now he knows, doesn't he? Where going against the grain gets you. Do you think he realised that? Or did it all happen too quickly?'

I felt my body stiffen, catlike, all the hair standing up. Fury locked me in place even as the boat rocked under us. 'Shut up.'

'Why? Who's going to make me now that dashing Harry's lifeless body is bobbing in the ocean? You?' Olly laughed.

I threw the bottle. I didn't think about it, didn't even really notice what I was doing. I just wanted him to stop. The bottle hit the glass in Olly's hand and both shattered, raining glass and whisky over him. I sucked in a breath – to scream or to apologise, I wasn't sure – but before I could decide, Olly's fingers were around my throat.

The sudden jolt drove my teeth into my tongue. I tasted blood, reached up and tried to prise his grip loose. It was no good. Olly's hands bit into the flesh of my throat and wouldn't let go. My eyes were watering, vision blurring, but I could still see his face. He wasn't blinking, the only sign that he was aware of what he was doing was the smile playing at the edges of his mouth and the snake-like flaring of his nostrils as he fought my weakening efforts to escape.

I tried kicking out at him, but it was impossible to get enough leverage. Even trying to throw myself out of the chair had no effect. A horrible gurgling sound bubbled up out of my mouth and Olly bared his teeth.

The room behind him was growing dark, his pale face fading into the shadows. I couldn't move my fingers anymore. My arms fell to my sides, limp. I'd lost the fight. It was over.

Then the pressure was gone and Olly with it. I tumbled out of the chair and landed on my hands and knees, coughing and retching as blood rushed to my head and air flooded my lungs. I was trying to crawl away, but didn't know where to. My palms pressed down on broken glass and I whimpered.

As the roaring in my ears subsided, I heard Olly struggling with someone, swearing and snarling. I held my injured throat in my hand and turned to find him locked in a struggle with Maggie. One she was losing. She must've run in from the stairs and tackled him, but without the element of surprise he was close to overpowering her.

I floundered to my feet and grabbed the nearest shard of whisky bottle. Stumbling over the broken glass as the boat heaved through another wave, I reached Olly and grabbed his hair with one hand. With the other I pressed the shard of glass to his neck.

'Stop!' I managed to wheeze.

He froze mid-struggle. Maggie, who was crying openly, slithered away from him and hauled herself up using a chair. I waited for her to circle around to me, then dropped the glass and pushed Olly away as hard as I could. He tripped and fell against the mostly empty bookcase, crushing the fake books on the floor underfoot. Immediately he started dragging himself to his feet, hands grasping at book covers as he hunted for a weapon. Finding nothing, he squared up instead. There were two of us and one of him, and I could tell he wasn't willing to test those odds.

'Stop it! Both of you!' Maggie dodged my hand when I reached out to steady her. 'Did Harry make it yet? When are we getting out of here?'

'He's dead,' Olly spat. 'Just like the pair of you will be if you don't start listening to me.'

'You tried to kill me,' I wheezed. 'Just like you killed Libby. He needs to be locked up, Mags.' I turned to her, pleading, because she was the one person on board who might possibly back me up. She'd just saved my life, after all.

'That was self-defence,' Olly retorted. 'She threw a bottle at me because I dared criticise her precious Harry. Who, by the way, just wasted our one possible means of escape on his suicide mission.'

'Shut up.' Maggie covered her ears with shaking hands. 'Both of you, just shut up!'

'She just threatened to slit my throat.' Olly gestured to a tiny spot of blood on his neck, where the broken glass had nicked him. 'And she said she never wanted to see Libby again, right before Libby vanished.'

Maggie turned her red-rimmed eyes on me. 'Is that true?'

'No!' I said, automatically.

'Liar!' Olly said triumphantly. 'You see, Maggie? You can't trust her. Come here, let me protect you.'

'Maggie, don't!' I pleaded. 'Look . . . I said I never wanted to see her again and that I was never coming to another one of their stupid parties,' I corrected myself, hoping Maggie would be able to see I was telling the truth. 'I wasn't going to be her poor friend anymore, but that doesn't mean I did anything to her. I want to keep you safe, and I'd have done the same for her. Despite everything.'

Maggie looked between the two of us, a scared animal unconvinced by bribes and promises. She was in survival mode. We all were. Trust wasn't as easy anymore.

'I want the key. To the cupboard,' She said, holding a trembling hand out to me, gesturing to the exposed elastic band on my wrist.

'Mags . . . you know I can't let you have it. You'll let Leon out and he'll just make everything worse.'

'I know that I can't trust either of you right now.' Her voice quavered and she looked ready to burst into tears again.

'And you can trust him? After he hit you, twice?' I said.

'Give me the key,' Olly ordered. 'Neither of you can be trusted with it.'

'Hannah, give it to me,' Maggie said, straightening up as

211

if trying to regain some of her previous glamour, and with it, some authority.

'No.' I took a step back from both of them. 'No, and if you try and take it, I will throw it overboard.'

'I'll pick the lock then,' Maggie said. 'Or . . . or take the door down with the tools we found.'

I was fairly confident that neither she nor Olly could do anything of the sort. Picking the lock was definitely out of the question. As for using tools or brute force, well, they could try, but Maggie didn't have it in her and Olly had as much reason as I did to want to keep Leon under lock and key. He probably only wanted the key so as to use Leon as a bargaining tool to keep us in line.

'He's staying locked up and I'm holding on to the key.'

'See, we can't trust her,' Olly said. 'She's out for revenge.'

'I don't trust either of you.' Maggie backed away from us and towards the stairs. 'I'm going to shut myself in my room and if either of you try and get in, I'll make you sorry. I will. You' – she pointed at me – 'better stay away from Leon. I'll take care of him.'

'Maggie, I'll need to check on him, make sure he's—'

'Stay away!' Maggie ordered, dashing down the gloomy stairs. 'I'm warning you.'

'Looks like you're on your own, Han,' Olly said, sneering my nickname.

'So are you, Olly,' I said, grabbing the remaining bottles off the bar as I headed for the stairs. 'So are you.'

CHAPTER TWENTY-TWO

I descended to the lobby, keeping an ear out for footsteps. If Olly tried to come at me from behind in retaliation I wanted to be ready. I was also wary of the darkness below. The glass walls let in a lot of greyish winter sun but there were plenty of places to hide in the shadows of the furniture draped in duvets and blankets. Maggie was paranoid, acting irrationally. I wasn't sure she wouldn't try to jump me for the key, or if she thought I was coming after her.

Fortunately the lobby was quiet. The fire was mostly dead and giving out only a tiny amount of red light. I wanted to stay by it and keep it going but there were too many ways in and out of the lobby to be safe. I wanted somewhere I could defend myself if necessary. I'd just have to be cold whilst I did it.

I picked my way though the room and headed down into the cabins. There it was truly dark, there being no windows in the rooms or the hallway. It also stank down there; unwashed bodies, unflushed toilets and rotten food blending together into an odour that hung thickly in the air. It was particularly strong outside Leon's cupboard.

Harry's lighter and one of the candles was still outside the linen cupboard and I grabbed them, tucking my two bottles under one arm.

'Who's out there?' Leon called.

I flinched, startled by the sudden noise. I decided it was best not to say anything. I didn't want him kicking off or Maggie coming to investigate. Instead I shuffled quickly past.

'Is that you, Hannah?' I heard him shaking at the door, shuffling around in the dark. 'Mags said Harry's dead. You better let me out, otherwise it's not going to be good for you when I do get out of here.'

I ignored him, though he was making my stomach churn. As soon as I got to my room I shut the door and wedged the heel of one of the Dior shoes under it, just as I'd done on the night of the party. That felt so long ago. I crept about in the darkness, looking for other things to secure the door with. In the end I heaved the whole vanity over to barricade myself in. I put the candle on the bedside table and lit it. By its flickering light I saw the dirt and blood under my nails from several days without showering, followed by my fight with Olly. I felt filthy, my hair was lank and under my borrowed, sea-damp clothes I was sticky with sweat. In the gloom I felt like I was trapped in a musty burrow. I could see that the room around me had been searched – drawers were open and my things were all over the place. Olly had been through everything before he'd found the whisky. With so little food and fuel on board it looked like it would be every man for himself from now on.

If I got out of this, which just then seemed like it would take a miracle, I was going straight to the coastguard to get them out searching for Harry. I was not going to give up on him. He wouldn't give up on me. Right after that, I'd tell the police about Libby's disappearance and how Olly was responsible for her death. Or Leon, or both of them.

The boat lurched and I wished I had a window so I could see outside. Though if I'd had one, it would have been below water level. It felt like another storm was coming. I only hoped we would make it through. Without a life raft we were screwed if anything happened to the yacht.

I didn't feel safe going back out there, which meant I had no way of knowing if any boats were passing. After so long without seeing one though, my hopes weren't high. Weighing the odds of being attacked versus seeing another ship, I knew I was better off staying where I was.

I tried to keep calm by taking stock of my resources. Back at home, when the rent went up or my energy bills suddenly went through the roof, I'd collect anything I could sell and go through it. Taking stock of what I had at my disposal helped me feel in control, gave me something to focus on. On the boat, my resources weren't monetary but more vital. I took everything to the corner furthest from the door, putting the bed between me and it. Sitting on the floor, I spread things out and tried to make a plan.

Maggie had taken the jars of cocktail garnishes and as far as I knew all the party food on board was gone. I hadn't really looked at the bottles as I'd grabbed them. They were of grenadine and mint syrup, respectively. Cocktail syrups weren't food, but they did contain calories, quite a few of them, and I reasoned that with both bottles I had enough sugar to keep me energised for a few days. No nutrients though, except for the vitamin gummies in my overnight stuff, and those couldn't provide me with protein or complex

215

carbs to make me feel full or fight brain fog. At best, I would be staving off starvation.

As for water, I didn't have any in the room. The wet room's tap was out of action like everywhere else on board, and there was no loo in there, so no cistern to dip into. Most of the bottles of water were still in the kitchen as far as I knew, though I hadn't been keeping track of them. I didn't put it past Olly or Mags to have hidden a stash of them away somewhere. At least the syrups I'd taken from the bar contained water, if I wasn't able to get anything else. Having secured the room, I wasn't in a rush to go back out there into the dark, cramped corridor. Maybe I'd chance it once everyone else was asleep.

There wasn't much else of use in the room. I'd packed for a weekend getaway, not a lengthy survival trip. I had the candle and lighter, and a book, which I'd brought along in case there was time to read. At least I wouldn't die of boredom. After searching the pockets of my handbag and turning out all the small pouches inside I found a reusable metal straw, two paracetamol tablets, a weathered-looking maxipad and a lip balm. I remembered reading somewhere that if you wore lipstick every day you'd consume somewhere around four pounds of the stuff during your life. No, wait, Libby had told me that. She'd read it in a magazine. I remembered her looking up and being so disgusted at the idea. It was summer and we were down by the lake, tanning and drinking two-quid Slushies from the union, topped up with white rum. She'd wondered aloud just how many calories that was, because lipstick's mostly oil and fat, isn't it?

Thoughts of Libby and the idea that I was considering how long I could survive on a lip balm tipped me over the edge. A shrill little giggle bubbled out of my bruised throat and I had to clamp a hand over my mouth to smother my laughter. I didn't want to risk attracting attention from one of the others. I couldn't stop though. I couldn't breathe and tears were sliding down my cheeks. My chest hurt and my stomach muscles were stiff as piano wire, but I couldn't stop laughing, until it turned to sobbing.

Libby was gone, Harry, too, though I was hoping he was still out there, alive. The luxurious yacht felt like it was closing in on me, getting smaller by the minute. It had seemed so grand and expansive on the night of the party. Now I felt like I was trapped inside a freezer. The ocean around us appeared bigger every day, as if it expanded for every metre we drifted, keeping us at the centre of its endless expanse. I was starting to get a strange feeling every time I looked out across the water to the sky, an irrational fear that this was all there was. That it wasn't us who'd gone missing, but the world itself.

If we weren't rescued soon there was a real possibility that I was going to go mad, or that we were going to starve to death on the imported marble floor. Or die of thirst surrounded by empty champagne bottles. The idea was so perverse that it prompted another wave of hysterics.

I cried until I felt sick and then curled up in an exhausted ball on the floor. My duvet was still in Maggie's room and without it I was shivering. Cold to the bone. With the last bits of effort I could muster I pulled the mattress, sheet and all, off the bed and propped it against the wall, making a sort of tent for myself. Then I blew the candle out. Inside my shelter I wrapped myself in guest towels and the faux sheepskin rug from the floor. Too many nights of broken sleep and stress were catching up to me, and I'd barely rested my head on the plush carpet before I was out for the count.

I woke up some time later, my stomach grumbling resentfully. I had no idea what time it was. The timer I'd been using to wake me the previous night was still in the hallway, somewhere. I hadn't left the candle burning, and I had no window, so there was no way to estimate how long I'd slept. I listened, straining to hear even the slightest sound. There was nothing. Nothing but the roaring of the sea, slightly dulled by the hull around me.

If the others were still awake, they weren't down in the cabins. I couldn't hear so much as a footstep. This was, I realised, as good a chance as I was going to get. If I wanted water or to check for extra food, it had to be now. Secondary to that pressing thought came the realisation that I should probably also check on Leon. He'd need his pot emptying and maybe some blankets as the temperature continued to plummet. I had responsibilities as his one remaining jailer. Ones that I couldn't in good conscience ignore.

After dragging myself upright I downed a few mouthfuls of mint syrup. It was vile, like trying to make a meal out of toothpaste. It didn't even leave me feeling full. But at least my energy levels felt a little higher afterwards.

I didn't want Olly or anyone else snooping and taking what little I had left, but there weren't many places I could hide my supplies. In the end, I pressed the metal straw against the wall and used all my strength to force the mattress back against it. The straw punctured the fabric covering the insides and I quickly made a hollow that could hold the syrup bottles and the rest of my supplies. They'd be exposed if someone turned the mattress over, but it was the best I could do.

After a second's thought I slid the metal Boba straw into the pocket of my borrowed joggers. It wasn't that sharp,

218

but it was thin and strong. With enough force I could potentially use it as a weapon. It was all I had until I could retrieve a knife from the kitchen. Though if the others were lying in wait outside my door, I'd never make it that far.

With my neck prickling with fear I moved my barricade. After each item I paused to listen. There were still no signs of movement outside. Not even a cough or bang from Leon's cupboard. Maybe they really were all asleep? Or maybe Olly had cornered Mags and killed her?

The thought made me move faster. How could I have left her, vulnerable and alone, whilst I slept? She was going out of her mind with fear and paranoia. Ironically, that meant that she might not be thinking clearly enough to keep herself safe.

I pulled the shoe out from under the door and opened it. At the far end of the corridor a faint amount of greyish light told me that it wasn't fully daylight outside. Maybe I'd slept right through until morning? Or else it was early evening. There was no way to be sure without going up there.

The stale air from the corridor oozed over me. The stink was even worse now, or maybe I'd just become more aware of it after escaping it for a while. Leon's temporary toilet definitely needed emptying. I could also do with using the facilities and I wondered what Olly and Maggie had been doing. My heart sank as I realised they had probably been using the toilets and thus the only supply of fresh water that could not be hoarded away. I paused as I went past the powder room and let myself in. I was intending to check the cistern to make sure we still had clean water but one look at the toilet – overflowing with wet, soiled paper and no water in sight – confirmed the worst. Still, I reached for the 'drain' button to flush it automatically. I was operating on pre-disaster logic – see a mess, dispose of it. It was only as I pressed the button that I thought of the noise and water waste. But nothing happened.

I pressed the 'fill' button, hoping for something, but no. The toilet wasn't working. Either it was out of water, as I'd feared, or something about it was electrical and therefore not working. Either way, I doubted there was any water I could get at via the cistern. There wasn't much else I could do except add to the fetid bowl.

Once I was done, I escaped to the comparatively airy corridor. Still no actual sign of Maggie or Olly. I crept down the corridor and finally reached the kitchen. I wanted a knife before I did anything else. That and some water; my bruised throat was crying out for it. Inside I found the kitchen in disarray. Clearly someone else had searched it since I had – maybe more than once. Cupboards had been left open and pots and pans were scattered everywhere amidst broken crockery. Someone had thrown a real tantrum in there. Or else the motion of the boat had thrown things about. The mess didn't concern me, but the empty knife racks did. Every single one was gone. Someone had taken them before I had a chance. Olly? Maggie? I had no idea.

The doors of the fridge were hanging open, the inside dark and empty. On the floor were the remains of several water bottles. They'd either fallen out and smashed or someone had thrown their empties down. Every other bottle of water was gone. I gritted my teeth so as not to swear aloud. I didn't want to chance waking anyone. I'd been right. Olly or Maggie – perhaps both of them – had hidden the water away somewhere.

The boat rocked slightly then, and I heard a sloshing

sound. There was water, somewhere. It didn't take long to pin it down as coming from the fridge itself.

I opened the door all the way. The water reservoirs in the door were about a quarter of the way full. Apparently it was too much effort for whoever had come through there to take them out and empty them. I cast around for something that could hold water and grabbed the nearest saucepan. Once I'd filled it, I quickly moved to carry it back to my room, trying desperately not to trip in the darkness. At least I now had water. Before leaving the kitchen, I gulped down a few mouthfuls. It tasted stale and plasticky, but I didn't care. I'd have gladly paid twenty dollars for a bottle of it at that moment.

Going back out into the corridor made me feel anxious. I didn't like the silence, especially not now I knew about the missing knives. Knowing that I had to check on Leon only made things worse. There was nothing I wanted less than to look in on him, but it had to be done. No one else was going to be much use to him; Olly because he didn't give a shit and Mags because she didn't seem to be thinking too clearly at all.

I was so aware of the choices I was making and of the time each action was taking. Was I doing the right thing? Had I already made a mistake? I couldn't let those thoughts take hold of me. If I did, they'd stop me in my tracks, terrified of doing or not doing anything.

At the cupboard I stood on tiptoes and peered into the dark. I was tense, expecting him to appear at the vent, eyes inches from mine. It took a moment before I could make out Leon's sleeping form, propped up against the left wall. A strong smell wafted up to meet me and I again felt guilty for allowing him to be locked up. Having lost Harry, I was less certain that he'd meant to intimidate me into helping him. Perhaps I could have made him listen. Apparently Maggie wasn't the only one suffering from paranoia. But now that Olly had attacked me, and with Harry gone, I couldn't quite bring myself to give Leon free rein. It was too dangerous for all of us.

I stood there, debating whether or not I should open the door. What if Leon was pretending to sleep? What if he woke up and overpowered me? He could easily force me into the cupboard and lock me in as revenge. That was the best-case scenario. He might be so furious he'd just attack me outright. My hand hovered over the handle, key clamped between my fingers. The smell was disgusting. I couldn't leave him like that. If I did, I'd be no better than Olly. I took a few more seconds to watch Leon, assuring myself that he really was asleep. No indication that he was poised, waiting to strike. I just had to be quick.

I unlocked the cupboard door and edged it open, listening for anyone coming up behind me or any slight shuffle as Leon moved. The large gold stew pot I'd supplied as a toilet was on the right side. The lid was on it but the smell was still stomach churning. I tried to pull it towards me so I wouldn't have to get too close to Leon. The pan slid a few centimetres, then hit an uneven bit of floor and started to tip. I pushed it back and managed to avoid tipping it over, but the lid fell off with a clang. I jerked upright and looked down at Leon. He didn't twitch, and I let out a sigh of relief. Then I sucked in a tiny, foul breath.

I couldn't hear him breathing.

I was on my knees within seconds, shaking him and slapping lightly at his face. He didn't flop as I did so, like he had when he'd been unconscious. He was stiff. Stiff and cold as the breath that rose from my lips and not his. I flinched away from him, from the feel of freezing, waxy skin on my hands.

'Leon . . .'

The unexpected voice made me jump backwards, knocking over the pan in my desperation to escape. But it was too late. Maggie was behind me in the corridor, silent and pale as a ghost, clutching a knife to her chest.

CHAPTER TWENTY-THREE

'Leon . . .?' Maggie repeated. Her voice was so strangled and so hoarse that it sounded like a cat imitating human speech. It made the hairs all over my body stand up. I couldn't take my eyes off of the knife in her hands.

'Mags? Leon's . . .' I swallowed. 'Something's happened to him.'

'No!' Maggie snapped out of her ghostly gaze and rushed me, shouldering me out of the way so she could get into the cupboard. Not noticing or caring about the mess she was stepping in, she dropped the knife and grabbed Leon's shoulders. As soon as she felt the mannequin-esque stiffness of his body she howled and collapsed onto her knees.

I backed away and glanced to the side, ashamed to be spying on her grief. I nearly jumped out of my skin when I saw the pale shape of Olly's face looming out of the shadows. He came padding up the corridor and stopped only feet from me. Maggie was sobbing and calling Leon's name, but Olly didn't seem to hear her.

'You're in my way,' he said, flatly.

I wondered, for the first time, if being stuck out here was sending him off the deep end, just as it was preying on all of us. Only this was Olly's reaction to it, this refusal to let go of his status and breeding. This wasn't just his usual callousness and haughty disdain for others. This was psychotic. He seemed unable or unwilling to acknowledge the squalor we were currently in, or the deaths that had rocked us. It was like he was still seeing everything as it had been. The party, for him, hadn't ended. We were all still his glittering, ungrateful guests.

Perhaps that was why I flattened myself to the wall to let him glide past. I'd finally realised that there was no point trying to engage him, and that doing so was dangerous. Olly left us, climbing the stairs without acknowledging Maggie's hysterical sobbing over the corpse of one of his guests. I was alone with this new horror.

My strongest impulse was, shamefully, to leave Maggie to it. Her sobs had an edge to them and this whole situation screamed 'danger' to my frayed nerves. Not to mention being near Leon's body, which frightened me on another level entirely. One that felt evolutionary. A fear of the presence of death.

I squashed the urge to flee though. Maggie was clearly on the edge and if I didn't do something she'd go spiralling off of it. If she hadn't already. That didn't mean I wanted to take any chances. The first thing I did was slide my slipper over the knife and kick it back, out of her reach.

'Mags? Maggie?' I tried to keep my voice level and calm. 'I think you should come away now. I'm sorry, but . . . he's gone.'

As Maggie wailed something unintelligible and clung to Leon, I backed away slightly and tried to think what to

225

do. I wanted to see what had happened to Leon. Needed to, really. If this was my fault, I needed to see it. If he'd been murdered, I wanted to know how and by whom. I needed to know in case they had the same thing planned for me.

Not 'they' – Olly. With Leon's death it was clear that, if he had been murdered, it was Olly who was doing this. The three of us were the only ones left. It had to be him. I wasn't sure if he was responsible for setting us adrift in the first place or if he was just taking advantage of the situation. Maybe this had been his plan from the beginning, or perhaps he'd just lost his mind. Whatever the reason, I wasn't going to wait for him to get round to Mags and me. We had to know what we were dealing with.

'I'm going to get a light, I'll be right back,' I promised Mags. She didn't respond and I hurried away.

In the dark cabin I stumbled around trying to find the candle and lighter. My mind was whirling with possibilities. I had the only key to Leon's makeshift cell. Olly couldn't have gotten in, but that didn't mean he wouldn't have been able to kill Leon anyway. He might have given him a cocktail laced with any number of cleaning chemicals from the kitchen. Or perhaps Leon was begging for drugs and Olly mixed his coke with drain cleaner or something else.

My fingers caught the edge of the lighter and sent it skittering. I clawed it back and found the candle, tried to force my shaking hands to cooperate and light it. The scent of lime and basil cut through the musty air. It felt so alien in that place. I shielded the flame as I hurried back to Maggie and Leon.

Only, Maggie was gone.

'Mags?' I called out, turning and scanning the hallway

226

behind me. My eyes darted down and I relaxed a tiny bit when I saw that the knife was still on the floor. I could also see some foot prints where she'd walked through the pot's spilled contents and then run down the hall. Maybe she'd gone back to her room to hide?

I leaned into the cupboard and held the candle as close to Leon's face as I dared. The sight of his stiff, waxy skin made me feel sick. I wasn't really sure what I was looking for – cocaine around the nose, foam on his lips, the signs of overdose I'd seen in films and on TV. There was nothing like that, though it looked like he'd gotten vomit on himself. Was that a sign of poisoning, or that he really had developed a concussion? Either way, I was certain it was Olly who'd killed him. Though hadn't I also let this happen, by allowing Leon be locked away?

The sound of running footsteps rapidly approaching had me on my feet in seconds. Maggie whipped past the entrance to the cupboard and I exited it in time to see her stumbling up the stairs to the deck. She dropped something large and soft as she went, then turned and snatched it up. She spotted me and cried out in panic before fleeing.

'Maggie! What are you doing?' I hurried after her, using the candle to avoid the clutter that had accumulated in the hallway.

'Stay away from me!' Maggie shouted at me as I arrived in the lobby. She shouldered open the door to the deck and a freezing wind almost threw it back at her. She had to fight to get outside onto the deck. The weather out there had turned foul – bruise-coloured clouds stretched from the horizon in all directions and the sea was working itself into a fury, throwing up waves and spray, which lapped onto the deck.

'Mags, come back inside, please,' I called from the

doorway over the howling of the wind, my heart thundering. 'It's not safe out there.'

Maggie ignored me and stumbled over the heaving deck to the side of the boat, her feet slipping on the wet planks. I put the candle down on the filthy table and went after her. I couldn't stand by and let someone else die.

'Maggie, stop!' I shouted, struggling to keep my footing as the yacht was tossed about on the waves.

She finally turned towards me and I could see what she was holding. I stopped short, more afraid now than I had been at the sight of the knife, just not for myself this time.

'Maggie . . . don't. Please, just listen to me.'

'No!' Maggie waved the life jacket and took another step towards the side of the yacht. 'I don't trust you, either of you. You killed Leon!'

'I didn't do anything to Leon, I swear. It was Olly, OK? Olly hit him in the head and I think he had a brain injury or a bleed . . .'

'He was fine!' Maggie bawled, teetering as the boat rocked. 'He was talking to me yesterday and he was fine. You did something to him. One of you did something!'

'It wasn't me,' I said, trying to sound as calm as possible despite my thundering pulse. If Maggie was planning on jumping into the water with only that life jacket, she was a dead woman, just as surely as if she were to jump off a bridge. 'Please, Maggie, just . . . come back inside and we can shut ourselves in somewhere safe.'

'There's nowhere safe.' She fumbled with the life jacket and pulled it on over her head. God only knows where she'd found it or why she'd kept it hidden. Maybe for this exact reason.

I darted forwards and tried to grab her but she slapped

me away. The lighter flew out of my hand but I didn't dare leave her to look for it. I backed out of range of her hands but tensed, ready to leap for her again.

'Please.' My voice came out shrill and the wind shrieked with me, mocking my attempts to talk her down. 'Maggie, if you go into that water, you are going to die.'

Maggie just looked at me, shoulders shuddering as she hiccoughed. She looked half-dead already – her tiny body stippled with bruises and dark circles under her eyes. Her hair, like mine, was matted and greasy and there were stains on her clothes. Her eyes were huge with fear, raw from crying.

She glanced down at the churning water. 'At least this way I have a chance.'

'No, you don't, you—'

It was too late. Maggie was there one moment and in the next, gone. She'd rolled herself over the side of the yacht before I'd taken a step.

I heard the splash as she hit the water. By the time I reached the spot where she'd been standing, she'd floated out several feet, thrashing and gasping in the freezing cold waves.

'Swim! Swim back to me, come on!' I stretched out my arm as far as I could. 'Come on, you can do it, Maggie. Please, come on.'

She made a ghastly sound, a cross between a cough and a retch. That was when I realised that she was drowning. Her head was above water and she was floating, thanks to the life jacket, but she was drowning all the same. She must have gasped as she went in – automatically, because of the unimaginable pain of the cold water. She'd sucked in water and couldn't bring it back up, not whilst she was being tossed around like a cork with all her muscles cramping from the cold.

My eyes stung as I reached out so far that my muscles burned. My fingertips brushed hers, her hands desperately seeking help, but her wet fingers slipped through mine as the waves pulled her back. I screamed in frustration, looking around for anything that I could use to pull her in. There was nothing. I looked back just in time to see her bobbing up out of the water, having been sucked down, life jacket and all, by the rough sea. Her mouth gaped open and the cords on her neck were standing out against the reddened skin, but she wasn't making any noise. Her arms flailed and her lips were turning purple. Her bulging, bloodshot eyes begged me to help her, then they unfocused entirely as her body seized violently.

I was screaming, crying, shouting out her name and begging for this to stop, just stop. Then suddenly it did. Maggie's body went limp in the life jacket, her head lolling down until her face was under the water, still contorted in pain and fear.

I let go of the side of the yacht and collapsed onto the deck, where I threw up minty bile and sobbed. When I managed to get upright and looked again, Maggie's body was being dragged out to sea by the greedy waves. Tossing her here and there excitedly, as if she was a prize they'd won.

CHAPTER TWENTY-FOUR

Something was broken inside me. I couldn't bring myself to get up, not even when freezing sea spray slapped me across the face. I was numb, inside and out. Libby, Harry, Leon, Maggie, all of them taken, all of them gone with me powerless to stop it. Only that wasn't true, was it? I could have stopped Harry from getting in that raft. I could have stopped Maggie from throwing herself into the sea, if only I'd tried harder, been faster. If only I hadn't second-guessed myself. As for Leon, I hadn't dissuaded Harry and Olly from locking him up. I had helped them do it. Maybe he'd be dead either way, but now I'd never know, would I? If it could have been prevented. If I could have prevented it.

I tipped my head back against the side of the yacht and let the churning emotions in my chest burst out in a horrible wailing sound that flew out of my aching jaw and was almost immediately stolen by the storm. When I opened my eyes and looked up, a jolt passed through me. There was a dark outline at the viewing room window, looking down at me. Olly was watching me fall apart, watching and making no attempt to help me. Had he also watched Maggie drown, not bothering to come and help? Just how far gone was he and what was he capable of now, after days at sea with little hope of rescue? He'd already killed Libby and that was when he was saner, with more to lose. Now we were both desperate. Both facing a slow death.

The knowledge that I was now alone with him was like a slap to the face. Perhaps Olly wasn't the raging thug that Leon had been, but that didn't mean he was any less capable of violence. He'd just be smarter about it, sneakier. Less a charging bull and more a python slipping soundlessly, strangling his prey as it slept. As I slept.

Fear gripped me, leaving no space for grief and guilt. I dragged myself upright and ran across the deck, nearly slipping over as I did so. I dropped to one knee, my hand outstretched on the deck, and I spotted the lighter. I grabbed it and shoved it back in my pocket. I was racing to secure a safe space and resources for myself. I was trapped with a selfish murderer who could end me at any time, for the sake of anything; a bottle of water, a crust of bread, a disposable lighter. Just because he wanted to. Just because he was bored and didn't like me.

On my way to the cabin stairs I grabbed my candle. In doing so I sloshed hot wax over my hand, but I ignored it. In the hallway below I passed the cupboard and then stumbled to a halt.

If Olly was going to look for me, it would be in my room. Or one of the other bedrooms. I needed somewhere more defensible to hide. Quickly. Options flew through my mind one after the other. The kitchen was too open, the powder room too small and disgusting to stay in long term. The cupboard was . . . out of the question. That left the engine room.

I ran to my bedroom and snatched up a pillow. Into the case, alongside the pillow itself, I stuffed my few supplies. I had to go back for the knife that Maggie had dropped on the floor. Standing there I listened for any sign that Olly was coming downstairs to meet me. I couldn't hear anything, but then again, my own thundering pulse was pretty deafening. Anyway, he didn't need to come and get me right away, did he? There was no escape. He could take his time, wait until he wanted something from me. My stomach flipped over. I grabbed some spatulas from the kitchen to wedge the engine room door closed and found another pot to use as a toilet. With those dumped by the door I hurried back for my duvet, pillowcase and water pot. The duvet snagged on dropped junk in the hallway, making me struggle and swear, slopping water over myself.

Once I was inside the engine room I wedged the en suite door and the inner one closed with the spatulas. If Olly wanted to get at me, he'd have to make it through both doors. I'd also locked the en suite door, not that the lock was up to much and it did have a keyhole on the outside. Still, at least I'd hear him coming.

Once again I was unable to watch for land or passing ships. But those things both felt so distant now. It had been five days and we'd seen nothing except the sliver of coast that had prompted Harry's desperate escape attempt. I wasn't sure I'd trust anything we did see. It felt as if any sign of rescue was tainted now by Harry's disappearance. As if he'd been lured away and now anything might be used to draw the rest of us out.

I extinguished the candle as soon as I'd sorted everything

into place. The engine might have been empty of fuel but that didn't mean there weren't fumes or other flammable substances around. I wasn't taking any chances. In the dark I cautiously positioned myself opposite the door, with the duvet around my shoulders. It was just as cold in the engine room as it was in the rest of the ship – possibly colder, or it might have been my imagination. That, or shock was setting in. Either way, I couldn't stop myself from shaking.

Images of Leon's stiff face and Maggie's awful, bulging eyes refused to leave me alone, and in the dark there was nothing else to focus on, so the memories came at me vividly. I pulled the duvet tightly around myself and rested my forehead on my knees. All the fight had gone out of me. I had nothing and no one to help me, no plans or escape routes to seize on. I was trapped in the very bowels of this stinking boat, waiting for a killer to come and find me. When he decided it was time.

When would that be exactly? What was he even doing? I could imagine him idly searching the bar for something to drink. Maybe he'd find a bottle or two that I'd overlooked? With nothing much left to eat he'd feel the effects quite quickly. Maybe he'd pass out? Or else he might have found some cocaine in Leon's room. Perhaps he was giving my terror time to breathe, like a fine red wine. Perhaps he had forgotten entirely that I existed, and would only remember once he was hungry enough to wonder if I had food.

I sat there, waiting to see what would happen. Tensed for the possibility that he would arrive at my door at any moment. I passed the endless minutes in complete darkness, shivering with fear and cold. The waiting was its own unique kind of torture, one I couldn't believe Olly was inflicting accidentally.

Finally, the wait ended.

'Hannah!' Olly slurred. I could hear doors banging open as he yelled my name. He was searching the bedrooms, one after the other. I heard him kicking at the mess on the floor of the rooms, cursing as he stumbled into things, knocking them over. Something shattered and I heard something else explode against a wall as it was thrown, the shards tinkling to the floor.

'Hannah? I know you've got more food hidden somewhere – more of those chocolates, maybe? Hmm?'

I gripped the knife tightly and tried to work out where he was by sound alone. It seemed like he was in one of the bedrooms, possibly mine. How long would it take him to check his room and find the locked en suite door? I realised, far too late, that I ought to have left it open. If I'd done that there'd be a slight chance of him not finding the engine room door, and going elsewhere. Now he'd know where I was as soon as he tried the outer door.

'It's very rude to leave a party without saying goodbye to the host,' he called, his voice suddenly much, much closer. 'I've got water – do you want some? I'll let you have a bottle if you share your food, maybe make me a coffee?'

He sounded somehow both exactly as he always had and more deranged for it. I crawled out of the duvet and groped my way around one of the hulking engines. There was a space beside it just large enough for me to slide into, pressed against the outer wall. I did so, taking the knife with me.

Olly was definitely in the master bedroom now. I could hear him quite clearly despite the two doors between us. I heard the thud of the mattress turning over, then a bone-shivering bang as something was thrown against the wall. It sounded like the vanity stool, or something else large and heavy.

'Hannah?' Olly didn't sound so casual now. His voice was laced with suspicion and wariness. 'What are you up to, hmmm?'

Then I heard the rattle of the en suite door. Then silence. He'd found me. The door rattled again, more violently, and I heard the latch clicking repeatedly. He was pulling against the lock, trying to shake it loose or just not realising it was engaged. The aggressive shaking stopped and I heard rustling, like he was moving away. I held my breath, hoping that he hadn't been lying before, about not having any keys to the rooms.

A bang reverberated through the wall and I nearly bit my tongue, the sudden battery against the door making me jump. He was definitely hitting it with something. Maybe the stool or one of the bedside tables. I heard a cracking, splintering sound. Was that the door, or whatever he was hitting it with? Then I heard the unmistakable sound of the inside of the door being ripped apart. He was close. So close that I could hear his laboured breathing as he stood there. Was he listening for me? Could he hear me breathing too?

I pinched my nose closed with the hand covering my mouth and waited. I was begging whatever powers that would listen to keep him from spotting the little latch for the engine room door. Let him just think the door was stuck, not locked. Let him think I went over the side like Maggie.

Maybe that was where he was going to dump me, when this was all over. Just like he'd done to Libby.

Don't think that. Don't think at all, just listen. I strained to hear him. There were small shuffling sounds, like he was moving things around. There was a cabinet under the sink. Maybe he was checking that or just biding his time, waiting for me to give myself away.

One moment it sounded like Olly was just idling his time away in the bathroom, the next, the door to the engine room struck the improvised doorstop. He'd found the door and shoved it, hard. I heard the wooden spatula grate against the rough floor as he tried the door again.

'Should have known you'd feel more comfortable in steerage,' Olly said, in a cold, dead voice. He sounded like a slowed-down recording of himself. He didn't seem connected to anything anymore. He'd gone adrift from himself, from sanity. 'At home with the rest of the rats, are you? Gnawing away at what's mine.'

I let go of my mouth and sucked in air, shifting back as far as I could to try and hide behind the engine. The knife slipped in my sweating hand. He was probably armed, too. There'd been so many knives in that kitchen, he had to have stumbled across one whilst he was looking for me. Even without one, I was sure he'd find a way to hurt me. He'd already stoved Leon's skull in with a fire extinguisher, attacked him on the mere suspicion of taking something from him. As if Libby was just a bottle of water for him to hoard. He could use any number of things against me.

Olly jerked the door back and forth. Each swing pushed the doorstop, and I heard the short, grating sounds as it moved, giving way little by little. Finally, I heard it skitter across the floor. The door flew open and rebounded off the wall behind it. Olly was in.

He'd sounded so scarily calm that I'd expected him to prowl the room, hunting. Instead he charged in and threw himself at the duvet I'd abandoned. He tore it aside and I heard something metal scrape horribly over the rough floor. He'd tried to stab me.

I was trying so hard to stay still that my whole body was

on fire, every muscle burning with the need to run. To fight. To save itself. The image of Maggie's body flashed before me; her bulging, terrified eyes and her body locking up as it fought to expel the water from her lungs. I felt like that, like my body was shutting down, painfully, one cell at a time.

A sound vibrated through the walls but I was too focused on my heartbeat to make sense of it. My pulse was going so fast that my ear drums felt the pressure. I was listening to Olly as he stumbled over the duvet, disturbing the air only inches away. He started feeling around the engines, looking for me. I couldn't just hear him breathing, I could also feel the heat of his breath in the air as it passed my cheek. I heard his weapon glancing off of the engine itself, metal on metal. I tasted metal, too; my tongue was bitter with it. I couldn't breathe. Sweat poured off me and I wasn't still anymore but shaking, shaking so violently that I couldn't keep hold of my knife.

Then I heard it. Or rather, my brain finally made sense of what my ears were telling me. It was a metallic scraping so much louder and larger than a knife on pipes. It was the sound of cars crashing one after the other in a tunnel deep under the earth. A rockslide of sound that got inside my chest and made it ache, a thumping bass from the depths of the sea. The noise registered with a part of my brain that was still trying to function, the part that was screaming at me to do something. Anything.

Cold fingers brushed my ankle, then stilled momentarily before seizing hold. I screamed. Olly pulled hard and I slid down the wall, hitting my head on the floor.

'Just like a rat,' Olly hissed and I yelped as the tip of his knife nipped my thigh.

Then the noise was everywhere, deafening. Metal on metal on stone on water. Olly was gone, and the wall became the floor, became the thing that I'd hit my face on. The darkness spun around me and I could hardly hear Olly's furious screams over the roar of the ocean.

CHAPTER TWENTY-FIVE

With a mouthful of blood I clawed my way out from behind the engine. At any moment I expected my hands to encounter clothes, flesh, a knife. But Olly wasn't there. I staggered to my feet and the same sense that tells you you're home alone told me that he was gone. Fleeing the floodwaters like a rat.

Already several inches of water were foaming around my feet. Nothing about the room I was in felt familiar. Everything had shifted. The layout of things was the same but I was at the wrong angle, listing sideways with the yacht itself. The floor that had been under my feet was now angled up, leaving me clambering along the wall. I'd just made it out from between the hull and the engine when the boat lurched over again, sending me stumbling into the waterlogged duvet. We'd righted, but everything felt unsteady.

Dimly I realised that we must have hit something. I felt a flash of hope that perhaps we had reached land at last. That this would finally be over. I needed to get up and away from the water but I was still, despite the new danger – the new hope – fearful of Olly. He had been a hairsbreadth from killing me and that had flooded me with adrenaline. I felt for the wound but couldn't tell how bad it was through the wet fabric of my trousers. It hurt but I wasn't sure how deep the cut was.

I staggered into the en suite and on into the bedroom. I had my arms out and desperately waved them from side to side in the dark, attempting to either locate Olly or ward off an attack. He was already gone, far ahead of me. Despite the floodwaters I was relieved. Just then he was more frightening to me than even the freezing currents. I fought my way past the overturned mattress and reached the door.

In the hallway it was as dark as the cabins themselves. Night again, I suspected, or else the storm had gotten very bad indeed. I could hear waves crashing and the wind howling above. Deep in the engine room I'd been mostly insulated against the chaos but now it was inescapable.

I didn't need light to know that water was rushing into the cabins. I could feel it tugging against my legs, trying to pull me down. I was up to my knees by this time, wading up the corridor towards the stairs. Along with the seawater came the reek of backed-up plumbing. The water was sweeping through, overturning and swamping everything on this level, including the toilets. I gagged at the smell but kept going, half sobbing in panic as the water continued to rise and my fear of it replaced my fear of Olly.

I was halfway to the stairs when the yacht listed again. I was slammed against the wall as it rolled on the waves. I could hear metal and plastic being torn apart. We were stuck on something and it felt like I was at the centre of a tug-of-war between the sea and whatever we'd hit – one which the boat was rapidly losing. The water was coming in so fast I knew I had to get out of the cabins and above sea level. I tried to fight my way to the bottom of the stairs, finally finding them with my outstretched foot. They were tilted at a forty-five-degree angle along with the rest of the boat and, worryingly, water was running down them. Was that rain or were waves swamping the deck above?

'Help!'

I turned automatically at the scream, one hand maintaining a death grip on the banister. Olly called out again, coughing and spluttering somewhere further down the corridor, back towards the engine room. Had he tried to reach the stairs and become lost in the dark, blinded by panic? Fear knotted my guts, but after a moment I found my tongue, unable to simply abandon him. In spite of everything, no one deserved to die like this.

'Olly! It's this way! We need to get out!' I tensed, ready to run up the stairs if he came at me too quickly, if this was a trick.

The only answer was a strangled cry of pain.

My fingers were turning numb on the railing. I was at the stairs. I was nearly out of the fetid, flooded cabins . . .

A frustrated growl burst out of me as I threw myself back and started frantically wading down the corridor. Despite everything in me wanting to get the hell out of there, I couldn't just leave him. Not in that hellish flood.

'Where are you?' I shouted, shaking my head to get the wet strands of hair out of my eyes.

Olly didn't reply. I stumbled to a stop. What if he was luring me back so he could kill me? Was he so far gone that he didn't care whether he lived or died, so long as he took me with him? The icy water was up to my thighs now and if I hadn't been full of adrenaline I'd have been breathless with pain from the cold. My teeth were chattering and I knew I didn't have long before my muscles would seize, leaving me unable to escape. Still, I wavered. I didn't want to leave Olly behind down there to die. Even after everything.

A hand brushed mine in the water and I flinched away with a shriek. The water around me was rising and falling with the waves outside and the motion of the boat. Had Olly fallen under the water? I grasped the hand but even when I got a grip on it, there was no response. It was as cold as the water itself. I looked down and could just see the waxy skin of the pale fingers under mine. Leon's fingers. I screamed and let go, tried to back away and blundered right into Leon's body. The rising water had carried him out of the cupboard, floating past me with bedroom clutter and cloying strips of used toilet paper. I floundered away from him, my whole body locking up at the remembered feeling of his hand. I felt things bump into me and brush my hands as I waded away, shuddering.

'Olly!' I shouted, my voice by then shrill with panic and sounding strangely dampened in the half-flooded cabins. 'Where are you!?'

Someone gasped to my right, then flailed in the water. I turned towards the splashing and choking and waved my hands, searching for the source. Cold hands clawed at my waistband, my sweatshirt. As soon as he got hold of me he gripped hard, as if he meant to pull me down with him. I fought him off, prising his fingers loose. He was floating, as though the current had taken his feet right out from under him, so I had the advantage of height and footing. I grabbed handfuls of his clothes to pull him above the water line. He spat a mouthful of foul water and retched into the flood, still trying to climb me and escape the water.

'. . . Foot,' he managed. 'Foot's stuck.'

I swore, still trying to get my breath back. 'Stuck how?'

Olly was gasping down air, shivering so hard I could hardly understand him. 'Went through . . . the floor. Can't get out.'

I had to look, find a way to get him out of there before the water rose over his head. I ducked down into a sitting position, buoyed by the water. Olly grabbed hold of me again but not so desperately this time. I wasn't in danger of being pushed under. For now. Feeling around, I found his leg and followed it down. There was his foot. He'd either staggered into a hole in the floor or had been sucked in by the pressure. Either way, his foot was trapped in the jagged hole in the jagged gap.

There was a grinding sound right before the boat shifted again and I only just snatched my hand away in time. The whole corridor tilted in the water, which slopped all around us, threatening to wash over my head. Olly's bellow of agony nearly deafened me. He started thrashing in the water, crying out. I wasn't sure what was going on below the hole in the floor, but whatever it was, the motion of the ship wasn't helping. His face was pure agony and all I could do was try not to get within grabbing distance as his foot was crushed or bent under the ship.

Olly sobbed in pain and fear as the boat rolled back with the tide, releasing the pressure. He was shaking and shuddering. The worst part about it was that we both knew it was going to happen again. It was only a matter of time until the ship rolled once more.

'I need you to pull with me here,' I panted, trying to get my hand into the gap so I could tug his shoe off. 'If I can just get this off, you might get back through . . .'

I wasn't sure if Olly just didn't hear me or if he was too

agonised to speak. He was struggling, but in no particular direction, just trying desperately to escape the pain, and he gave little sign that he was aware of my voice.

I stuck my hand back in the hole to get at the laces on his leather loafers. They were tight and the water was only making them tighter, suctioning the shoes to his skin. My fingers were too cold to feel properly and I was panicking, terrified that the boat would move again, crushing my fingers into chum.

The water swirled around us, swelling in waves up to my shoulders as I bent, working at freeing Olly's foot. Something crashed in one of the cabins and I heard the hull around us groan under the strain of holding back the sea outside.

'Hurry!' Olly managed to moan, snatching my hair as if to stop me leaving.

'I'm trying,' I grunted, awkwardly bending my frozen fingers to try and prise the still laced shoe off of his foot. 'I think I need something to cut it with.'

'Cut what?' Olly's voice cracked, shrill with terror. Looking up I could see the whites all the way around his eyes.

'The shoe. Where's your knife?'

'Dropped it.'

'OK . . . OK . . . I need to go and find it, or something else I can use.'

'No!' His grip on my hair tightened and his other hand leapt to my still bruised throat. 'I won't let you go.'

'Get the fuck off of me!' I had to dig my fingernails into his hands to make him let go, and before he could try again I pushed myself out of range. 'I'll come back. I can't help without something to cut the shoe off with!' I avoided his snatching hands and swam away from him until I could get my feet under me to wade. The water level had risen and even when standing it was now up to my waist. I glanced upwards. The ceiling only just cleared my head by a couple of inches. The inside of the boat was luxurious but still a boat, so it was lower than a normal ceiling. How long until the space filled with water?

'I'll be back,' I said, hearing the uncertainty in my own voice as I struggled against the water, trying to make my way back to the engine room.

'Hannah!' Olly's outraged roar followed me as I thrashed my way through, but I didn't stop. He didn't know what he was saying, most likely. I had to find the knife; it was the only way to get him out of this.

I was halfway across the master bedroom when the ship rolled again. Olly's angry shouts for me to come back dissolved into screaming and begging. The sound of his screams went right through me and it was so awful that I couldn't help bursting into tears. I had to get him out of there. Get us both out.

I took another step forwards into the dark and was blindsided by something heavy hitting me hard in the side. I fell and whatever it was acted like a battering ram, shifted by the rolling of the ship. It drove me across the floor and pinned me to the wall. I went under the water, choking and clawing for air. The cold seawater felt like white-hot needles all over my skin. The real agony was in my shoulder, though; it felt as though two hands were pulling the joint apart. White spots danced across my vision and I thought for a moment that I was about to black out and drown.

Mercifully, the boat rocked once more and the weight pressing on me slid away. I struggled out of danger, coughing and spluttering. My nerves were shredded with terror. I felt stretched out of shape, my body and soul torn beyond the limits of human endurance. My lungs felt like they'd been scrubbed with wire wool. My shoulder was half-butchered meat, and I was frozen to the bone. My teeth were chattering from cold and shock as I groped my way towards the bathroom. The water was up to my chest now, even when standing. I began to hiccough as panicked tears fell, desperate to be out of the water, to finally feel safe again. If I left it much longer, I was going to be trapped down there.

Finally back in the engine room, I tried to find my knife. I ducked under the water repeatedly, reaching down to run my fingers over the floor. I found bits and pieces from the bedroom, my other supplies bobbing in the water. But no knife. I surfaced, desperation thundering in my blood. The only warmth came from the snot dribbling down my face as I cried in pain and frustration.

'Hannah!' Olly yelped, his voice distorted by the flooded space between us, guttural and groggy with pain. 'Hannah—' He was cut off by a weird hiccoughing noise and I realised he must have gone under.

Without a knife I knew the odds of getting his foot free were against me. But if I had to, I'd break every bone in his leg to do it. I was not going to watch someone else drown. It was the worst death I could imagine and even Olly didn't deserve it. No one did.

I struggled against the water flooding in from the bedroom door. It was almost over my shoulders now and I could swim in it instead of wading. I made it back to the door and clung on to catch my breath. I couldn't see far in the dark, but I could hear Olly splashing around as his hands broke the water's surface, clutching the air he couldn't reach with his mouth.

After sucking in as much air as I could, I ducked under

and swam towards where I'd left him. I caught his flailing hand and he gripped hold of me tightly. A blast of bubbles hit my face as he tried to either say something or let out a breath he couldn't hold anymore. I had to pull away from him to feel my way down to his leg. When I found it, I grabbed hold and pulled as hard as I could. My shoulder exploded in pain, but I gritted my teeth and ignored it as best I could.

Olly immediately began to thrash against me, kicking with his other leg. I knew I was hurting him and that he couldn't help it, but when he caught my shoulder, I screamed. My breath spiralled upwards in bubbles. I could feel my nails slicing into his skin as I tried to drag his foot free. It moved a little, but not much. Out of breath and out of time, I rose to the surface and sucked in air, then ducked down to try again.

I heaved on Olly's leg once more and felt his body go limp. Had he passed out from the pain or was he out of air? I gave one final heave on his leg and then surfaced. My gasping mouth was only inches from the ceiling, my feet off the floor as I chased after oxygen. The pressure of the water outside must have been widening the holes in the hull. It was coming in faster and faster. It was no good. I had to leave him. I had to get out.

I found myself blubbering apologies that no one else could hear as I fought the swirling water to reach the stairs. By the time I swam to the end of the corridor, only my eyes were above the water line, stinging with salt. I made it to the stairs and hauled myself out of the water, feeling boneless. I climbed up the few unsubmerged steps and reached the lobby just as the boat tilted again. The movement made me stagger and I barely managed to get out of the way as one of the sofas barrelled across the lobby floor towards me. It smashed into the already fractured glass wall and broke free onto the deck.

As the wind howled in, I finally saw what we'd hit. Between the stormy sea and the black clouds that were doing their best to keep the dawn light from me, there was a jagged spine of wet rock. Not land, or even an island. Just a lonely strip of stone, with waves crashing over it.

I looked at the slick rocks and realised that we weren't any closer to being saved. That was followed by the sickening thought that there was no longer a 'we'. There was just me. Alone.

CHAPTER TWENTY-SIX

The groaning of the boat below me shocked me back to reality. I had to move. Even above the water line I wasn't out of danger. Though most of the yacht wasn't yet underwater, it was still being torn apart by the current. I could feel it shifting unsteadily, pitching to and fro as the sea rushed at it. It wasn't safe for me to stay aboard; I'd already been hit by falling furniture once.

A resounding crash made me jump and I turned in time to see the shell of the helicopter topple to one side. The end of the deck beyond it was already submerged, angled down into the churning sea. The boat was going under, and I didn't want to go with it.

I didn't think, just ran to the hole the sofa had punched in the glass wall and clambered out onto the deck. The wind took my breath away, cutting through my soaked clothes immediately. I couldn't feel my hands or feet. I was so cold from being repeatedly submerged, even the burning pain in my shoulder was deadened by it. I tugged the top of my sweatshirt aside to get a look at it. My skin was red raw from the icy water, and it was hard to tell if there were bruises forming. There was, however, something off about the dips and bulges of my shoulder. It made me feel sick to see the familiar shape of my body twisted like that. I let the sweatshirt go and looked away. I was badly hurt but I needed to get to safety before I could do anything about it.

The adrenaline from Olly's attack was wearing off and I could feel myself succumbing to the shock of my injured shoulder and of witnessing his death. If he even was dead. Perhaps he was still down there, drowning. The thought almost made me turn back, but I stopped myself. Going back inside was suicide and I had already tried and failed to free him.

I forced myself to keep going, across the deck, to the side nearest the rock formation that had sunk its teeth into the yacht. Although the rocks rose up about level with the deck, I couldn't see them that well, just their outline against the pre-dawn grey light. I pulled myself up over the side of the boat and swung around, feeling for land with my feet. At some point I'd lost both my slippers to the water and my bare toes were numb. Still, I felt them hit the rock and tried to lower myself to solid ground. It was hard, holding on with one arm, and I lost my grip halfway down, landing hard on the rocks. I rolled awkwardly to my feet, trying to avoid using my injured arm.

It felt strange to be back on land after several days of the slight motion of the yacht underfoot. The wet rocks under my feet felt weirdly dense and motionless. Dead. I shuffled away from the yacht and felt my way over the seaweed and barnacle studded stone, climbing out of reach of the sea.

I hadn't gone far when I slipped and fell. A scream of

pain tore itself out of my mouth. I'd hit my injured shoulder and felt it come apart. I tried to get up and realised I couldn't really move my arm now. I had to drag myself up with one hand and then try to get out of harm's way whilst cradling my injured arm.

Finally, wedged between two chunks of stone, I checked on my shoulder. The configuration of bones was even more off now. I started to cry, the shock of it hitting me. When I raised a tentative hand to probe the injury, something inside my body grated like a rusty hinge. I dropped my hand and glanced away, trying to regain composure.

I looked at the yacht. The sun was finally rising and despite the mass of storm clouds I could see a little better now, especially as the light was coming from behind me. The front end had broken up on the rocks. I had no idea what the situation was under the water line, but chunks of white debris were being swept up in the waves. The boat was being torn to pieces. The yacht was tilting with the waves as they broke against it, rolling it over towards the rocks. Everything from the lower deck upwards was still clear of the water, though it looked as though the yacht would capsize before too long.

Soaked to the skin and shivering uncontrollably, I curled in on myself. My shoulder burned with pain. I was fairly certain my fall had dislocated it, or worsened a minor dislocation into full ripping it apart.

The muscles in my shoulder twitched violently and I winced. I couldn't leave it like this, but I didn't know what to do. I'd seen people in films resetting broken noses and shoulders, but was that even possible to do to yourself? What if I made it worse?

My shoulder spasmed again and I bit my lip hard against

a fresh wave of pain. I couldn't cope like this. It was tearing me apart.

Hesitantly, I took hold of my shoulder with my good hand. It hurt, just doing that, but I then pressed slightly and tried to shift my arm back into my shoulder – like popping the arm back on a disarticulated Barbie. My yell of pain carried across the water, a shrill sound of human agony that caused every hair on my body to rise. But my arm was still limp. I'd accomplished nothing except increasing the numbness. It obviously wasn't working.

I got my breath back and again asked myself if this was making everything worse. If I was just hurting myself for no reason when I ought to have been attempting to get warm. But just the idea of trying to manoeuvre around in my current state made me feel ill. I could hardly stand to sit still with my arm like this. There was no way I could get up and move.

I gently tried to feel my way around the separation in my shoulder. Maybe if I tried getting my arm behind me and pulling it? The way I'd stretch it out if it was aching?

Knowing how much this was probably going to hurt, I took my arm in my good hand and slowly lifted it up. The pain was immediate and completely blinding. I was sobbing before I got my arm halfway up to my head. It was excruciating, and I kept wanting to stop and give up. But just the idea of having to go through that pain in reverse made me keep going. If I stopped now, I'd only have to try it again later.

When I got my arm over my head, I felt my shoulder grinding together and that, plus the pain, made me vomit. I wasn't in a position to bend over, so it dripped down my front. The convulsions only made the pain worse. I bent my good arm behind me, as if scratching my back and pulled down on my tingling, numb hand.

I heard the sound it made. Like an apple being ripped in half. A wet crunch that registered before I temporarily blacked out and then jolted back to myself, bent over on the rocks. I was still in pain, but my arm wasn't numb anymore. It hurt, a lot, but I could just about move it. My shoulder itself felt like it had been scooped out with a red-hot spoon. I untied the scarf I'd taken from Maggie and awkwardly fashioned a kind of sling for my arm. Then, exhausted, I propped myself against the rocks.

I didn't sleep, but I sort of . . . drifted. I was aware of what was going on, but mostly as though it was a slideshow. The cold faded from my body and I experienced flashes of the yacht slowly capsizing, interspersed with sudden blackness. Eventually the dark flashes grew longer, and I realised I was losing my grip on consciousness. A tiny burst of panic failed to stave it off and I felt my eyes droop closed as awareness slipped out of my grasp.

I wasn't out for very long. Or at least, I didn't think it had been that long. When I prised my salt-crusted eyes open the sun was barely risen. The storm had blown itself out, mostly, and the remaining grey clouds let in more light. However, the sight before me had changed dramatically.

The yacht was in pieces. The battering sea had driven it into the rocks and I guessed the weight of all the water inside it hadn't done it any favours. Only a large white chunk of hull remained, and I could see all sorts of furniture and debris in the water, slowly sinking. The helicopter had vanished, presumably swept away, and I could see what looked like part of the bridge sticking out of the sea about twenty yards from where we'd crashed. Only half the lower deck remained stuck on the rocks. The lobby was completely missing – torn off and sucked down with the cabins.

I tried to move and found my body felt heavy and numb. I wasn't shivering – I didn't even feel cold – but my fingers looked blue. A tiny splinter of fear wormed its way into my sluggish mind. I needed to do something, to move. If I stayed where I was, the next time I closed my eyes would be the last time.

But, would that be such a bad thing?

Looking at the furious sea and the remains of the yacht, the hopelessness of my situation sank into me with the cold. We'd not seen a single sign of rescue the whole time we'd been adrift. Survival had looked bleak enough on the yacht; what were my odds now? I was stuck on a rocky spit far, far out to sea. No fire, no bottles of water, no walls between me and the elements. I wasn't moving anywhere, so the hope of simply drifting into view of land was gone. I didn't have any food or shoes and my only clothes were soaked through.

I was going to die. Why not let it be now, when I would barely feel it? Why go on struggling just to meet a worse end later? Because despite all my struggles and attempts to fix things since we went adrift, things had only gotten worse.

I closed my eyes and the image of Harry's laughing face on that long-ago hungover morning brought me to tears. I could almost feel the warmth coming from him as he perched on the edge of his bed, bringing me tea and toast.

'How is it that you were the one drinking and you look like that, whilst I look like death?' he'd said, then ruffled my hair, trying to mess it up. 'You're too cute, that's your trouble.'

I should have told him, years ago, how I felt about him. How stupid had I been to believe that by shutting myself

255

off from anything serious, I could spare myself from heartbreak? That my mum's grief and pain could be avoided if I kept everyone at arm's length? I'd only cheated myself. All that time I could have spent with Harry had been wasted. Now I'd never get the chance to tell him, because he was gone.

I opened my eyes and looked out across the steely sea. Only, perhaps there was a chance, still, that he wasn't. That he had made it ashore. And if there was a chance, then I had to try and make it back to him. I had nothing to lose anymore. I just had to try and survive.

Slowly, by inches, I eased my stiff and unresponsive body onto its feet. I cautiously removed my makeshift sling and felt as if I'd be fine without it. I needed both hands for climbing over the rocks and the scarf would be more useful for carrying things in anyway. I needed to get warm. To get something to shelter under, out of the wind. It had abated a little with the easing of the storm, but it was still stealing the heat from my skin.

A fire. I needed a fire.

As soon as that thought penetrated the fog in my brain, I started patting myself with my one good hand. I'd fought for my life, been submerged in water and fallen on the rocks – what if I'd lost the lighter? Had I even put it in my pocket when I was rushing down to hide from Olly? I turned out my sweatshirt pockets and felt around in the joggers. Nothing. Then my fingers brushed hard plastic. Harry's lighter was jammed into the seam of the pocket. I nearly cried with relief. It was like a sign. He was out there, and he was saving me. I pulled it out and tried to strike a light, but nothing happened. My brain was still struggling to wake up, but after a few seconds of confusion I realised that the lighter wouldn't work now that it was wet. I'd have to let it dry out and pray that when it did, it could hold a spark long enough to make a flame. Which wouldn't help me unless I found something dry to burn.

I tucked the lighter into my bra to keep it safe. I was hoping that the heat from my skin would help it to dry, though there was precious little heat coming off me at that moment.

With my arm in better shape, though still aching, it was easier getting back to the yacht than it had been getting off of it. Once I reached its level, however, I saw that there wasn't anything of use on what remained of the deck. The only thing I'd be able to get was wood from the smashed-up edges. There was some stuff floating in the water, but it looked like most of the yacht's contents had sunk. Meaning if I wanted it, I'd have to go diving. The idea made me shiver, not just with cold but also at the prospect of finding Leon or Olly's remains down there. I didn't want to go back down into the cabins. I didn't want to find myself underwater again. I also realised I might not have a choice.

For now, though, firewood was my main concern. I cautiously climbed onto the slick hull where it jutted out of the rocks at an angle. I made it to the deck, which slanted down into the water on the other side. There, I inched my way around to the lowest point, where I could reach my good arm out and grab for flotsam in the sea. Chunks of wood floated past me and I gathered them, keeping them separate from the drier pieces I pulled from the boat wreckage itself. At least the scouring wind was good for something.

On my way back to the rocks I realised I still didn't feel cold. Which was worrying. I wasn't too familiar with the symptoms of hypothermia, but it seemed like not feeling cold after having been submerged in the sea in January was a weird thing and not a good sign.

I made it back up to the dry point of the rocks and looked around for a place to start a fire. Between one spine of rock and another there was a tiny scrap of flat ground. It was about the size of a bathtub, but it at least looked dry, and there were curls of crisp seaweed stuck in amongst the pebbles and shards of driftwood. I was hoping it was high enough out of the sea that it wouldn't get wet.

After clambering over to the crevice, I dumped my wet wood aside and set up the pieces that looked like they'd light. My fingers weren't shaking anymore, but they were bloodlessly white and I was having trouble moving them. I scraped together some seaweed and driftwood, then tried the lighter. It was hard to get a grip on it and even when I managed that, it wouldn't produce a spark.

'Come on,' I growled. 'Please . . .'

It didn't want to work. I needed to dry it out somehow. After considering it for a moment, I tried to prise off the metal cap on top. It was probably wet underneath. I tried a few times with my hands, but it wasn't happening so, in the end, I had to use my teeth. The strike wheel grazed my gum and my mouth filled with the taste of blood and metal. Once the cap was off, I blotted the mechanism on the edge of my jumper, which the wind had blasted semi-dry. Then I held the lighter up and blew into it, the same way I'd cleared dust from Sega cartridges as a kid.

I struck the lighter and a lone spark pinged off the wheel.

'Yes!' I struck again, and again. Sparks came, but that was it. I held my breath, striking the thing over and over again, feeling tiny darts of dying heat as the sparks landed on my hand. A flame appeared between my fingers and I laughed, caught by surprise and drunk on relief.

I carefully coaxed that flame over to the pile of wood. It went out just before it touched the kindling. I growled in frustration, tears spilling down my face. I struck again. Just sparks.

Again.

Nothing.

Again.

The flame popped up and I managed to get a piece of seaweed smoking before it blew out in the wind. I tried again, curled over the firewood and almost nose to nose with the sand. This time, I got the seaweed to catch. I had a fire.

I knew that I should try and find something to shelter under – pieces of wreckage or something that could act as a roof in case it rained again. But I was so tired. Making that fire had taken the last of my energy and even though I knew I should try and stay awake, I just couldn't. I lay down and curled around the fire like a cat, then passed out on the sand.

CHAPTER TWENTY-SEVEN

When I woke up I saw it was getting dark. It took a while for me to rouse myself fully and to realise where I was. I felt groggy and exhausted, almost hungover. Gradually I eased myself into a sitting position.

My shoulder ached but thankfully it wasn't in blinding pain anymore, and I was uncomfortable in my clothes, which had dried on one side but not the other because I'd been lying down. My hair was stiff with salt and my skin felt scoured raw, pitted with tiny stones from where I'd been lying. My muscles ached from wading and swimming, and I was starving, but I was alive. That in itself felt like a miracle. I wondered if I'd still feel that way a day or even an hour from then. I'd have to see.

I still wasn't sure what I was hoping for. Rescue was out of the question, and in all likelihood I was going to die on that rock. But if I focused on the now, on what I needed in order to keep going from moment to moment, I could convince myself that there was still hope. I could believe that I'd see Harry again and get the chance to fix the mistakes I'd made before getting on that yacht.

I was lying to myself, and I knew it, but those lies were all there was between me and the prospect of my death.

The fire was down to its embers but picked up when I added some more wood. I'd have to keep it going, no matter what. I'd carefully wedged the lighter into a crevice to keep it safe. Harry had probably only paid a few quid for it, bought it without thinking as a little novelty, but now it was priceless to me, in more ways than one.

I was cold again. It felt weird to be grateful for that, but I was. Each shiver meant that I was reacting to the temperature normally. I never wanted to feel that awful false-warmth again. I knew I needed to collect more wood to keep my fire going. My stomach snarled and I realised that I'd also need something to eat; fuel to heat my body from within. Where I'd find something to eat was another issue entirely.

The sea had calmed down whilst I was asleep. That was a bonus.

I picked my way over the rocks, bare feet smarting from the cold and the sharp stones. As I went, I picked up pieces of driftwood or seaweed and threw them back towards my spot. I'd store them properly later.

When I reached the shoreline nearest what was left of the boat, I found it littered with junk washed up from the wreck; wet clumps that were once clothes, toiletries, most of a champagne bottle and one of the oil paintings of the yacht itself, though the wooden supports behind the canvas were smashed. I grabbed what I could use and took it back up the rocks.

After a few trips I had some bits of clothing drying over the rocks and a reasonable pile of firewood. I'd managed to drag a chunk of plastic or fibreglass off the beach, and it was wedged over my camp. Not exactly a shelter, but it was better than nothing. I'd also emptied out a few bottles of shampoo to hold water in case it rained. I hoped it did soon. I was desperately thirsty. Still no food though.

I stood on the narrow strip of pebbles at the base of the rock spine and looked into the freezing sea. I was thinking of the bottles of cocktail syrup I'd had stashed in the engine room. They'd still been mostly full so were too heavy to float to the surface, I was guessing. As far as I knew, those two bottles were the only source of calories on the whole ship. Maggie had taken the jars of cocktail fixings, but I didn't know what she'd done with them or if they'd survived the wreck. It would be like searching for a . . . well, for a jar of olives in an ocean. But I knew where the syrups were, sort of, and they were in thick, quite durable bottles. If I could locate the engine room, I'd be in with a chance of finding them.

Standing there I tried to weigh up the odds. I'd meant what I said to Maggie; going into water that cold was suicidal. I'd only just survived the wreck because the water had leaked in slowly and I'd had time to get somewhat acclimatised. And even then, I'd nearly gone hypothermic afterwards. If I dived into the sea now the shock would probably kill me – as it had killed Maggie. But what choice did I have? If I didn't risk freezing or drowning, I'd starve to death, slowly. We'd been gone for days on quite a large yacht and still no one had found us. What chance did I have now on this tiny rocky spit, too small to even be considered an island?

I stood and looked out to sea, trying to reach a decision.

Eventually I had to admit to myself that I'd rather die trying to live than live waiting to die.

Risk wasn't the only thing I had to face though. I knew that there was a strong possibility I'd find Olly's body down there. Maybe Leon's, too, though he hadn't been trapped on anything and might have floated free in the storm. The idea of swimming into the deep, dark sea and being confronted by Olly's corpse filled me with horror. But I knew I had to do it. If I didn't, I'd be joining him soon enough.

I prepared carefully. The fire needed to be fed so that it would still be going when I emerged, frozen to the bone. I stripped off my clothes and weighted them down near the boat so I had something dry to put on. Lastly I sorted through the wet things I'd found until I came across a t-shirt. It was one of Harry's and just seeing it made me want to cry, but I held it together. With the arms and neck tied shut, it would make a good enough bag to hold what I found. If I found anything.

Finally there was nothing left to stall me. I had to face the sea. The cold numbed my feet as I paddled in but quickly started to burn. I stopped when I was in up to my knees and held my breath against the pain. I counted to ten, then moved forward. By the time I was up to my neck I was shivering. The shore looked so tempting, but I knew I needed to do this. I let the water take my weight and began to swim out to sea.

When I was reasonably far out, I took a deep breath and ducked under the water. The salt stung my eyes but I was terrified of losing my sense of direction so I forced myself to keep them open. The water was fairly clear, and I quickly spotted the shape of the wreckage below. I surfaced and swam out a little further until I was right over it, then ducked under the water again.

Large parts of the yacht had been sheared off but I could just about see the entrance to the cabin level. I'd need to go down there to see how much of the cabins remained attached. Thankfully, it looked like submerged rocks were keeping the wreckage from sinking right to the bottom. I'd have had no hope of reaching it there.

After gulping down more air, I swam down. My first attempt failed because I panicked and turned back. I had to surface and calm myself down. I didn't have much time so I needed to be as quick and efficient as possible.

This time, when I went under, I sank as quickly as I could and found myself at the top of the stairs to the cabins. I used the banister to pull myself down as the water tried to buoy me up. In the corridor below it was actually lighter than it had been before, thanks to several holes in the ceiling where the sea had torn up parts of the deck. Unfortunately, the watery light enabled me to see Olly at the end of the hall. His foot was still trapped and his body was floating, making it seem as if he was slowly turning in a pirouette.

My first instinct was to freeze but my lungs were already burning. I didn't have time to give in to my fears. I had to plunge forward and get on with what I needed to do.

Thankfully, I didn't need to get past Olly to reach the door to the master bedroom. I did, however, have to get closer to him. On my way along the corridor I made myself look straight ahead. I didn't want to risk spotting Leon as well.

I caught the edge of the bedroom door and used it to propel me forward, kicking off of anything solid I could reach. I made it to the en suite and through the door to the engine room. My things were suspended in there, the duvet swaying slightly like a jellyfish in the water. I batted it aside and tried to make out the shapes of objects in the shadows. I found my book and bagged it for kindling. There was the pot I'd had my water in; potentially useful. I swept my hands out and felt around, finally snagging the neck of a bottle. I didn't look at it but could tell it was full from the weight. I stuffed it into the t-shirt bag and momentarily considered trying to find the other. I was desperate for air by then. Tiny bubbles kept slipping out as my body fought to expel the useless breath I'd taken. I had to go. Immediately.

In a panic I thrashed my way back into the bedroom and on into the corridor. My vision was going spotty and I knew I'd waited too long. Against my instincts my mouth opened, and I had to fight to close it. A large silvery bubble passed me by and I reached out, desperate for the feeling of air but knowing it was still far, far away.

Naked and freezing, I swam up from the wreck. The water was helping me, pushing me up, but it wasn't enough. My body started to cramp and convulse as I rose. I only just kept hold of the bag.

When I broke the surface the air was like hot knives in my lungs. Every breath hurt all the way down to my diaphragm but I sucked the air in greedily anyway. My teeth were chattering and my eyes burned from the salt water but I was alive. I floundered my way to shore and pulled myself onto the rocks. For a while I couldn't move. I was too exhausted from the swimming.

As soon as I could stand, I put on my dry clothes. Even that small amount of comfort was utter bliss. My fingers were blue tinged and I just wanted to collapse by the fire.

I just about made it, thrusting more wood onto the fire to get it going fully again. Leaning heavily against the surrounding rocks I went through my bag and pulled out the bottle I'd found. Part of me was afraid that it was going to be something useless – a £170 bottle of conditioner or something – but it was the grenadine syrup. At least I had one of them. There was no way I was going back to look for the other one. Not after that close a call. I'd just have to make do and try not to think about what I'd do when it eventually ran out.

CHAPTER TWENTY-EIGHT

I spent the rest of my first full day on the rocks recovering from my dive into the wreckage. I kept by the fire, drank some grenadine and tried not to think about anything other than the present.

Sleep wasn't so easy to come by after darkness descended. Fear and hunger kept me awake, and nightmares about Olly woke me up whenever I managed to drift off. I kept imagining him rising out of the sea, pale and glassy eyed, coming to get me for leaving him to die. By the time morning broke I was curled up tightly by the fire, slowly going to pieces.

At least in daylight I could find ways to occupy myself. In the dark I couldn't leave my camp or I risked falling on the rocks. When I wasn't jerking awake from nightmares or reliving them as I tried to sleep, I thought of the yacht and the missing mooring rope.

Which one of them had done it? That was the question that kept me most distracted, so it was the one I returned to over and over again. Nothing cut through my hopelessness like anger; it was useful, warming. By turns I blamed Olly, for trying to avenge himself on his cheating wife. Leon, for setting the yacht loose to humiliate his rival for Libby. Even Libby herself didn't escape blame. I imagined her untying the rope, grimly satisfied that Olly would be forced to admit that he couldn't sail. That he'd be humiliated just as his mismanagement of their finances had embarrassed her.

I lived from moment to moment, trying to cope with one need after the other. On my second day out there I examined the seaweed and clinging shellfish. My belly was an aching pit and sugar water – though it gave me energy – wasn't going to keep me full. I had no idea what I was looking for and I wasn't too sure about the shellfish. There were limpet, barnacle type things, but I didn't know if they were safe to eat or how to prise them off the rocks. Shellfish was out then, so I focused on the seaweed. I'd never heard of 'poisonous seaweed', and I knew some seaweed had to be edible because it was on sushi and deep-fried at Chinese buffets. Though the day we'd skipped our lectures to go see an action film and stuff our faces at the buffet afterwards, Harry had told me that was just lettuce. The thought of that wet October afternoon made me so homesick, so desperate to hear his voice, that for a second I stopped craving food. My hunger pangs returned moments later though, almost doubling me over.

I had to eat something so I rinsed both the pot from the boat and the seaweed in the sea. Cooking the stuff seemed the way to go. At least if I ate it hot it might warm me up before it made me sick. I balanced the pot over my fire and put some choice bits of seaweed in to heat up. The end result was a sort of green mulch with brown jelly ribbons in it, but it didn't make me throw up or give me any worrying symptoms – though I did get sand in my teeth – and even though I had to make myself eat it, because it tasted disgusting and the texture was vile, it at least filled me up. Some types were definitely less horrible than others so I tried to remember which sort of shapes and colours to look out for to try and make meals bearable. I had to keep myself going, no matter the discomfort. It was all I had to do and yet I had to keep reminding myself: *Survive, Hannah. Just keep surviving.* It was the only thing I could do.

Despite trying to conserve energy, I did have to get some things taken care of. I used the side of the boat's wreckage as my loo, feeling gross as I took care of business over the sea. I also had to make adjustments to my shelter; adding bits of debris to strengthen the roof and drying out more bits of clothing and bedding as they washed up on the rocks. I needed as much insulation as possible because the temperatures barely seemed to climb above zero, even in daylight, and my shelter did almost nothing to keep heat in. Even right by the fire I was struggling to keep warm.

That night I shivered my way to sleep with a bellyful of rubbery seaweed. My eye had been itching since the dive, probably irritated by the salt water, but aside from that I wasn't in terrible shape. I wasn't exactly thriving but I just needed to hold on a little longer. That was the phrase that kept circling my brain, like a fish in a bowl: a little longer. *This'll just last a little longer. I'll be OK for a little longer.* As though I was debating whether or not to give up waiting at a rainy bus stop and just walk. Five more minutes, then I'd think about whether or not I was ready to give up on life.

I wanted to think I was keeping myself together, but the endless repetition felt increasingly panicky every time it passed through my thoughts. I was a train about to derail. All it would take was a little thing to throw me off.

I was half asleep when the rain started. Almost immediately, my makeshift roof began to leak. A steady drip in several locations, which quickly soaked into my clothes and bedding. The rain was freezing, sharp and heavy. The worst kind. I heard it sizzling into the fire and rushed to protect my one source of heat and light.

As it continued to beat down, stinging my face as it blew in under my roof, I held a towel I'd found on the beach over my head and hunched over the fire. My arms began to ache soon after but I couldn't let the fire go out so I sat there and sheltered it as the rain pummelled my refuge.

I stayed like that for what felt like hours – cramped and uncomfortable, with no way to mark the time. The towel helped to keep the leaks from getting to the fire, but the compromise was freezing rain running down my back and coursing over the sand to seep into my trousers. There was nothing to listen to except the rushing of water and the crackling of my fire, and nothing to look at except the flames and the rock opposite me. My mind couldn't find a distraction in that, couldn't conjure memories of Harry to keep me company. There was nothing to occupy my thoughts except my own misery. No escape even into sleep. In those hours I started to wish it would all just end. That the life I had fought so hard to keep hold of over the past few days would just slip away from me. Anything to put a stop to the seemingly endless hours of anxiety and pain.

The rain stopped shortly before dawn. I lay down on the wet sand and tried to get some sleep, but the temperature had plummeted and in my soaked clothes I couldn't get warm again, despite the fire doing its best to keep the chill away. Eventually, once the sun had risen enough to see by, I gave up on sleep and went to look for anything that might help improve my shelter.

I was at the edge of the rocky outcrop, looking for debris and gathering seaweed, when I took a step and felt something soft under my foot. I stepped back and nearly fell over backwards in my attempt to scramble away.

Leon's body had made it to the surface. The rain and wind the previous night must have driven him to the shore and swept seaweed and sand over him. Enough that I hadn't noticed he was there until my foot landed on his thigh. All I could see of him was that one thigh and the knee below. Everything else was covered up. I wasn't sure whether that was a blessing or not. There was something about that disembodied leg that was worse than seeing him dead in the cupboard had been. Seeing that was a reminder that we were all just meat and bone. That eventually our names and faces wouldn't exist anymore and we'd be gone.

My own knees buckled and I sat down heavily on a rock. The exposed leg looked like some kind of obscene sea creature, dredged up where it ought never to have been. The flesh was mottled grey and green, reminding me of a frog's belly. How had he been brought to the surface? It was a long way and he was a big guy – literal dead weight, I realised, and nearly threw up my morning sip of grenadine. He'd been dead for several days now, and his body was bloated with rot – he was being digested into gas and that gas had brought him to the surface.

Overhead a sharp cry cut through the endless TV static of the sea. I craned my neck back and squinted at the pair of gulls that had appeared, wheeling in a circle like vultures. The thought of them coming to rest on the island, and doing what gulls did best, filled me with horror. I looked down at Leon's mottled leg and quickly scraped sand over it with my foot, being careful not to touch him again.

I couldn't really escape Leon. We were trapped together again, the rocky outcrop so small that I couldn't get more than ten metres away from his body. Slightly further if I clambered over onto the boat wreckage. Having him there was a constant pressure in my head. A spider I had to keep a wary eye on or a stranger in the corner of my eye, watching me. I was already too cold and too hungry to sleep, giving me long dark hours in which to think about how all this might end for me. Now I had a constant reminder. He might have been buried, but I could feel him there, under the sand.

That night it rained again. I'd added some more debris and some of the less tolerable seaweed to my roof and covered it with a bedsheet to hold it all together. This at least helped to keep the leaks under control, though the added weight made it sag in the middle until it touched my head. Rain still blew in from the sides with the occasional slicing wind, but it was better than before.

I sat up most of the night, feeding my fire and thinking of Harry; bringing me toast in the morning, chatting with me on a bus as the rain hissed off the road and our laughter fogged up the windows. Harry calling to me from a boat as it moored off the rocky spit. Harry wrapping me in a warm blanket and telling me that everything was going to be OK.

I didn't have much of a routine. I slept when I could and when I couldn't I either watched the fire or tried to read my one and only book by its flickering light. I had decided to save it in case the fire went out and I needed kindling. Had I known it would be the only distraction I'd have on a tiny rocky island, I might have spent longer choosing it. I could remember buying it, actually – I'd gone into town to buy the expensive chocolate for Libby's present and popped into Smith's for a Boost bar. It was my lunchbreak and I had nothing to rush back for, so I did one of those time-wasting sessions you can only really do in a WHSmith, or an airport. I was looking at stuff I didn't even need and wasn't interested in – printer paper, puzzles, a whole pile of laptop bags. I didn't want to go back to the office and I was enjoying the slightly tinny sounds of S Club 7 on the speakers. The book was on a table near the self-checkouts. The cover looked interesting and it was half-price. I had four quid on me, so I bought it, mostly for the serotonin boost.

I wanted to be that Hannah again. The Hannah who could walk into a well-heated shop on a whim and buy calorific snacks and any other little thing she fancied. I wanted to stroll home, buy a latte on the way and think about what I was going to watch on TV when I got in. I wanted to sit on my sofa and make art just because I felt like it. I wanted to think about rent increases and shopping lists and what to wear to work tomorrow instead of whether or not I was going to die soon.

The idea that I had ever seen my life as not measuring up, or not being good enough, was absolutely insane to me in my current state. Who cared about what kind of shoes I wore or could afford to buy? I had been without shoes since the shipwreck. I had been without a bed, without hot water and dry clothes and proper food. I would never, in my whole life, take those things for granted or be ashamed of how and where they came from. I would never compare myself to those who had more than me. I would never shut myself off again, believing I could avoid pain. I would be happy and contented and make art even if it didn't bring in any money, even if someone was going to steal it. Because depriving myself of the pleasure of making wasn't worth it. I would live my life, if only I could get back to it.

I offered these promises up as if hoping that something in the universe would pay attention. That if I could say I'd learned a valuable lesson, I might suddenly be rescued. Nothing happened though. I'd told Libby where to go, stood up for myself against everyone else and made peace with a humble, normal life. I'd admitted the depth of my feelings for Harry, at least to myself. I'd stopped thinking about my creative side as a failed business instead of something I loved – and I was never going to get the chance to do anything about it.

I had wasted my life, and now it was almost over.

I ate when the hunger pains were intolerable. I slept in a ball on the sand and shivered by my fire – no matter the time of day. I only got up to fetch firewood. A few days after my diving expedition I woke up to find that my itchy eye had swollen – some kind of infection from the water, I was guessing; a painful bump had formed on my eyelid and swelled to the size of a pea. I had nothing I could look at it with, but it felt awful. Gradually it began to prevent me opening that eye at all. I probably needed antibiotics. I needed a lot of things.

I'd been afraid for so long that I'd started to become numb to it all. The only thing that brought me comfort was closing my one good eye and imagining a boat reaching me. Harry up on deck, bedraggled from his swim but determined to rescue me no matter the odds.

I dreamed of Harry and had nightmares of Leon and

Olly. I dreaded the latter and gladly threw myself into the former, and I was safely buried in such a dream when a repetitive crashing woke me. For a moment, jerked out of unconsciousness and into blackness, I forgot where I was. My first thought was that something was wrong with the ship. Then I remembered and tried to sit up, only to be dealt a sharp blow to the head. I curled up low and squinted through my one good eye, realising as I did so that it was so dark because my fire had finally gone out.

Inside the shelter it was freezing cold, worse than it had been since I'd first dragged myself onto the rocks, and the loud crashing was coming from right above me. The roof of the shelter. I could sense movement in the darkness as it was lifted by the wind, then released to crash back onto the rocks. Accompanying the crashing, occasionally blocked out by it, came the shrieking of the storm.

The wind was buffeting against the rocks and screaming through the gaps in my shelter. Rain lashed down and the sand underneath me was already waterlogged, with actual pools forming at the outer edges. This storm rivalled even the one that had destroyed the yacht, and I was trapped right at the centre of it with nowhere to run to.

I screamed when the roof was lifted off my shelter, thrown away in an instant by the wind. The rain had me soaked to the skin almost immediately. My arms, which I'd held up instinctively to shield myself, did nothing. I grabbed the nearest piece of fabric – a robe – and held it up over my head, lurching to my feet. Then I realised I had nowhere to go that was any more protected than I was there. I sank back down onto the wet sand and draped the robe over my head. There was nothing to do but wait out the storm.

The wind howled and snatched at me, and the rain

continued to pummel the sand and sting my exposed skin where the robe couldn't cover all of me. I closed my eyes and hummed, long and low. I hadn't decided to do it but it made me feel a little calmer in the centre of the onslaught. I shivered and hummed and bit at my fingers to sting feeling back into them for what felt like hours.

Eventually the storm ended. The rain didn't stop, but did ease down to a light mist, and the wind dropped entirely, leaving me to climb up into the pre-dawn light and assess the damage.

My shelter was gone. Around me were a few remnants – a sheet, some seaweed, shards of wood and fibreglass. But the bulk of it was missing. I couldn't even see it in the water. It must have been carried off by the waves. Worse still, the last visible part of the wrecked yacht had finally sunk. If anyone was looking for us, for the yacht, they'd have no reason to look twice at this place.

The rocks were slick and as I climbed about at the highest point, I slipped. I didn't fall far but I did scrape my legs on the jagged rocks and razor-sharp barnacles. I was already covered in cuts and grazes from clambering about on the rocks over the past few days, but this on top of everything else broke my fragile calm. I sat on the wet rock and cried in great gasping sobs like a child with a grazed knee.

Everything was pointless. I had tried so hard to regain so little and now it was all gone. The idea of gathering what I had left and trying to hang on until the next storm felt insanely useless. I might as well have never dragged myself out of the sinking boat, for all the good it had done. I was still going to die, just slower.

I looked out across the unfeeling expanse of water. It felt personal, this destruction. As if somehow Olly and Leon's hatred of me had seeped out into the sea, turning it against me. If I was going to die anyway, wouldn't it be better to get it over with? Shouldn't I be stripping off and lying on the shore, allowing hypothermia to take hold? Only the memory of Mags' terrified, rigid face prevented me from swimming out as far as I could and waiting to drown. I'd rather starve than go through that.

When I looked down at the shoreline I saw that the storm had stripped away the coarse sand and leathery seaweed to expose Leon's corpse. I shut my eyes tightly as soon as I realised what I was looking at but it made no difference. The image of his bloated, mottled body remained, inside my eyelids. In that quick glimpse I'd absorbed every detail, right down to the gulls pecking and ripping at his flesh. Five horrid gulls, one with its beak inside Leon's empty eye socket.

I turned myself a full 180 degrees and looked out to sea. I knew that despite how useless it seemed, I ought to be searching for my things in all the debris. I needed to start a fire and get warm and dry as soon as possible. I'd need to find my bottles, if any were left, and see if they'd managed to hold on to any drinking water. I was hungry and I'd have to gather seaweed to cook. I knew I had to do all those things if I wanted to go on living. I just didn't know if I had the strength to do them. I wanted to live, but not like this.

In the end, bloody and shivering, I caved to the pressure from my survival instincts. I mindlessly collected what little had survived the storm and returned my things to the area where I'd made my shelter. With nothing solid to make a roof from, I did my best with the bathrobe and some rocks to weigh it down.

The lighter had fallen from its little niche and was wet again, but I managed to dry it out enough to light a new fire. As I did so, I noticed that it wasn't Pac-Man on the plastic case, but Ms Pac-Man. I hadn't spotted the tiny red bow on the yellow circle before. How many other things had I failed to notice when my life was busier and fuller than it was now? In the chaos of the days after the yacht went adrift, perhaps I'd missed something important. Something that might have led to us being rescued. The idea was unbearable, so I pushed it away.

Somehow my book had stayed slightly dry, possibly because I'd been sitting on it, and it burned well enough to get some wood going as well. I'd found some splintered planks on the shore, but with my main source of wood gone, I'd have to rely on whatever washed up. Which meant I'd probably have to keep relighting the fire instead of keeping it going. Eventually the lighter would be empty and that would be that. It wouldn't matter that some evolutionary spark was driving me on, forcing me to survive. Without fire, I'd be dead within a day.

Hunched over the fire I waited for the small amount of seaweed I'd collected to heat through. Sitting there I listened to the howling wind, the sea and the gulls fighting over Leon's most tender pieces. The fire crackled and I heard a soft thumping sound, like wind beating on a sheet of plastic in the wreckage. Only the wreckage was all gone.

Torn between numbness and hope, I leapt to my feet and followed the sound.

CHAPTER TWENTY-NINE

There. It was silhouetted against the sky, where it had just started to turn blue-black at the edges. A helicopter sweeping across the sky, dotted with flashing lights. Was it the coastguard or some kind of rescue helicopter? Or was it just coincidence that it was here and they weren't looking for me at all?

I waved desperately, screaming at the top of my lungs. It was hard to tell which way it was pointing, or where it was going. For a moment it seemed to hover in place before heading back the way it had come. Then it came closer again. It was hard to tell but I thought it might be circling. It was looking for me, I was almost sure of it. They were looking for me and for the first time in days they were close to finding me.

'I'm here!' My salt-blasted lips cracked and my voice sounded ragged. I realised I was crying. 'I'm here! Harry! I'm here!'

I waved even though my body ached, watching the helicopter as it moved in slow circles. It was definitely getting nearer. At the same time though the sky was getting darker. I couldn't see it as clearly anymore; the dark blur of the helicopter kept disappearing against the sky. Only the flashing lights helped me to locate it.

Feeling sick with desperation I reached down and snatched a smouldering stick from my fire. I waved it in the air like a flare, trying to attract their attention.

'Here! I'm here, you bastards! Please, help me! Help!' I screamed a mixture of pleas and obscenities until I realised that I hadn't seen the lights for a while. I stopped moving and shouting. The only sounds were the sea and the gulls. The helicopter was gone.

Exhausted, I collapsed by the fire and buried my face in my hands, hunched over my knees. They hadn't seen me. How could they not have seen me? I was right here! Right sodding here and they'd just left me behind. I screamed my frustration into my scratched palms and pounded my feet against the sand like a child. I'd been scared or numb for so long that feeling angry was a giddy release. It was the most energy I'd had for days. I didn't stop screaming and stomping until I ran out of energy completely and went limp.

As the heady anger subsided, I asked myself the only question that mattered: the helicopter was gone, yes, but was it going to come back?

The more I thought about it, the more likely it seemed that it would. They were searching for me and had probably gone back because it was too dark to do so. If they were planning to continue searching, it was reasonable that they'd begin where they'd left off, near my island. I had to be ready when they came back. I couldn't bank on them seeing me on my pinhead of a rock formation. It was also unlikely that they'd hear me yelling over the sound of the helicopter itself.

I had no idea what kinds of technology they'd be using, but I needed to try and make myself as visible as possible.

That night, heedless of the dark, I climbed all over the island and hunted for anything I could burn. I cut myself on the rocks and grazed my palms on razor-sharp shells. My feet were shredded and I felt more than one scuttling crab flee across my bare toes. I didn't care. Come morning, I would be ready and waiting beside the largest signal fire I could muster. It would use all the fuel available to me but this was the moment to do it. If I didn't get rescued now, I never would, and the fire wouldn't be necessary for much longer. I knew deep down that if the helicopter failed to see me or didn't return, I was going to give up my last shreds of hope. Come nightfall, I'd be lying naked on the shore, letting nature take its course.

When the sun began to come up I searched again, looking for anything I'd missed by the light of a single smouldering stick. The hollow at the top of the rocks, where I'd climbed to right after the shipwreck, was packed with driftwood, the last of my book, some dry clothes and handfuls of seaweed. I climbed up there and sat by it, holding the lighter in my sweating palm. I was ready. The only thing that mattered was whether the search would continue, or whether they'd given up. I refused to allow myself to consider if I might be mistaken. If that helicopter hadn't been for me, then what I was about to do would spell the end for me. I had to be right.

It seemed like I waited for hours, holding my position, scanning the sky and listening, until, eventually, I thought I heard the whoop of helicopter rotors on the wind.

It was so faint that as I listened for it, I worried it was coming from my imagination. It wasn't until the sound grew louder and a speck appeared on the horizon that I was sure I wasn't going mad. They were coming for me and I was ready.

I waited, tense and fearful. If I started the fire too soon, it might burn out before they saw it. Too late, and they might pass over me entirely. I didn't know when the right moment would be. It was all just guesswork. I waited and then, finally, I couldn't wait any more.

I lit a spill of paper with the lighter, then pulled the top off of the plastic base with my teeth. I splashed the tiny amount of fuel inside onto the pyre I'd built. For a second the spill guttered and nearly blew out in the wind. I shoved it into the lighter fluid and held my breath. The orange embers on the paper crumbled into the puddle and dimmed. Then a bright yellow flame rippled out and the wood began to catch.

As the fire grew, the damp seaweed I'd piled on began to smoke. Dense clouds rose upwards and forced me down off the peak – coughing and choking. I reached a safe distance and cupped my hands around my mouth.

'I'm HERE!!'

The helicopter was still circling and I watched as it completed a rotation and began another. Had they really not noticed the smoke from my fire? I looked up and saw that the dense cloud at my level was trailing up into a tiny wisp above the island. Could they even see it up there?

The helicopter seemed for a second to go completely still in the air. It looked to me like a dog catching a scent and freezing as it focused on it. Then the black shape broke its pattern and began to move in a straight line, right towards me.

I dashed down to the tiny slip of shore and snatched up

a t-shirt I'd found a few days before. Waving it like a flag I jumped up and down and called up to the helicopter as it arrived overhead, deafening and majestic as an alien craft. A rope spiralled down towards me and overhead I heard a man's voice, calling out. My knees went from under me and I hit the sand, already sobbing. Everything I'd pushed down, everything I'd blocked out just to survive, hit me like a wave.

I was still sobbing when a pair of feet landed in front of me. Firm hands looped me into a harness and held onto me as I was winched to my feet and then up into the air. I clung on to this man, this stranger, and cried so hard that I could barely breathe. He was shouting over the noise but I couldn't hear what he was saying, or I could and my mind just couldn't latch on to the words themselves and what they meant. We were lifted back up into the helicopter and as he bundled me in I looked back at the rocks that had been my world for several days, and saw how small they looked from above. Hardly a difference between them and the dark water, were it not for the fire, slowly dying on the peak.

The man who'd brought me up to the helicopter and a woman inside began asking me questions. It felt like they were fighting over me – one removed the harness whilst the other bundled a foil blanket onto me and attached wires to my hand, then shone a torch in my eyes. Then a third body broke through them and flung itself on me, gripping me so tightly that I felt barnacle cuts reopening under the strain. It was all so fast and so loud and confusing that I could hardly stand it. A tiny part of me was almost longing for the sea's hushing quiet I'd just left behind.

'Hannah! Han, Oh my God. You're here. You're really here – we found you.'

For a moment I thought I really had gone mad. That I'd

blink awake and find this was just another dream. I gripped back just as tightly, wracked by full-body sobs. I'd been waiting for a miracle and had received not one, but two. I'd been found and rescued from the edge of nothingness. A scrap of land in the endless sea. But I'd also landed in the arms of someone I'd thought I'd never see again.

'Hannah?' Harry pulled back to look at me. 'It's all right – it's over. You're safe. We're safe now.'

I nodded, unable to speak. He was wearing another one of the shirts I'd hand-printed for him – faded and slightly too small, worn soft from a thousand washes. I buried my face against it and continued to sob. Harry held me tightly and I could hardly breathe for relief and happiness at being there with him.

The rest of the helicopter journey passed in a blur. I was only conscious of the occasional touches of the rescue team and Harry's soothing voice. Eventually we landed and I was escorted from the roof of a hospital down into a private room overlooking a sea of buildings and roads.

'Can I stay with her?' Harry asked.

I'd thought 'you're safe' was the best thing I'd ever heard him say. I was wrong.

After some rapid-fire French between the helicopter medics and the hospital staff, this question was turned over to me. I nodded and Harry stayed in the room whilst a doctor looked me over and called out instructions to several nurses and more junior staff. Once she'd done that, she stood over me and assured me in a calm, clipped voice that I 'had been in the wars' but was 'holding up well'. I had an eye infection and lots of cuts, which would be treated with IV antibiotics. My injured shoulder had been noted and would require some scans later to check for damage. I was also malnourished and suffering from a touch of hypothermia. Both of which would be brought under control in no time, I was assured. Suddenly, all the problems that had been insurmountable were easy fixes. I was back in the world again, where electricity, running water and antibiotics would make everything OK.

Once the doctor left, a nurse arrived to drape my bed with blankets and I was frogmarched into a warm shower in the neighbouring room.

The figure in the bathroom mirror was like a fever dream hallucination. A pinched face stared back at me from one red eye, the other swollen shut with a pus-filled cyst in the lid. My skin was chafed so red raw I looked sunburned, and my hair was stiff as seagrass with salt. My lips were white and peeling, my face marked with crusts of tears and snot. My body where it had been covered by clothes was still fish-belly white, but scoured with scratch marks and grazes. My shoulder was mottled green and purple with bruises. I could hardly believe that I was looking at myself and not some sort of waxwork from the London Dungeon – plague victim number five, perhaps, or the little match girl frozen to her stoop.

I didn't look much better after a warm shower, but I could at least feel my fingers and toes properly – as well as every cut on my body, now ruthlessly cleaned and stinging. Once I was in bed with a meal replacement shake in front of me and the promise of solid food to follow, the nurse left Harry and me alone. He came to sit beside the bed, staring at me as if he'd never seen me before. Or perhaps more accurately, as if he'd never expected to see me again. I reached out and he took my hand in his, thumb stroking over the cuts and grazes on my skin.

'What happened?' he asked eventually, in a hushed voice, like he was scared I might hear him and then answer.

'What happened to you?' I croaked back, not willing or able to conjure any answers for him just then.

'Me?' He looked shocked, as if he hadn't even considered that he had a story to tell.

'I couldn't see you, from the boat. I thought . . . I was afraid you'd gone under.'

'Oh!' Harry seemed surprised, as if he couldn't remember what I was talking about. 'Sorry, it's been . . . well, we've been out searching for over a week. A lot's happened since then.'

Yes, it had.

'I went off in the raft and it was OK for a bit but then this wave just took me out. I got thrown in and I probably would have drowned if the current hadn't got me. I went under and it carried me towards land. I'm not sure how long I was in the water, or how far it took me, but I was spotted by this fishing trawler and they got me out. By then, though, I couldn't tell them what direction I'd come from, and they couldn't see the yacht. They radioed in and a search started but the weather's been awful, storms too dangerous to go out in – and then when they could go out, they couldn't find you.'

'We were out there until . . . I don't know. It's been a while since the boat sank, five days, six?' It hurt to speak, and Harry passed me a cup of water to help ease my throat. It tasted like plastic and steel, reminding me of school water fountains.

'They'll want to talk to you about what happened, get as much info as possible like they did from me. Before they go back out, to look for the others . . . We saw a body, on the island where we found you. I couldn't tell who—'

286

'Leon.'

'Christ.' Harry rubbed a hand over his exhausted face. 'He was so . . . How? I mean . . . were you two there after the wreck? What happened to Olly and Mags? Are they still out there somewhere? We need to tell the rescue team if they . . .' He trailed off when I shook my head.

'Leon was dead before the wreck, and the sea brought him up. Left him on the beach. I tried to cover him, but the storm didn't let me.' It was a struggle to find the right words in my brain. I wasn't sure if it was the cold or the lack of food and proper sleep, but I was finding it hard to get my mind running at its normal speed. Everything felt slowed down and soft around the edges, foggy. A feeling I was used to by now.

'What about the others?' Harry asked, then interrupted himself. 'You don't have to tell me, if you don't want to. If it's too hard . . . But the police have already questioned me about what happened. They're probably going to ask you, too.'

'Mags tried to swim. She got . . . She went kind of crazy when Leon died. She was scared of me. Scared of Olly. She had a life vest and she tried to get away but . . . It was awful. I couldn't help her.' I wiped my nose with the back of my hand, not caring what Harry might think of me. I hadn't had to think about what I looked like for a while, and it was hard to get back into the habit. 'Olly, he was . . . he went strange. Like he didn't see what was going on all around us. Like it was still New Year's Eve, and we were being bad guests. He chased me down to the cabins and he nearly killed me but then the boat hit the rocks. We were both trying to get out and he got trapped. He's still down there, in the boat, as far as I know.'

'Fuck . . .' Harry breathed.

We sat in silence for a moment, then Harry squeezed my hand gently. 'Did he ever admit to it? To what he did to Libby?'

I shook my head. 'I don't know that he even knew himself if he'd done it. He was losing it. Have they . . . have they found her?'

Harry shook his head, still looking completely devastated from learning about the others. 'You're the first person we found and I guess Leon was the second. I don't know if the others will ever be recovered. No one's saying it, at least not to me, but I think they're giving up. It's kind of a miracle that we made it.' Harry squeezed my hand tightly. 'I'm so glad you made it out.'

'Me too . . . I thought I'd lost you.' I could feel my eyelids drooping as exhaustion took hold. I squeezed Harry's hand back and let myself go, thinking, *this is how I want to fall asleep forever.* Wondering if he felt the same way.

CHAPTER THIRTY

I was woken a few hours later to speak to the rescue coordinator, a tall, leathery-skinned woman with kind eyes. She was the one who finally filled me in on where I was – I'd already guessed that I was in a French hospital – and how the rescue teams had charted the tides from where we'd gone adrift in order to find us. The yacht had drifted from Italy, bypassed the Spanish coast and made it into the Atlantic. The storms had then driven it northwards and I'd ended up being shipwrecked off the north-west coast of France. I told her everything I could remember about the wreck, how Maggie had gone into the water before that and about Olly being trapped in the boat. With the news that everyone was confirmed either dead or rescued aside from Libby, she told me gently that the search would be scaled down. She didn't say it but we both knew it – Libby had likely died over a week ago.

I had to repeat everything all over again to the French police. Then I was finally allowed to go back to sleep.

I was laid up for a week, during which Harry stayed with

me as much as possible. The only times he left were to bring extra food from the canteen or to speak with the police. They'd had divers go down into the yacht and had recovered Olly's body. There were questions to answer about his and Leon's deaths, and only Harry and I were left to answer them. The police seemed most interested in Libby's disappearance and I told them everything I knew, right down to the vanishing bloodstain. I wasn't sure they believed me. They probably thought we'd all gone completely mad. To be honest, I wasn't sure we hadn't. Being in the hospital was like waking up from a fever dream.

After a week of antibiotics my eye was mostly back to normal, if sore, and I was feeling stronger after proper rest and food. Finally I was allowed to leave my room and move about the hospital. Harry had warned me that there were press people outside and even in the hospital, prowling the corridors. The story had blown up online with Harry's rescue and the hunt for the rest of us garnering national attention. So, I avoided crowded spaces and settled for staying mostly on my own floor.

I didn't have a phone but Harry had seen to it that some of his things were sent on to the hospital. Using his tablet I read articles about the search, in disbelief that all this had been going on whilst I hung on the edge of despair. Ironically, it seemed like the only thing that had saved me was being on a boat with the others in the first place – no expense had been spared in the search for them. Each article detailed the yacht's occupants – missing socialite, miraculously rescued artist, deceased podcast star and his much mourned fashion mogul wife and lastly, the end of the Bathurst line, as only son and heir, Oliver, was found dead.

I was mentioned in several pieces as well – I was 'and a

sixth guest' in a few, and even had one credit as 'a childhood friend' on a Libby fan blog. I didn't care that much, though it didn't escape my notice that Harry's survival was a lot more newsworthy than mine. I was just glad to have made it. I didn't need to 'make it' too.

Eight days into my hospital stay, Harry suggested I come out for a smoke with him, to get some fresh air. He smiled as he said it, faintly joking. He still seemed not to know how to act around me. Like he was stunned by my existence. To be honest, I felt the same way – not just about him, but also about myself. I'd been so sure that I was going to die that I'd sort of forgotten to imagine a future in which I escaped. I'd only clung to the fantasy of rescue, not what came after. I told him so as we sat in plastic chairs on a fire escape, watching the cars below as they trundled noisily past.

'I honestly can't imagine it,' Harry said. 'I mean, what happened to me was so fast, I guess I didn't really have time to react. I just kept thinking "oh fuck" and then it was over. I was being rescued. I don't know how you got through nearly a week on that little rock we found you on.'

I wanted to tell him. The words 'It was you. You kept me going' sat on my tongue, waiting for me to say them. Hadn't I promised myself that I would if I got my miracle?

'I just did it, I suppose. Because there wasn't anything else I could do.' I took a breath. 'I kept thinking about you. About how if you were out there, you'd come and save me. And you did.'

There. I'd done it.

Harry's face softened. 'Don't be all humble about it – you survived a psycho, a shipwreck and being stranded on an island in the Atlantic, in the coldest month of the year. Take a bow, Han. You earned it.'

I smiled, but I was annoyed with myself that I hadn't said it better. That I hadn't managed to make him understand how much he meant to me. Harry was right, though, I had survived and that was worth holding on to. Despite everything, I'd made it home. Now I just had to put myself out there, open up.

'I wanted to give this back to you,' I said, digging in the pocket of my dressing gown. It was one of several things Harry had ordered in for me to make the hospital stay more comfortable. I'd told him not to worry, but he'd gone ahead anyway.

When I held up the empty plastic lighter, now without its metal top, Harry looked confused. 'Is that . . .'

'Yup. Your lighter. I kept it with me, and it literally saved my life, more than once. Without it I'd have frozen to death before anyone found me. I . . . It wasn't just that it was useful. It meant something to me, too. To see it and to think about you, how I hoped you had made it to the shore and that you were coming to save me. I just . . . I needed to survive, to get the chance to tell you that I . . .' I paused. 'That's . . . a Pac-Man lighter.'

'What? Oh, yeah,' Harry said, gesturing to his cigarettes and the new lighter on top. 'I got it downstairs, can you believe – they sell them right outside the hospital. I don't know why I picked the same one again . . .' He sighed. 'Listen, Han, I know what you're going to say but . . .'

I was staring at the lighter. The two of them looked really similar; both blue, both with the signature yellow pie-chart outline in a repeating pattern. The only difference was the tiny red bow on the broken lighter's Ms Pac-Man – so worn and faded from constant handling that I'd convinced myself I hadn't noticed it before. But I knew now that I hadn't missed it. It just hadn't been there when he'd handed it to me. I hadn't kept hold of the lighter Harry had given me on the yacht. I'd ended up with a different one. A matching one. Which meant someone else on board had brought it with them.

Harry cursed, stubbing his cigarette out before he reached for my hand. 'I'm so sorry. You're great, but I'm just not in that place right now and . . . Han?'

'It's Libby, isn't it?' I said.

Harry's hand dropped from mine as if I'd burned him. He didn't say anything, which was proof enough. Looking back now, I realised it was kind of obvious. The way he'd butted heads with Olly, how hard he'd gone after him when Libby went missing. Libby had even asked him for a loan to bail Olly out. The very fact that she'd gone to Harry, when she and Olly had worked so hard to pretend to all of us that they were doing great, should have tipped me off.

'The two of you had matching lighters. The one you had, that you gave me, was Pac-Man, hers was this one.' I reached out and tapped it.

I could see it now, all too clearly – Harry and Libby meeting for secret trysts, reverting to their student ways. So quaint and kitsch for Libby, to drink cheap alcopops and smoke roll-ups with Harry. He was the one who probably bought the lighters. A last-minute gift, a sort of in-joke . . . or maybe a sign that he resented her marriage to Olly. Mr and Ms Pac-Man. Never Mr and Mrs.

'Where did you find it?' Harry finally asked, softly.

'I grabbed it right after Maggie . . . after I lost her. I thought it was luck that I found it again. But I didn't find it. I found this one instead. Libby's one.' My voice cracked a little as my disappointment and humiliation caught up to me. 'You two have been together . . . for how long?'

'A while. Uh . . . about a year, actually. On the quiet.'

My whole body shuddered, as if by rejecting the information it could protect me from harm. I felt so stupid. So small and sad and just . . . idiotic. How had I ever convinced myself that Harry and I were some kind of meant-to-be love story? I should have known better. There was nothing and no one that Libby didn't have first refusal on. I wasn't even second best. I didn't even register.

Harry picked up his lighter and looked at it. 'I don't know why but it just felt like remembering her, you know? To get the same again.' He sniffed and I realised he was crying. 'Because I don't really have anything to remember her by, and we've been looking but . . . I don't think she's coming back.'

Hearing his heart break for her only made mine ache. I had been protecting myself from this pain for years and even as it gnawed at my insides a part of me realised it wasn't as bad as I'd always assumed it would be. It was agony, but I could survive it. Just as I'd weathered the pain of resetting my shoulder. The pain was temporary, necessary. A part of healing. Even as my world came down around me, I could appreciate that these awful feelings were proof that I was alive – that I had survived – just as my awareness of cold had returned as I escaped hypothermia. Numbness was the sign of losing the battle, and I never wanted to be numb again.

'You let me think it was Leon,' I said, some anger creeping into my voice. 'That she was sleeping with him. Why would you . . .'

'Libby didn't want anyone to know,' Harry said, apparently

experiencing his own share of pain. 'Taunting Olly was the closest she came to telling him. I couldn't tell you. Then, when she was gone . . . I was embarrassed. Humiliated, really, to be her dirty little secret. No. She liked Olly's money and his name too much to throw him over for me. Even with their money problems, he still had the estate, the prestige.'

My heart thumped painfully, shock zinging through my nerves. I needed something to do with my hands, so I helped myself to one of Harry's cigarettes. I started to peel the filter, dropping the tiny pieces over the edge of the fire escape.

'I have told the police,' Harry said, interrupting my thoughts. 'About me and Libby. I didn't want it coming back to bite me and . . . I suppose I just wanted to talk about her. About what she meant to me, because there was no one else to talk to about her. I didn't think I'd ever see you again.'

It shouldn't have hurt, that he was still thinking of her, but it did. Any romantic ideas that had occurred to me when I fell asleep with his hand in mine that first night in the hospital were well and truly dead. Harry would only ever see me as 'Libby's friend', even now that Libby was gone and that, by the end, I hadn't even been her friend.

'Do they think Olly killed her?' I asked. 'I suppose you told them that they were arguing the night she vanished?'

'I did, yeah. But now I think that . . . maybe it wasn't him.' Harry rolled the empty tube from Libby's lighter between his fingers. 'That night, the night she disappeared – she came to see me,' He said. 'I was on watch, up in the bridge. She'd been arguing with Olly, who was blackout drunk, and she was pissed off. So she came upstairs to . . . spend some time with me.' Harry glanced at me and I saw him wince, probably imagining the image he'd just created in my mind. I nodded at him to continue, but inside I felt empty and sick.

'Once we were, um . . . done, she bummed a cigarette and left. Said she was going back to bed. It was already really blowing up outside. The boat was swaying and waves were breaking over the side of the lower deck. I never thought she'd go outside. But you said you found her lighter on the deck. I'm just thinking . . . what if she went outside to smoke, so Olly wouldn't smell it on her as bad? You know how he was about that. He made her quit, before.'

I knew that and I could see in my head an image of Libby, dressed in an expensive pyjama set, giddy and ruffled from her time with Harry. I pictured her, laughing and twirling in the high winds on the lower deck, where the spotlights were still on, and everything was still normal. Feeling invincible as a wave came over the side and took her away, her screams lost in the noise from the storm. The plastic lighter could have gone into any number of cracks and crevices, eventually coming loose before I found it.

'You think whatever happened to her, it was an accident?' I said slowly. 'We all thought it was murder, or manslaughter at least, and it was just a freak wave or the wind that took her? What about the blood?'

'Dunno. Maybe it wasn't blood, or Olly got so drunk he hit his head on the wall when the ship moved in the storm and then forgot.'

'But it disappeared. Someone cleaned it up.' Even as I said it, my mind was turning over the events. Now that I wasn't trapped on board the yacht, afraid for myself and everyone else, I could see it clearer. Maybe Maggie had cleaned the blood up to protect Leon, if she'd believed he'd done it. Or else Olly might have been so drunk that he didn't know if he'd killed Libby or not. Come to that, Leon was so coked up that he might have had his doubts about his own involvement. Any of them could have wanted the blood gone to protect themselves.

Harry shrugged and I saw him pocket Libby's lighter, along with his.

'I suppose we'll never really know, will we?' he said. 'Unless they find Libby, and they don't seem to think they will. The whole boat's been torn apart and sunk. Any evidence is gone with it.' He clenched his fist and looked down at his white knuckles. 'Such a fucking waste. All of it.'

'There might still be a way to prove it. Or at least, prove something,' I said, slowly.

'How do you mean?'

'The boat's gone, Libby's gone and they'll probably never find her or Mags in the sea, but what about the rope?'

Harry just stared at me. 'What's a rope got to do with what happened to her?'

'The mooring rope. It wasn't on board so it's probably still partly tied off at the harbour. It'll have DNA on it – skin or hair or sweat. Maybe even fingerprints if there was any plastic or metal on it. If Olly knew Libby was cheating and was planning to kill her, so he set us adrift, there'll be some evidence.' I rolled the body of the cigarette between my hands, crushing it. 'Not that it'll mean much, with him being dead. Still, at least we'd know who was responsible for what we all went through. For everything we lost.'

Harry didn't say anything, and when I looked at him I was shocked to find him completely white, face drained and drawn, as if he was the dead one, not Olly. His bloodless lips moved as if he wanted to speak, but couldn't. The hand holding his cigarette trembled and he had to rest it on the railing as it scattered ash everywhere.

'Harry?'

'I . . .' Harry's eyes flicked to me and for the first time I could remember, he looked afraid. No, not afraid. Terrified.

I realised, then, what he was about to say. I wanted to stop him, to run so that I wouldn't have to hear it, wouldn't have to know. But I was rooted in place as he swallowed and finally managed to dredge up the truth.

'Hannah . . . I never meant for this—'

'It was you.' The words were barely a whisper.

'You have to believe me.' His voice rose and he reached out to grasp my arm, but I jerked it away. 'I swear it wasn't supposed to be like this. I didn't know Olly couldn't sail! And I didn't know about the fuel.' He was talking fast and low, voice straining, pleading. 'I just needed time.'

'Time for what?' I felt horribly exposed on the fire escape, alone with him.

'She was pulling away from me. Asking for the loan, it was . . . it was the beginning of the end. She was using me to keep up appearances with him. I could see it then, that I'd never be good enough for her. I was moving up in the world but it was me she was embarrassed by. Me and my art and my background and . . . I couldn't make her see that we could be together, that it would be all right. That I could now give her everything he could, and that I loved her more.'

'What does that have to do with sabotaging the boat?' I hissed, trying and failing to understand what the hell he'd been trying to do.

'She was always running from me. Every time I tried to

talk to her about it she'd cut me off – block my number, leave me stewing. It wasn't like I could just show up to his bloody mansion to see her. I needed to get her somewhere she couldn't brush me off. Somewhere she'd have to listen.' He clenched his hands in the air and shook his head. 'It was only meant to buy me a few hours. Everyone was asleep. I thought if I undid the rope we'd float out far enough that it would take a while to get back. Everyone else would be distracted, hungover. I could get her alone.'

'Is that what happened the night she disappeared?' I said. 'You "got her alone"?'

'No!' Harry glanced behind us in case anyone was listening. 'No, I swear! She . . . she was done with him, all right? After all that stuff came out about the boat and the helicopter and the fight they had, she was done with Olly. She told me that when we got back she was going to come and live with me. I don't know if she got taken by the storm, or if Olly did something to her, but it wasn't me, Han. I'd never have hurt her. Never.'

It was like looking at a stranger. Harry, my friend for so many years. My secret crush. Harry the liar, my rescuer, a manipulator, my one defender.

I stood up.

'Hannah . . . Hannah, please, you can't tell anyone.' His voice cracked, turned shrill. I cringed away from him, avoiding his grasping hands. He disgusted me.

'They'll find out, but you should tell them first – they might look more kindly on that. Call the police and tell them what you did.' I looked down at him. 'Tell them, before tonight, or I will.'

Harry looked a mess. He must have been keeping it all buried, trying to hold it together. Now the cracks were showing.

'Hannah . . .'

'And I don't want you coming to my room after this. I don't want to see you again. Ever.'

His eyes were pleading, one hand fluttering near my arm, not daring to make contact. 'But I still care about—'

'I don't think you do. If you did, you wouldn't have endangered my life to corner Libby, and you wouldn't have lied to me about it. I do think that you were perfect for her though. You both use people, and I'm done with it.' I was still trembling, but I made the effort to make my voice sound strong. It helped that I meant every word. I didn't need defending – I was strong enough to do this for myself. I left the balcony.

'Hannah!' Harry called after me as I went. He sounded desperate, but he didn't raise his voice or try again. He cared more about being overheard than he did about getting through to me.

I didn't look back. I didn't want him to see me cry.

EPILOGUE

Harry never called the police. I checked, because I'd learned the hard way that he couldn't be trusted. It still hurt to be proved right. I had to tell them about what he'd done. It hurt more that he was making me do it instead of sparing me that. He was arrested a few days later – I imagined the police had needed to verify my story before they acted on it – and the arrest made the news. I saw it on the huge TVs at the airport on my way home. That was one good thing to come out of the whole affair – I didn't have to drive all the way back. My car was impounded somewhere in Italy and I wasn't too fussed about it. It was time I let it go and moved on to something newer, more reliable.

I wasn't sure what they'd charge Harry with – criminal damage? Kidnap? Manslaughter? I didn't want to know. I'd meant it when I told Harry I never wanted to see him again. He was on his own with whatever happened.

My flat was exactly as I'd left it, though my milk was off and the place felt musty and damp. My wardrobe was open and discarded options from when I'd packed littered the bed; my dressing table was covered with makeup I hadn't bothered to take with me. The box that had held my Dior heels was open on the floor.

Seeing the flat after so much had happened brought home to me how small I'd allowed my life to become. Ever since I'd lost Mum two years before, I'd been steadily losing bits of myself as well. First had been my painting and printing – anything creative, really. Then I'd stopped cooking, stopped looking for better, more fulfilling jobs. I hadn't done anything to make the flat my own – it was a grey box for a grey little life – and I'd stopped wanting things because the idea of losing them was too much. I'd stopped trying, because I couldn't bear the thought of failing.

That first night back home, I cried myself to sleep on my unmade bed.

The next day, I pulled out the crates of decorations and artwork I'd packed away and filled the flat with them. I sent Rin an email telling him I was handing in my notice and then I applied for any job I could find that involved actually doing something or making something – from cleaning to paint mixing. I didn't want to sit in an office answering customer service calls anymore. I wanted to be able to end the day knowing I'd achieved something, no matter how small. I wanted to move my body, too, and not be stuck behind a desk.

That night I ordered Chinese and ate it on the floor of my living room. I'd put my hair up in a colourful scarf to get it off my face and I had my art supplies out and a half-formed idea for a lino printing block in my head. I wanted to carve the lines of the sea and the jagged rocks out, print them in stark black ink on textured, handmade paper. I wanted the seaweed coiled like serpents and gulls in the air – five of them.

By midnight I'd turned one of my worst memories into something beautiful. In doing so, I'd fed the part of me that had been starving long before I ever set foot on the yacht. It didn't matter that no one would ever see the print I'd made. That I wouldn't be able to sell it. That I was never going to get rich and famous off of my art. I wasn't measuring with that yardstick anymore. I just wanted to make something; to do it for myself, not for anyone else, and certainly not for money.

It hurt, making those things, but it hurt in the way that growing a new tooth in place of a sore gappy gum hurt. The pain wouldn't last forever, but what I got from it would. Or so I hoped. So, for several weeks, I printed designs with carved lino and made screen printing stencils. I drew and painted and sent out job applications. I cried and ate homemade curry and listened to my mum's CDs. I created disturbing images, seascapes, smears of colour and movement, pictures of my mother, of Libby and Mags as the kids we'd been together, and each one felt like I'd carved a tiny bit of hurt out of myself and stored it somewhere safe.

A month after my return I was starting to have job interviews. Some of them went well and some were awful. One left me sobbing on the train home, convinced that I'd only made my life worse in the time since it was saved. I was rejected by several companies and left hanging by others. I worried about where I'd find rent money when my small amount of savings was gone. For the first time in a while, I found myself inventorying my belongings and working out what I could sell. There wasn't much but I made it work and soon I was ferrying eBay parcels into town and spent one afternoon hauling bags of designer gifts to a swanky second-hand shop in Bath.

'You're sure?' the woman at the counter asked approximately fifty times, as she looked from my dungarees and Crocs to the pile of silk, leather and cashmere in front of her.

'Really sure,' I repeated, over and over again. 'I need the space. For something new.'

What that would be, I still wasn't sure. But I had earned myself one more month to figure something out.

After offloading my bags I went for a long walk in Victoria Park and took photographs in the botanical gardens. I ended up sitting on a bench under some wooden sculptures. It still felt surreal, being back in the real world. A world with traffic noise, squirrels and people everywhere. I bought an ice-cream because I could and relished it all the way back to the bus stop. By the time I got home, I realised that no matter how hard things got, even if I didn't find a new job, I'd survived far, far worse. Of course I'd already known that, logically. But it was something else to feel it inside. To know it about myself.

That night I sent messages around to my old art fair friends, and a few of us met for drinks a couple of days later. They were aghast at what had happened to me. We drank wine and one of them, Elle, said she had a stall now, selling dresses made from vintage bedding. We got talking about it and she said she liked my shirt. Before I'd have probably said 'thanks', and left it at that. Now I told her how I'd made it and the inspiration for the seaweed design. She seemed to find it interesting and eventually she asked if I was looking for a local stockist, because if so, she could use someone on the stall.

'It doesn't pay that much,' she warned. 'But on top of that we could do a split on the profits for the shirts . . . say . . . sixty-forty?'

'Seventy-thirty and you have a deal.'

Elle smiled. 'Tough negotiator, huh? Well, you're worth it. I can already tell.'

She was right, it didn't pay much, but once I moved out of my flat and into a house share with some friends from my old crafting circles, it was enough to cover my expenses. We did a lot of group cooking – I ate enough chickpeas in those months that I started to worry I'd turn yellow – but it was a laugh. Literally. I had never laughed as much as I did in that house, drinking Lidl wine and playing Monopoly in front of *Bake-Off*.

A few months later, whilst tending the stall, I met a guy who sold old console games elsewhere in the market. We got talking about sharks, of all things, and later met for wine. Elle initially said she would join us, but sent a text to say she couldn't make it after all, with a winking emoji.

I'd been certain that I'd die on that rock, and maybe I had in a way. The Hannah I'd been before the yacht wasn't the one who came back. I felt sorry for her, the old me. But I loved her, too, and I forgave her. I forgave myself for being her. For being small and lost and scared to open my heart.

My heart felt like an open wound now, but it felt. And I was glad.

ACKNOWLEDGEMENTS

I'd like to thank my parents and brother for supporting me this year as I attempted to write three books and edit two more. It's been tense, but we got there in the end! You all laughed at my sketch-map of the yacht, but that's in the past now. I won't mention it again, except for here, in print.

Thank you to everyone at Avon, starting with Rachel Hart. Rachel, your enthusiasm for this novel was contagious and I appreciate everything you added to the process of making this ridiculous boat come to life. It has been such a pleasure working with you, and I'm already looking forward to working on the next book together (which is a tiny lie, because at time of writing, we are already working on it!).

I am always blown away by the cover design and art assets produced alongside it, and *The Yacht* was no exception. Thank you to everyone at Avon who worked on them – you absolutely nailed it.

Enormous thanks are due to Laura Williams at Greene and Heaton, my incredible agent. Your input on *The Yacht* was as always, very much appreciated. I will even forgive you for recommending *The White Lotus* with no content warnings, which led to me watching it around my 60+ year old parents. That was super awkward!

Further thanks to Kate Rizzo, also at Greene and Heaton, for her continued efforts on the international front. Every time a translation of one of my novels lands on my doorstep, it always feels like a fever dream.

Lastly, thank you to everyone who has read and reviewed my previous books. It really helps the book to reach a wider audience and I try and read as many as I can, because I want to make each book better than the last. I hope you enjoyed reading *The Yacht* just as much as I did writing it, and that you're just as excited as I am for the next one.

Loved *The Yacht*?
Turn the page for a sneak peak of
The Festival . . .

PROLOGUE

I can feel the pounding music in my chest, racing along with my frantic pulse. My eardrums rebel against it and send sharp throbs of pain through my skull. Even my teeth are vibrating as the headline act takes to the stage.

All at once everyone is screaming, leaping up and down. They're completely focused on the act going on at some point behind and above me as I struggle away from the stage.

"Ari! Carla!" I yell, but it's no use. I can barely hear myself.

I breathe in dust from the ground beneath a hundred thousand shuffling feet and cough. I don't dare stop moving though. I'm tensed for a hand on my shoulder, a sharp sting in my back, it could come at any time. I can hardly move in the crushing crowd. Can't get away.

"Carla!" I try again, clawing my way past a wall of sweaty dancers, all as plastered as I am in yellow-brown dust. "Ari!"

Someone blows a whistle and it sounds like a scream.

I'm surrounded by faces – all baked red and brown, slathered in glitter and flaking face paint. None of them are familiar. None of them look concerned, just annoyed as I grab at them, elbow them in my rush to get past. I feel like an ant clambering over a whole nest of its fellow insects. An ant which knows a bird is hovering above, its sharp beak about to strike.

Something sharp does get me then. I feel the cold metal against my skin and scream, preparing for the pain, the blood. I feel hands pushing at me and I turn to find that it was just someone's sunglasses. The sharp hinge has raked against me, there are tiny beads of blood welling all along the scratch.

"What the fuck is her problem?" I hear someone yell.

"Bad trip," a voice says over my head as I blunder into a man's chest, sunburned and covered in blurry tattoos.

"Must be that shit they were warning everyone about . . ."

"Please," I'm clinging on to this stranger's arm. "You have to help me."

"Go to the medical tent," a girl practically bellows in my ear, shoving me away. "Get lost!"

I stagger away, exhaustion and heatstroke competing to see which can take me down first. My skin is frying under the sun and I'm breathing in the hot air of the crowd, laced with the smell of weed, stale sweat, too much body spray and overflowing toilets. Inside though, I feel ice cold. I wish this was a bad trip. At least then none of it would be real.

I've turned gotten turned around by all the shoving and elbowing. I can't tell which direction I came from anymore. Even the main stage, my one landmark in all the heaving bodies, has sunk into the tide of people. I'm too far away from it to see and the speakers all around us are confusing me – the music is coming from everywhere all at once.

"Ari! Carla!" I scream again. "Help!"

I spin on the spot, trying to spot Ari's sunflower crown or Carla's pink space buns, but there are so many other girls who look exactly like them. We're all just part of the crowd now.

There's no one else who looks like him, though.

My heart seems to stop, my chest echoing with the sound of the music, as I turn and spot him, heading straight towards me I scream and try to claw my way through the crowd behind me. Around us, the first song of the headline act comes to a close. A voice comes bursting from the loudspeakers.

"Lethe Festival! Get ready for the ride of your life!"

Cheers burst out around me and before I can try and make myself heard, my foot tangles with someone else's and I go down, hands outstretched to stop my fall. Before I've even registered the pain of landing, a foot crushes my fingers. My scream is absorbed into the opening of the next song.

"This one's for all the lovely ladies of Lethe! Make some noise!"

CHAPTER ONE

"I'm baaaack."

Carla's voice, always loud enough to reach me on the top floor of our odd little house share, seemed even more so today. Maybe it was because I'd been alone with my thoughts since she and Ari left that morning. I'd become used to the deafening silence.

I heard her dump her coat and umbrella in the hall, then come pounding up the three staircases between the hall and my room on the top floor. Two flights carpeted, one painted concrete and finally, the wooden ones – which were basically a ladder – up to my bedroom under the eaves. Her head and shoulders appeared in the hatchway and she peered up at me, where I was curled up on my bed.

"Cuppa?" she panted, her long blonde hair still thick with rain. "They had doughnuts at the office but everyone's on a diet so some of them came home with me. The doughnuts. Not Marjorie from accounting."

I managed a smile, though it felt foreign on my face. "Sure. Be down in a sec."

Carla stayed there for a second too long, looking firstly at me and then at the dirty clothes overflowing my wash basket, the empty plates on my desk chair and, finally, at the packages she brought up for me yesterday, which I still hadn't opened.

"Jody . . . have you been in bed all day?" she asked, so gently it makes me want to cry.

"Just since *Doctors* was on," I said. It came out defensive, even to my own ears.

Carla didn't look thrilled with this answer. "You'd let me know if there was anything I could do, right?" she asked.

"Yep," I smiled back, knowing that I would literally rather throw myself in the Thames than have my housemates do any more for me than they already had.

"Alright, I'll go make some tea – you, pop some proper clothes on. You'll feel better," Carla instructed me as she disappeared back downstairs.

I wasn't in my pyjamas, not exactly. But she did have a point. I'd had the same jumper and leggings on for three days now. I also hadn't had a shower. It wasn't that I didn't want to be clean, it was just the thought of getting all my stuff together and going down to the second floor bathroom. Then having to get into the shower and go through the whole routine, dry off, come back up and put more clothes on. It was too much. I could barely bring myself to go downstairs to grab some food twice a day.

Dressed in a cleanish t-shirt and jeans with a hoodie thrown on over the top, I descended to the first floor, where the kitchen was. The ground floor being just the entrance hall and a storage space for the mouldy washing machine, mammoth fridge freezer, several car boot sales worth of junk and the landlord's project motorbike. Ludlow House was affordable even on my tiny bursary because it was tall, narrow, practically derelict and shared between the three of us. Carla had been the first one of us in residence, when her housemates moved on to other things she brought in Ari, then I moved in three months ago, with what I could pack into the car in an hour. While Nick was at the gym.

As if I'd summoned her, Ari came up from the entryway, also wet through. It had been raining all day. The perfect August in my opinion, especially given my current mood.

Ari's long dark hair was shoved into her hood and she was carrying a bag of books that had left red rings on her arms where the handle had cut into her. I took the bag while she stripped off her coat.

"Did you leave anything in the library?" I asked.

"Just the Kant. I'm not taking that module." She offered me a smile that tried and failed to hide her assessment of my greasy hair and wrinkled clothes. "How are you?"

"Fine," I lied. "Carla's making tea."

Ari followed me into the kitchen, where steaming mugs were already clustered between her bags and the mountain of junk mail and actual post she must've picked up on her way in. A slightly battered box of *Krispy Kreme* doughnuts was balanced on top of three different coloured local directories.

"Anything vegan?" Ari asked, hopefully.

"The box? Maybe?" Carla said, doubtfully. Then she grinned and extracted a packet from her handbag. "Got you a strawberry ring on the way home."

"You are a saint," Ari said, already tearing into the cake. "I've had back-to-back lectures and two seminars since nine."

"Beats my all staff meeting and a full three hours crawling

316

around the filing room," Carla said. "Though I think my day was worse on the knees – those shitty carpets have shredded my tights."

I let their domestic chatter wash over me. They've been so great about everything, so supportive of me. I wasn't exactly new to London when I moved in, yet they practically fell over themselves 'introducing' me to city life. I was happy to let them.

I'd been scared of my housemates at first. These women who had their shit together, but they've been so kind, almost too nice. In the three months since I moved in, Carla has given me a list of safety tips and helped me get hold of some furniture and clothes on the cheap, since most of my stuff was still at Nick's. Ari showed me the places near us to get free Wi-Fi, the best but most affordable coffee and how to make most efficient use of the nearby laundrette, because the machine downstairs was permanently stuck on the wool setting.

"This one's for you," Carla said, sliding an envelope over to me. "And this one – someone's popular."

Her forced jolliness was well meant but it only made me feel worse. I smiled back and pulled the envelopes towards me. My heart sank. One of them had my university's logo on it. The other had the address written in my mother's handwriting. Neither seemed likely to cheer me up. I ripped open the one from Mum first. It was a card from one of her 'correspondence sets' with wild foxes on it. Inside she'd written the latest on her neighbour's bunion (worse) and the state of the roads (improving). She signed off by asking how school was going and when was I bringing Nick down to meet her? The last line asked me to phone her. The idea of hearing her voice, of having to explain without telling her the full story, made me feel like there was a weight pressing down on my chest.

I slowly opened the letter from the university, as if what was inside might sink its teeth into my fingers. My eyes skipped over the niceties and landed on a bolded paragraph halfway down the page.

Your attendance has become a cause of concern in the latter part of this term. Please contact your head of department with any issues relating to any prolonged absences in future. Please note that, if your overall attendance falls below the threshold outlined below, following the summer break, your bursary for the next academic year may be affected.

"What's the matter?" Ari asked.

I realised I was shaking, the paper shivering in my hand. I slapped it down on the table and reached for the steadying influence of my cup of tea. Half of it sloshed over the table, but Ari still managed to see the paragraph that had nearly reduced me to tears.

"Oh, Hon," Carla said, reading upside-down from her side of the mountain of post. "You need to get in touch with them, explain about . . ." her eyes met Ari's and she bit her lip, clearly unsure how to finish that sentence. They didn't know the half of it. To them, I was just taking a break-up really, really badly.

Ari took over from Carla. "No one can blame you for needing some time away. For not being able to focus after having to move and everything."

They were clearly trying to be kind but that's what made it worse. I felt as if my skin was on too tight, like it might split open and all the awfulness inside me would spill out. I was emotional roadkill, getting more rotten by the day.

"Maybe you should try and get away somewhere, you know, for summer break?" Ari said, hovering nearby with a bottle of water. "You could visit your mum?"

I shook my head. The last thing I wanted was to have to look Mum in the eye and tell her I was failing off of my course after she worked so hard to support me during my bachelors in veterinary medicine. I was meant to be qualifying as a proper veterinary surgeon, making her proud. Instead I was hiding away in my tiny attic room day after day. I didn't want to tell her that all her predictions about me moving to London had been right – I wasn't ready for the real world.

"Or we could go somewhere," Carla said. "What do you think, a girl's trip?"

"I can't afford it," I said, still looking at the letter. "I'd barely be able to afford the fare down to Dorset, never mind booking a hotel abroad, flights, going out . . ."

Neither of them seemed to have an answer to that. None of us were exactly rolling in it. Ari was only one term into her Philosophy Masters and Carla was on the second rung from bottom on the corporate ladder. A surprise holiday for their depressed roommate was definitely not something they could afford.

"Well, you never know," Ari said, sounding slightly less positive than before. "I might be the next person to win Lethe tickets – I entered a draw on Twitter and about twenty sponsored giveaways on Instagram."

"Sure, and I'll get invited to the Royal Wedding," Carla said, nudging me to include me in the joke. "Besides, even if you did win tickets for the festival – we'd still need to afford flights to Greece."

While the two of them shared a fantasy of using all of

the air miles Ari had racked up visiting her family, I sat and looked down at the college letter. In only a few months I'd managed to completely fuck up my entire life plan. I'd wanted to be a vet, like my Dad, since before I could remember. I'd fostered animals in my teens, done work experience and wildlife rescue volunteering. My GCSEs, A Levels and degree had all been aimed at getting me here. I'd put nearly every single one of my twenty-eight years on the planet into this dream. Now I was probably going to lose my bursary and end up having to drop out of the course. What would I do then?

"I think I'm going to go back to bed," I said, causing a tense silence to descend on the kitchen.

"If you're sure," Carla said. "Let me know if you fancy that doughnut later, OK?"

I nodded, forced a small smile for Ari and then left the room, heading for the stairs. The kitchen door swung closed behind me and if I hadn't been moving so slowly, I probably would have been gone by the time Carla spoke again.

"Do you think we ought to call someone, her mum maybe?" she murmured to Ari.

I paused on the carpeted stairs, tears stinging my eyes.

"I don't know . . . if she doesn't get better soon I suppose we have to. She won't tell us what's wrong."

"It's definitely that guy. She never talked about him much when she moved in, but now . . . she reacts like you've slapped her if you even say his name."

I hear the chime of mugs being gathered up, then Ari heaves a sigh.

"She needs to be able to tell us what's wrong. We can't do that for her. I know it sounds harsh but . . . we can't help her, until she helps herself."

"What if she can't?" Carla asked.

There was a long silence. "Then she'll be stuck like this. I'm just worried that something will happen that'll push her over the edge."

I pressed my lips together to smother the sounds of my sobs and crept upstairs. Alone under the eaves, I looked at my pile of textbooks, the unopened packages and unwashed clothes, and crawled back under my duvet.

I wasn't sure when exactly I fell asleep, just that when I bolted awake again it was pitch black. My heart was pounding and I was confused, unsure what had dragged me awake.

Then, Ari screamed again.

You'll want to stay. Until you can't leave . . .

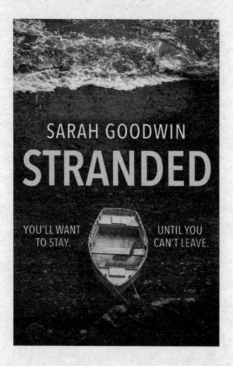

A group of strangers arrive on a beautiful but remote island, ready for the challenge of a lifetime: to live there for one year, without contact with the outside world.

But twelve months later, on the day when the boat is due to return for them, no one arrives.

Eight people set foot on the island. How many will make it off alive?

A gripping, twisty page-turner about secrets, lies and survival at all costs. Perfect for fans of *The Castaways*, *The Sanatorium* and *One by One*.

'Because he chose you. Out of thirteen girls.
You were the one. The last one.'

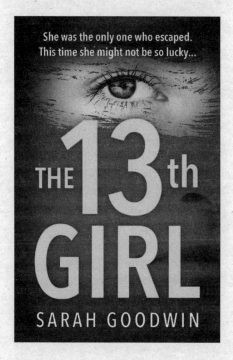

She was the only one who escaped.
This time she might not be so lucky...

THE 13th GIRL

SARAH GOODWIN

Lucy Townsend lives a normal life. She has a husband she
loves, in-laws she can't stand and she's just found out
she's going to be a mother.

But Lucy has a dark and dangerous secret.

She is not who she says she is.

Lucy is not even her real name.

A totally gripping, edge-of-your-seat thriller with twists
and turns you just won't see coming. Perfect for fans of
Girl A and *The Family Upstairs*.

It was a safe haven . . . until it became a trap.

It was a safe haven...
until it became a trap.

THE RESORT

SARAH GOODWIN

Mila and her husband **Ethan** are on their way to her sister's wedding at a luxurious ski resort, when the car engine suddenly stops and won't start again.

Stranded, with night closing in, they make their way on foot back to where they saw a sign for some cabins. They find the windows boarded up and the buildings in disrepair. They have the eerie sense they shouldn't be there.

With snow falling more heavily, they have no choice but to break into one to spend the night.

In the morning when Mila wakes, Ethan is gone.
Now she is all alone.
Or is she?

A totally gripping and spine-tingling psychological thriller. Perfect for fans of *The Hunting Party* and *The Castaways*.

You can't outrun the past . . .
. . . for what's done in the dark
will come to light . . .
. . . and someone wants revenge.

Summer. When Meg and Cat are forced to take a dangerous shortcut home one night, they notice two men silently following them. Suddenly running for their lives, they scramble into an abandoned building to hide and wait for help.

One year later. Attempting to escape the horrors of that fateful night, Meg barricades herself into a safehouse at the edge of a crumbling sea cliff. As a storm rages outside, a blackout plunges the house into darkness. But Meg's not alone.

Don't miss the new, totally addictive psychological thriller from Sarah Goodwin, with bombshell twists that will leave you stunned. Fans of *The Sanatorium*, *The Paris Apartment* and *One of the Girls* will be hooked from the very first page.